THE WEBS WE WEAVE

MICHELLE MORGAN

To my dear friend Helen. Thank you for letting me borrow your name. xx

I'll never pause again, never stand still,
Till either death hath closed these eyes of mine
Or fortune given me measure of revenge.
Henry VI, Part Three – William Shakespeare

1

2014

It was September. The sky was a bizarre orange colour, and I remember commenting to Craig that it looked like something out of one of those action movies he liked so much. I was in the kitchen, gazing out at the apple trees in the garden, and already looking forward to next spring. One solitary, straggling branch had found its way to the window, and every so often a gust of wind caught hold and sent it knocking against the glass. I made a mental note to go outside and trim it back, as soon as I'd finished making the lasagne.

Craig sat at the kitchen table, skimming through a car magazine. I always wondered how he could work with engines all day and still want to read about them at night, but that's just the way he was. I watched as he ran his oil-stained fingers down the *Vehicles Wanted* page, and tried not to be too concerned that he showed no sign of getting ready for our twentieth anniversary dinner party.

'Are you watching the time?' I asked, trying hard not to come across as a menopausal nag.

Craig looked at his watch and shrugged.

'I just want to finish reading this page. Bill, the window cleaner, asked me to look out for a van for him. He's written his old one off.'

Even though it aggravated me that Craig would rather look for a van than head to the shower, I couldn't help but be proud of everything my dear husband had achieved during the past two decades. Managing a garage was fabulous enough, but being in a position to own one was something else entirely. I reached over and planted a huge kiss on his cheek, causing his hair to ruffle in the process.

'I love you,' I said. 'But just don't forget the time!'

Without turning his attention away from the magazine, Craig's hand shot up and straightened his hair. Looking back, that was a red flag, but at the time, I thought he was being vain. His locks had always been his proudest feature, though I preferred his eyes if I'm honest.

'Rebecca phoned today,' I said. 'She's sorry she can't make it tonight, but she says she'll definitely be home for Christmas. I know that's looking ahead a bit, but you know what she's like – always the planner.' I looked for some kind of recognition from Craig, but nothing came from his side of the room. I cursed his preoccupation with the car ads and continued layering the lasagne.

One layer of white sauce.

One layer of lasagne sheets.

One layer of mince.

One layer of lasagne sheets...

And then it happened.

'Jenny, I've got something to tell you.'

I laughed.

'Well, it better not be that you don't want lasagne tonight, because I've got enough here to feed the whole of Cromwey!'

'No. No, it's not about the food.'

Craig's eyes flitted around the room, but never found my face. For an awful moment I thought maybe he'd received some bad health news or something. He'd recently been for an NHS health check, but as far as I knew, he'd passed with nothing more than a request to lose a few pounds.

'So, what is it? Are you okay?'

'Yes, yes I'm fine. It's just that I don't...'

His voice faltered, and the tiny hairs on the side of my face prickled. What was going on? The atmosphere was suffocating, and not at all what I expected on the night of our special anniversary.

'You don't what?'

'I don't think I can go through with tonight.'

I placed my spatula onto the counter, and thick drops of tomato juice dolloped onto the surface.

'Don't be silly! We've been looking forward to this for months. Why don't you want to do it?'

'Because I can't keep on with this charade, Jenny. I don't... I don't want to be married anymore.'

I didn't hear the words in my ears alone. Instead, they went straight to that space at the centre of my chest, just above my solar plexus. I had carried a variety of hurt feelings in that place over the years, but this? This had to be the worst. My breath caught at the back of my throat, and my ribs felt as though they were collapsing in on themselves, stabbing my heart in the process. This couldn't be happening. It must be some kind of misguided joke.

Except that it wasn't.

The man I'd been married to for exactly twenty years picked at the dirt underneath his thumbnail. I was standing next to the pre-heated oven, but I didn't feel any warmth at all. The room could have been made of snow and ice, I was so cold. I dropped the dish onto the floor – half out of astonishment, half fury – and it smashed into tiny pieces, sending pasta layers and mince all over the stone tiles and onto my feet and legs.

'Shit. Stand still, you'll cut yourself.'

Craig's voice sounded as though it was coming at me through a wave of water. I could hear it but there was no clarity, no tenderness at all. The words didn't even sound fully formed. Was he speaking in a foreign language? I felt his hands on the top of my arms, gripping my triceps as though trying to stop me from lashing out. I shrugged him off and then slapped his face, my hand tingling as it made contact with the stubble on his cheek. That was the first time I'd ever slapped him during our long life together and it shocked us both. Funny thing is I can still feel those pins and needles running through my hand if I think hard enough, but I've never regretted that slap. After all, I could have done far worse.

We both stood in silence and I tried to stare into Craig's eyes, but it was no use. He held my gaze for a second, before turning his attention to the branch, still tapping on the window.

'That bloody tree,' he grumbled. 'I always knew we should have installed double glazing.'

'We couldn't.'

'What?'

'We couldn't get double glazing. It was against harbour regulations. Remember?'

Craig rubbed his cheek. There was a crimson mark where my hand had made contact, but he didn't acknowledge it out loud.

'Yes.' He sighed. 'Yes, I remember.'

And then we both stood still again.

For what seemed like forever.

But at last words needed to be said. My breath was shallow

and when I opened my mouth, I prayed that I'd have the energy to speak.

'You don't want to be married anymore?'

'No. I'm sorry.'

Just like that. Those three words felt as though they were strangling me.

'But... But it's our anniversary! Twenty years ago, to the very moment, we were dancing to our favourite songs and thanking our family and friends for celebrating with us. And now... And now... those same friends are coming to visit us in just over an hour!'

Craig ran his finger across his eyebrow.

'You think I don't know that? Believe me, I didn't want to tell you like this. I didn't want to spoil your big day.'

Your big day? The words rattled in my brain. This was *our* big day, not just mine! Or so I had thought. I opened my mouth to tell him so, but then an unwelcome vision popped into my mind.

Just thirty minutes before I began cooking – when I was upstairs admiring the dress for our dinner party – there was a knock at the door. I looked out of the bedroom window and there was a woman in a yellow jacket, talking to Craig whilst thrusting her arms out in front of her. She had her hood up, and I could see nothing more than a shock of brown, curly hair sticking out at the sides. When Craig shut the door, he told me she had been a charity collector, passionate about the welfare of cats, or bats, or something. I had thought it odd that she wasn't wearing some kind of official uniform, but it was such an insignificant occurrence that I'd forgotten all about it.

Until now.

'Wait a minute! Does this have something to do with that woman I saw in the garden? She wasn't a charity collector, was she?' Craig shook his head, but stayed silent. 'Are you...? Are you having an affair with her?'

I asked the question, though heaven knows I didn't want to hear the answer. Craig's nostrils flared and I could hear his breathing from five feet away.

'Yes.'

The way he revealed this piece of information was just as if I'd asked if he wanted a cup of tea, or a slice of chocolate cake. How stupid I was. Of course he had another woman. Didn't they always?

'So, is that why you don't want to be married anymore? Because you love her?'

Craig slunk backwards towards the table. The shattered crockery broke further under his heels.

'Shit. I'll clear this up.'

Before he could move, I grabbed his wrists and held them down, the way I used to do with Rebecca when she was misbehaving as a child.

'Fuck the crockery, Craig!! For Christ's sake, you've just told me our marriage is over, and you're more concerned about a smashed dish?!'

Craig tore himself from my grasp, and grabbed the dustpan and brush from under the sink. He bent down to clean, but gave up after a few seconds and threw the pan onto the side. It clattered and a cloud of mince, dirt and pottery scattered along the clean surface.

'I need to know, Craig. Do... you... love... this... woman?' It took me a series of gulps to spit out that short sentence. I knew the answer, but I needed to hear it from his mouth. I needed to feel the agony of it.

'Yes,' he whispered. 'Yes, I love her.'

Blood rushed to my head, and I felt as though my arms were hanging by threads. The old branch continued its attack on the window and for a while it was in rhythm with my heart. It's bizarre what goes through your mind at times like that. I concentrated on that beat to stop myself from collapsing. All I could think about was my husband's lover, standing on my doorstep on our special day. How dare she?! How dare she?!

'Why, Craig? I thought we had such a happy life together. Why would you want to destroy it? Destroy *us*?!'

For the first time that evening, Craig's mouth turned up at the edges. Only it wasn't a joyful smile. Instead, it was an all-knowing grin, as though he was privy to some deep knowledge that I had yet to figure out.

'Come on, Jenny! We haven't been happy for at least a year. Maybe more.'

I breathed in so quickly that it hurt my throat.

'What do you mean?'

'You've hardly looked at me for months now! You're too wrapped up in creating your *business* to care about anything that's going on with me. I sit here some evenings, and the only thing you say to me is goodnight. I could stay at the garage and you wouldn't even notice.'

'Don't be ridiculous! I don't ignore you at all – I'm just trying to create a better job for myself, that's all.'

Craig made a harrumph sound and picked up his car magazine from the table.

'You know it's the truth, Jenny.'

I was stunned. First of all, the way Craig emphasised the word *business* was insulting, as though it was some kind of whim that I'd give up the moment I was bored. That was totally untrue. For the past seven months I had been doing an online course to become a genealogist, which I hoped would lead to me giving up my day job at the local library. It's true that I hadn't had much time to spare whilst working, studying and running a house, but Craig hadn't complained. Until today.

'I thought you were fine with me setting up a business! You even bought me a laptop so that I could study.'

Craig threw his magazine back onto the table.

'I was fine with it. But that was before I knew it was geneal-ogy. I mean, honestly – researching family trees? Seriously, Jenny? How can you ever make any money from that? You're going to bankrupt us if you keep up with this racket.'

I don't remember much about the next few minutes. Although there were many words and actions, I felt as though I was removed from it all. Everything was muted, surrounded in a cloud of sorrow, outrage and betrayal. I asked what we should do about Rebecca, but Craig shrugged and said that as she was now eighteen and at university, she wouldn't be affected by a separa-tion. At that moment I knew he'd lost his mind. Our daughter may not live with us full-time anymore, but she would never think this was okay. She would never get used to this new normal.

I sat down at the kitchen table – the same one where we'd shared family dinners and played Monopoly – and the fury continued to grow. My hands curled into fists and I realised that one of my nails had snapped. How did that happen? Was I falling to pieces outside as well as in? Craig wasn't about to stay to find out. He had broken the news and now wanted to head off to his fresh life. The life he planned with his new woman.

'I'll be back to pick up my things tomorrow,' he said and then headed towards the door.

'What's her name?'

Craig stopped and hung his head.

'Jenny.'

'I said, what's her name?! Or would you rather I call her the yellow-coated skank?'

My husband slumped down onto the kitchen chair, and I wondered if that would be the last time he'd ever sit there. Deep down I knew it would be.

'Her name is Helena Love.'

Helena. Helena Love? The name sounded familiar but I wasn't sure why. I searched my brain for a clue, and then it struck me.

'The Lovely Café.'

The words flew out of my mouth, and Craig blinked as though he couldn't believe I'd figured it out.

'She owns The Lovely Café; that garish little place, two doors down from your garage.'

He nodded, but didn't offer any further explanation.

'Is she younger than me?'

'I don't know. Maybe. But not much.'

'How much?'

Craig shook his head and shrugged as though he'd never even thought about it. But in reality, finding a younger woman was probably the most exhilarating thrill of his life.

'I don't know. Maybe four or five years.'

I snickered. It shot out of my mouth like a psychopathic clown impression.

'You don't know?'

'Okay, she's thirty-five.'

Thirty-five? I felt dizzy and embarrassed for being in my forties. How dare a wife reach middle age?!

'In that case,' I said, 'she's seven years younger than me. I'm forty-two.'

'I know.'

'So, you're just as shit at maths as you are at keeping your dick in your pants.'

Craig's shoulders hunched over and he became far too obsessed with a speck of pasta sauce on his T-shirt. Just an hour before, I had loved this man, and had looked forward to presenting him with the gold watch he'd coveted for the past six months. Now I'd have to return it to the store, unopened.

Before I could say anything else, my husband bolted from

the table. The chair legs screeched their way across the tiles and left black lines in their wake. Skid marks from a person desperate to leave the room – leave the marriage – as soon as he could.

When I heard the front door slam, my life shattered like the lasagne dish on the floor. Despite the outrage I felt through every inch of my body, I knew that our marriage hadn't been all bad. There were many days when I felt contented and happy. I had believed he felt the same.

But that was then.

And now he was gone.

I laid my head on my arms and stayed at the table for a long time, lost in my memories and ignoring our friends knocking at the front door. They'd have to go somewhere else for dinner. Darkness had descended into the kitchen and all I could see was the moonlight reflecting off the stainless-steel sink. At one point the phone rang, and then the letterbox clattered with the arrival of a leaflet advertising pizza or Chinese food. I didn't bother to look, before I threw them into the recycling bin.

When my upper back began to seize up, I lifted my head and noticed that my shirtsleeves were soaked with tears and snot. I dabbed myself with a piece of kitchen roll, then seized the dustpan, swept up the ruined crockery and made myself a cup of tea. That's what we do, isn't it? Tea makes all our troubles disappear. House blown up during the Blitz? Have a cup of tea! Been mugged in the street? Tea will make it better! Husband shacked up with some thirty-five-year-old café owner called Helena Love? Hell, tea will cure that too.

Only it won't, of course.

Afterwards, I swilled the cup out in the sink, dried it with the tea towel we'd bought from Bournemouth in 2012 and then placed it back in the cupboard. Craig's *World's Best Husband* mug stared back at me with a gigantic smirk on its face. I grabbed it, darted to the front door and took aim for the harbour wall, twenty feet away.

Bang!

The cup shattered and a seagull screeched overhead. A young couple glowered at me like I was a lunatic, and the old woman next door came dashing outside.

'Good lord, Jenny, what's going on? Have you and Craig had a falling out again?'

'Mind your own business!' I screamed, and I slammed the front door.

Before I got into bed that night, I went out to our backyard and trimmed the branch that had rattled on my window all evening. I broke off a crusty old leaf, placed it between two sheets of tissue and laid it inside my copy of *The Complete Works of Shakespeare*. When I opened the book a few months later, the leaf had disintegrated into a pile of dust and I thought that was ironic, since my marriage had ended the same way.

2

2019

Mrs Witkowski scowls at me over her teeny, silver spectacles. There's a deep crease in the middle of her forehead and I know that any minute now, she's going to question my research abilities.

'Are you sure there was nothing about a viscount in the documents you found? My mother always said there was a viscount.'

I knew that was coming. I smile and can't help but wonder how long I'll have to stand on the doorstep, before my customer accepts my findings.

'I am sorry, Mrs Witkowski. I did my best to find a viscount for you, but he was nowhere to be seen. I know it's disappointing, but I promise that if you read the documents, you'll still discover something interesting about your family. For instance, your great, great uncle once rescued four women from a burning factory. He was a real hero and I made sure to include his newspaper interview, in the files.'

I nod towards the folder but Mrs Witkowski doesn't seem

enthralled. However, she's polite enough to thank me, and then trundles off down the path. I close the door before she changes her mind, and tighten my cardigan around my chest. It may be late spring, but it's still too chilly to be loitering on the doorstep, discussing wannabe royal relatives. That's the problem with being a genealogist – everyone either wants to see a celebrity or a criminal in their family, and when faced with a tree full of servants, shopkeepers or farmers, they can't believe their bad luck.

Five minutes later and I'm slouched at my desk with a cup of tea in one hand and my latest commission in the other. This time it's the Carr family, which is filled with four generations of Durham miners called John. I love my job, but I wish that these old families were a bit more inventive in their choice of names. John Carr times four might be the project that propels me over the edge.

I grab my notebook and scribble the name, as if having it on paper will make everything easier. It doesn't, and I end up staring at the words until they become one huge dollop of blurred ink. When the telephone rings, I pounce on it.

'Gosh, that was fast! Were you sitting on the phone, waiting for me to call?'

The sound of my daughter's voice makes me smile.

'Rebecca! It's lovely to hear from you!'

There's a worried pause on the other end of the line.

'Is it? Why? What's wrong? Are you okay?'

I can't help but laugh. My daughter has always had a flare for the dramatic and I swear she only ever calls to make sure I haven't come to some kind of tragic end. I'm not sure what she thinks is going to happen though, because Cromwey isn't renowned for its serial killers or multiple murderers. In fact, I think the most scandalous event in recent years happened when a man was accused of peeping into the bedroom of an eighty-six-year-old widow. He was revealed to be a window cleaner hired by the woman's son, and that particular 'crime' became a washout – so to speak.

'I'm fine, Rebecca. Can't I just be glad to hear from you?'

'Of course you can, but you know I worry when I haven't spoken to you in a few days.'

I do know. The anxiety I have, knowing that my daughter lives 130 miles away is excruciating. I did hope that after university finished, she might come back to Cromwey for good, but I guess there's not much call for senior press officers in this sleepy town, so in London she stays.

'I was calling,' she tells me, 'because I have some good news.'

'Oh? What's that then?' I stare down at my George Michael mug and he smiles up at me. I grin back as though we share some kind of secret connection.

'I got a little bonus yesterday and I decided to buy a train pass with it. Now I can pop up to see you whenever I want, and maybe even bring you back here with me sometimes – if you want to. Won't that be fun?'

I listen to Rebecca's words as I pick up a photograph of her aged nine months. The glass in the frame is covered in a layer of dust and I have to wipe it with my finger to get a clearer look. I stare at the beautiful baby – *my* beautiful baby – and my heart glows. Her hair flops down towards her huge blue eyes, and her mouth is almost lost in the chubbiness of her cheeks. Where did the years go? How can my baby be twenty-three already? Once I was worried about her going to nursery for an hour a day – now she's living in London, all grown-up.

Rebecca coughs on the other end of the phone.

'Mum? Don't you think it will be great for me to visit you more often?'

'Yes,' I say. 'Yes, it will be perfect.'

~

It's Sunday morning. I'm still in my pyjamas, I haven't cleaned my teeth and my hair looks as though it's been styled in a wind tunnel, but that doesn't stop my doorbell from buzzing like a demented hornet. I pad down the hallway, stopping to straighten my hair in the mirror, but whoever's there doesn't appreciate the delay. Now instead of ringing, they start banging too.

'I'm coming for goodness' sake! Give me a chance!'

I release all the locks and open the front door. My best friend, Kate, stands with two takeaway hot chocolates in her hands and a bag of croissants dangles from her mouth. She thrusts the drinks at me and drops the paper bag into her hand.

'Thank Christ for that,' she snaps as she squeezes past me. 'The drinks are almost cold. What took you so long? And what's going on with your hair?' She stares at me over the top of her shades. It's overcast outside, but that doesn't stop Kate. The only other person who's ever worn sunglasses in rainy Cromwey was some random soap opera actress who turned on the Christmas lights in 2009.

I examine my mane in the mirror, but Kate has already disappeared through the living room, towards the kitchen. I tuck my hair behind my ears and when I reach the kitchen door, she has plonked the bag of croissants onto the table and is rifling through the cupboard for some plates.

'Have I got news for you,' she shouts over the spin cycle of the washing machine. 'Is that thing going to be on long? You need to engage all your senses to hear what I've got to tell!'

I place the cups on the table and gaze up at the wall clock.

'About five minutes,' I say, and then I watch as Kate reaches over and presses the pause button without even asking if it's okay to do so.

'That's better.' She removes her glasses and chucks them onto the table. 'Okay, sit your bum down, grab a croissant and listen to this.'

I do as I'm told in terms of sitting down, but I've already had two crumpets this morning and I don't want any more food right now. Regardless, Kate sticks a croissant on my plate and then scratches her eyebrow.

'I'll get straight to the point.' She sighs. 'Craig's left Helena!'

The sentence may be three words long, but the significance is encyclopaedic. I can't think of anything profound to say, so I reply with the first pathetic question that enters my mind.

'Are you sure?'

Kate bites her croissant and nods, wide-eyed.

'Positive.' She throws her hand up to her mouth, but crumbs still manage to escape. 'Craig told Pete last night. They had been to the late-night showing of that Queen movie. Yes, I know it's already out on DVD, but Pete wanted to see it on the big screen, because of the whole Live Aid thing...'

'Kate! Get to the point!'

'Okay. Well anyway, when they got to the taxi rank, Pete thought they'd be sharing a cab as usual, but Craig stepped back and said he'd have to take his own, cos he no longer lives in Harbour Rise. Pete didn't know what the hell he was talking about, but by that point he was in the taxi, so Craig just told him as fast as he could – he's left Helena, moved out of Harbour Rise and is now living in the new estate next to the butterfly farm. Hill View or something it's called.'

The words clatter into my ears like pennies being thrown into an empty well. Kate leans back in the chair, scrapes her hair from her face as though she's about to put it into a ponytail, and then drops it and throws her hands up in astonishment. Croissant crumbs scatter from her chin to her T-shirt, and she swats them onto the floor.

'Can you believe it?' she asks.

'No. No I can't.' My stomach is churning. I should be past caring about this by now, but in spite of myself, I'm hungry to know more. As if reading my mind, Kate shakes her head and grabs another croissant.

'I'm bloody starving. But before you ask, no I don't know anything other than what I've just told you. I walked past Helena's house on my way here, but the curtains were all drawn and there was no sign of life. I'd have called you last night if I'd had my way, but it was like 1.30am when Pete came in, and he insisted I wait until morning – didn't want you to think there was an emergency or something.'

I nod and gaze down at the floor... the same floor where I dropped the lasagne dish on the night Craig left me... and now he's left somebody else too.

'Jenny? Did you hear what I said? I didn't call late, in case you thought it was an emergency.'

'Yes, you were right. I'd have thought there was something wrong with Rebecca, or my parents. My mum hasn't been well – she's felt lousy ever since that cold she caught at Easter.'

I'm rambling, but I can't help it. All that agony! All that torture and torment, and for what? Almost five years after breaking my life into pieces, his new relationship is over. What was the point of it all?

'I wonder if he's got another woman,' I whisper, almost to myself.

Kate shrugs and throws the remnants of her croissant onto the plate.

'I have no idea. But I did wonder about that.'

I lean my head into my hands and great pools of tears escape from my eyes and splatter all over my cheeks and fingers. By the time I raise my head again, the plates are washed up, Kate has gone home and rain is pounding on the window.

3

It's two days since Kate's visit, and I haven't heard anything else about Craig's new life. Part of me tries not to care – his business ceased to be my concern some five years ago. But having said that, we did share over twenty years together and I can't help but be bothered that the woman he left me for didn't turn out to be his ideal woman after all. It leaves me wondering what the hell the last half-decade has been about.

Sex? I mean, I guess at the end of the day it all boils down to sex, doesn't it? And yet it's not as if he didn't get any at home. In spite of Craig's insistence that I barely looked at him while building my business, we made love right here in this living room, just the night before he left. I know the ramifications of that; don't think I haven't obsessed about his hands on that bitch one day, and me the next. And yes, the moment I found out about the affair, I went straight to the doctor to be tested for STDs.

I know it's distasteful to reveal such a thing, but when you're faced with the idea that your husband could have brought home all manner of diseases, you move pretty fast. Luckily for me I was healthy, but for months afterwards, the knowledge that I'd been having sex with a man who was screwing someone else tore my mind apart.

It's a rainy day in Cromwey and I have no intention of leaving the house. Instead, I'm going to tackle Mrs Carr's family tree again, and try not to dwell on Craig's latest scandal. I have no idea how Rebecca will react to all this, but then again, shouldn't that be something my ex-husband sorts out himself? Ha! Who am I kidding? He'll never tell our daughter about this development. It will be the furthest thing from his mind.

I scribble down some notes about the Carr family, but my pen dies halfway through the first sentence. I lean over to my pencil pot, but before I can grab another, there's a knock at the door.

It's 8.50am and I have a parcel due for delivery. I tuck my unwashed hair behind my ears and then shout a cheery, 'I'm coming!' at the figure behind the glass. As I open the door, the rain blows in and splatters my face and shoulders. I recoil and hold out my hands to retrieve my parcel.

Except there is no parcel.

Instead, there is a bedraggled woman wearing a navy-blue raincoat with the hood pulled tight around her face. Clumps of hair poke out over her forehead, and water dribbles down onto her cheeks. She's shivering and her arms are held around her middle. Her tight jeans stick to her legs like wet dish towels.

The woman stares at me through dull, heartbroken eyes.

'Helena,' I say, as though she may not be sure of her own name.

She nods.

'I wonder if I might be able to come in,' she asks.

My husband's estranged wife and I are perched at my kitchen table, nursing mugs of hot, milky tea. We don't speak out loud, but I imagine there are thousands of silent words swirling around like a cloud of grey fog.

At least from my side there is.

Why is she here?

What does she want?

She doesn't seem inclined to reveal.

I skim my finger around my cup and wish I could conjure up something polite to say, but I can't. What words can I share with this woman? This woman who turned up on the day of my twentieth wedding anniversary, and broke my family to pieces. There are no words... None that I can say out loud anyway. I forget about speaking and instead concentrate on attempting to stop my legs shaking under the table. I push down on my knees with as much force as I can muster without making it obvious, but still they move. The vintage, electric-blue clock ticks above Helena's head. Craig bought it about three months before he moved out, but it's pretty and reliable, so I'd never dream of taking it down.

The steam from our tea diminishes as time marches on. Helena has only drunk half of it anyway. I watch as she goes through a peculiar routine of chewing on her bottom lip, and then puffing air into her mouth and letting it go in tiny spurts. The look is anything but flattering. The silence between us is uncomfortable and awkward, but the one good thing – if you can call it that – is it gives me a chance to inspect my rival's face up close.

Helena Love is not an attractive woman. You could say that's just my opinion since I already bear a grudge, but I don't think anyone would disagree – well, except maybe Craig. She is a curly-haired brunette, though I imagine that at this point, much of that is to do with a bottle of dye rather than nature. Her eyelashes are huge, but her eyes are small. However, I couldn't tell you what colour they are, since she never looks up long enough for me to find out. The pores around her nose are enlarged, her jawline is weak and her neck has horizontal lines in keeping with someone who gawps down at her phone too often. When she opens her mouth, I notice she has one tooth darker in colour to the rest, but I have to admit that they're otherwise all perfect. I move my tongue along the surface of my not-so-straight teeth. Is that why Craig was attracted to her? Good teeth? What else is good about her I wonder?

'Thank you for the tea,' she says, and blows her nose on a pink, silky handkerchief. The suddenness of her words startles me, and she motions to the plate of biscuits in the middle of the table. 'If you don't mind, I won't have any shortcake. My appetite has disappeared since... since... y'know.'

I nod. Yes, I do know.

Thanks to her.

I stare at the plate where the biscuits reside. It's part of a set that Craig and I bought from Poole about ten years ago, after we sneaked off for a romantic weekend away. Rebecca moved in with my mum and dad for two days, but she wasn't pleased about it; feeling as though she was – at age thirteen – more than capable of taking care of herself. It was a perfect weekend, but apart from a handful of photos, my tea set is the only physical reminder of it. I hate myself for offering Helena tea and biscuits, and I despise myself even more for using that particular plate. Thank goodness she hasn't gone anywhere near it.

'Your house is in a great location.' She sighs. 'It must be fantastic to be close to the harbour. I haven't been down here in a long time.'

She smiles as though we're old friends, but I know better.

Husband-stealer.

Homewrecker.

'You just live up the hill. You could come to the harbour whenever you like.'

The moment the words come out of my mouth, I regret them. The hairs on the back of my neck prickle and my hands sweat. The thought of her making the harbour a familiar hangout is terrifying. This is my territory, not hers! But that didn't stop her from invading five years ago, when she came to give my husband her ultimatum...

'I know it's not far away,' she replies, 'but Craig...' Embarrassed, she stumbles over his name. 'He, err... He always complained that we'd never find a place to park beside the water and we couldn't walk because Smuggler's Steps are just not safe. In this weather they're lethal.'

Helena pushes away her cup and then heaves herself out of the chair.

'Do you mind if I use your toilet?'

Her words flummox me. Yes, I do mind! I'd rather see this woman wet her pants in the middle of the harbour than use my private space, but I can't say no when she's swaying in front of me like a newly potty-trained toddler.

'It's right at the top of the stairs.'

'Yes, I remember. Thank you.' And then she's gone.

Her words gather in the back of my brain and converge with my own paranoid thoughts.

Helena Love remembers where my bathroom is.

But she's never been inside before, so how could she know?

The question rattles around in my head and I try not to acknowledge it, because the answer is too painful. But I'm not naïve. Of course she's aware of the location of my toilet. Despite Craig's declaration that they'd never been in my home, it's something I've always worried about, and now she's confirmed it. Helena must have been in here during her affair with Craig. They must have... Oh God, they must have done it here!

All too familiar images dance in front of my eyes. I jerk up and my chair flies back and rattles off the cupboard door. I have no time to catch it before I throw up in a sink already filled with breakfast dishes.

What am I doing? Why is this woman in my house? What the hell does she want? I want to cry but I must not cry. Not until she's gone.

I wash my face and turn around, just as Helena arrives at the kitchen door.

'Are you okay, Jenny?' she asks.

She pronounces my name in that long-winded way Forrest Gump does – Jennneeeee. Why does she do that? She couldn't have heard Craig pronounce it that way, unless maybe he was making fun of me. He could have been doing a sarcastic impression.

'Jenny?'

Helena's voice invades my ears like a box of nails clattering on a tiled floor. I need to get her out of here.

'I'm afraid you need to go. I have a lot to do today – with my work.'

Despite my negative stance, Helena sits back down at the table and checks her eyeliner in a silver compact mirror.

'Craig said you're a family tree researcher. Sounds fascinating.'

'I'm a genealogist.'

'Isn't that the same thing?'

She stares at me with a genuine aura of confusion. I break her gaze by tipping the shortcake from the plate back into the biscuit tin.

'Genealogist is the proper term, but yes, I research family trees.'

'To be honest, that's why I wanted to talk to you.' Helena shuts the compact and then pushes her hair behind her ears. It's so springy that it pops back out again, but she doesn't appear to notice.

'Sorry, I'm confused. You want me to compile your tree?'

Helena raises her head just long enough to giggle and then she does the weird lip-biting, cheek-popping thing again.

'No, no it's not that. I... I wondered if you might do me a favour. Quite a big one, actually.'

I stare at Helena's long quivering eyelashes, and in that moment, I want to grab her by her bedraggled hair, drag her across the harbour and toss her in. She meets my eye and her mouth falls open, as if she can read my thoughts.

'*You* want a favour from *me*?! Don't you think I've given you enough?' I grab my cup and throw the tea down the sink. 'I'm sorry, but you have to go, before I say something I'll regret.' I wave my arm in the general direction of the front door, and Helena nods.

'I'm sorry,' she says. 'I'll leave you in peace, but I would love to see you again if you feel up to it.'

Helena Love drops her bright pink business card onto the table, and then disappears.

4

'But why though? I don't get it. Why did she want to see you?'

Rebecca stares at me through her thick, platinum-blonde fringe. Her hair is overgrown and I struggle to see her eyes. I reach over to push it out of the way and she bats my hand as though it's a wasp.

'Your fringe is too long,' I say, and my daughter tuts.

'I like it this way. And anyway, you're getting off the point. I know she must have been upset that Dad walked out – and I can't believe he left it to you to tell me, by the way – but why on earth would Helena visit you? What did she expect? Some polite ex-wife chit-chat?'

The prospect of my daughter knowing that I was soft enough to invite Helena in, and then offer tea and biscuits, makes my throat contract. I decide to keep that information to myself for as long as I'm able.

Together we amble along the lump of smooth concrete that makes up the popular Cromwey stone pier. It's a pleasant day and everyone is making the most of this unusual occurrence.

Kids with buckets stare at their captured crabs, while

amateur fishermen behave as though they're in a professional angling tournament. It brings back memories of when Rebecca and Craig used to come here almost every summer evening when she was little. Sometimes I'd go with them and watch enthralled as my daughter dangled her ten-foot line over the edge. The tantrums she threw when the crabs fell off the line were legendary. I smirk at the memory and Rebecca catches me.

'What's so funny?'

'I was remembering when you used to go fishing with your dad, and you'd throw a fit when the crabs stole the bacon and dived back into the sea.'

'I still get mad about that.' Rebecca gazes into a nearby bucket. 'We had some good times here though. I miss those days.'

'I do too. We had a happy life, for a while.'

We reach the blue-and-white bandstand, with its peeling paint and rust patches, and then beyond that are the Victorian railings that envelope the entire pier. The wind whips around our faces and below us the water swells and splashes against the cement wall that goes all the way down to the seabed.

A gigantic, pink jellyfish floats around next to the pier, ebbing along with the tide.

'Look at the size of that!' I shout. Rebecca holds up her phone and snaps a picture of it.

'So, you didn't answer my question. Why did she want to see you?'

'Who?'

'My wicked stepmother!'

'Oh. It was something about a favour. She began to tell me, but I cut her off and she left after that. To be honest, I'm kind of wishing that I had let her tell me. It's killing me not knowing.'

Rebecca scowls and stuffs her phone into her pocket. I pick

at a piece of peeling white paint, and the fracture reveals about a hundred years of different colours.

'Well, unless you want to open yourself up to a lifetime of moans and complaints, you should stay away. It was bad enough me having to put up with her whinging for the past five years, but I didn't have much option. You do though!'

'What the hell did Helena Love have to whinge about? She got what she wanted. She should have been ecstatic.'

Rebecca scratches her nose with the back of her hand.

'That woman could find something to complain about in paradise, believe me. It's just her nature, and exactly why I choose to stay away from her. As should you.'

She waggles her finger at me, but I flick her comments away.

'I'm just... I'm intrigued to know what I can do for the woman who stole my husband.'

'I can answer that for you. You can't do anything at all for her! She's no longer a part of your life – if she ever was – so just tell her to sod off.'

A young boy wanders over and thrusts his bucket under Rebecca's nose.

'Wanna see what I caught?' he asks. 'It's a gigantic crab!'

Rebecca stares into the bucket and whistles.

'Wow, you're right there,' she says. 'I used to come crabbing up here all the time and never caught anything the size of that. He's a whopper!'

The boy beams at my daughter and runs off to his grandparents. Rebecca laughs and then throws her arm around my shoulder.

'Do you know how proud I am of you, Mum?'

Rebecca's words take me by surprise. Where did this sudden change of subject come from?

'You're proud of me?'

She smiles and squeezes my arm.

'I've always been proud of you. Look at everything you've achieved since Dad left. Most women – including me, I imagine – would just give up after something like that, but not you. Look how far you've come! You've got your own successful business; you've transformed the house, and you look terrific, too. So just make sure that you don't risk everything by letting that moany bitch into your life. If Dad's decided she's not worth knowing, then the rest of us should follow. It may seem heartless, but it's also good common sense.'

I hug my daughter and tell her how much I love her. Rebecca's words have made my heart swell, and she's right; I shouldn't go anywhere near Helena again. It's just a shame, then, that while I truly want to take Rebecca's advice, I'm already planning my next move.

The Lovely Café is two doors away from Craig's garage, and in order to get there I have to head straight past the open frontage of the stark, 1930s building. The heavy stink of exhaust fumes and petrol wafts out in waves, and from inside I can hear the dull clunks and thumps of a mechanic – my ex-husband mechanic – at work. My stomach muscles contract.

Please don't let him see me...

Please don't let him see me...

Please don't...

'Jenny!'

Shit.

I turn my head and there is Craig in his oil-stained blue overalls, emerging from under the bonnet of an old Volvo. He wipes his ever-filthy hands on a grubby brown rag and throws it into the corner, where I'm sure it will linger for the rest of time.

'Hello,' I mumble, with an enthusiasm I would normally reserve for a trip to the dentist.

'How's it going?' He stuffs his hands into his overalls and leans back as though surveying a dilapidated old banger. I bob my head and try to stop myself gawping at his face, but it's hopeless. I look up and Craig's familiar green eyes stare straight back at me. His blond, messy hair is still as thick as it was when we met twenty-seven years ago, and even though it's now a little silver at the sides, he's still a good-looking bloke. In fact, it would seem that all age has done is enhanced Craig's natural charm. It's just a pity his personality doesn't match his exterior, but you can't have everything.

'I'm doing okay,' I gush, even though at this moment I feel anything but.

'I hear Rebecca was in town at the weekend,' he says. 'I was expecting her to come over but she didn't.'

'I imagine that's because she doesn't know your new address.'

Craig nods and shuffles his feet. They make a scratching noise on the filthy concrete floor.

'Right. Yeah... I'll have to get that sorted out. I did mean to text her about it, but y'know how it is – time gets away with you.'

He licks his lips and fiddles with the old earring hole in his left ear. I know he wants me to respond in kind, but I can't, because no matter what's going on in my life, I'll always find time to let my daughter know where I live. I should tell him so, but before any words come out, Craig speaks again.

'Where you off to? Wherever it is, you're all dressed up for the occasion.'

He runs his eyes up and down my body and I can't help feeling happy that he noticed. He's right though. I am dressed in my best spring coat, expensive checked trousers from Monsoon and boots that pinch my toes more than I ever care to admit. But

I love them and they add a couple of inches to my average five-foot-four height.

'You won't believe it, but I'm on my way to see your wife.'

Craig's face clouds over and he rubs his grubby hands all over his cheeks. By the time he's finished, great strides of dirt and grime are trailed all over his three-day-old stubble.I have an overwhelming desire to wipe it off, so I stuff my hands deep into my coat pockets.

'You're going to visit Helena?'

'Well, unless there are any other wives I should know about.'

He makes a snorting sound and scratches the back of his head.

'So, she's told you then? About the separation I mean.'

'Kate told me, which is how I knew you'd moved house.'

'Yeah, of course. I forgot for a second.'

The wind swirls down the promenade and an old chip wrapper whips into the garage. Craig reaches down, scrunches it up and lobs it towards the bin. It hits off the side and plops back onto the floor.

'You must think I make a habit of this.'

He stares at me as though expecting a denial, but he's out of luck.

'You mean being a dickhead? Yeah, I do.'

He plunges an imaginary dagger into his heart.

'Ouch! But I guess I deserved that. It's not what you think though.'

'I don't think anything.'

Craig smiles. He knows me too well.

'We hadn't been getting along for a while. Helena was so wrapped up in her café, it was as if I didn't exist. I'm quite surprised she even realises I've gone, to be honest.'

Jesus, this line again. His excuse for leaving me was that I spent too long on my business, and now he has the same problem with Helena. What a childish, self-centred little man. Why did I not realise this years ago?

'Didn't you say something rather similar to me, when we broke up?'

Craig's eyes dart to the floor and he sniggers through pursed lips.

'Hey, don't get me wrong, I'm not some 1950s bloke who hates his wife working. I loved that Helena had a passion – and you, too – but when it takes over your entire life...' I raise my hand to silence him, but instead of being offended, he flashes an infuriating smile. 'Listen, do you want to come in for a minute? I've just boiled the kettle.'

Craig motions towards the back room, but all I can do is glower at my ex-husband through a haze of resentment and sorrow. The last time we spoke, we were sitting opposite each other in my solicitor's office. Craig's representative was a long-haired monstrosity of a man, who tried to veto every tiny request from my side of the table. He even demanded my collection of 1980s albums, and that was long before vinyl came back into fashion. Luckily, my solicitor had a cheating husband history of her own, and was hungry to exterminate any man who dared question her. Still, that didn't stop Craig smirking whenever his lawyer managed to win even the tiniest victory. I couldn't believe that someone I had loved for over two decades could stare at me with such disdain, but in time I realised that any love he had for me, had been replaced with hatred.

And then I realised that I hated him too.

Or at least I told myself that.

And now here we are, face to face once more, and he's offering me tea in the back room. Who would have ever thought it?

I shake my head.

'I can't stop. Besides, I'm sure there's plenty of tea in there.'

I bat my head towards Helena's café, give my ex-husband something of a smile and then leave the pungent surroundings.

'So why are you going to see Helena?' he shouts from behind me.

I just keep walking.

5

I've never been inside The Lovely Café, but from the garish pink exterior I've always imagined it to resemble one of those brash, padded Valentine's cards that were popular in the 1980s.

I wasn't wrong.

The wallpaper is decorated in scarlet-and-pink stripes and there are framed pictures of teacups, teddies and carnations dangling from bright, bowed ribbons. On one side of the room there is a Victorian cake cabinet, and next to that the counter and an archway into the kitchen. It's a small space, but is crammed to bursting with tables and chairs, which would explain the abandoned pushchairs cluttering up the path outside. There is no room for such bothersome obstructions in The Lovely Café.

I hang around the doorway until Helena wafts out of the kitchen, wearing a flowery tabard over a blue, high-necked dress. Her face is caked in foundation, her eyelids are painted blue, and her lips are bright red, giving her a 1920s pout. Her dark curls are tied back into a messy bun and she's carrying two dainty china cups, balanced on delicate saucers. Despite my best efforts, we lock eyes.

'Sorry to keep you waiting... Oh, it's you.'

The painted-on grin disappears and Helena plonks the cups onto a nearby table, brushes her hands on her apron, and marches over.

'Table for one, is it?'

'Yes please.'

Helena's eyes dart around the crowded café and then she leads me over to a table in the window. It's cramped and tiny, but does have a pretty view of the prom so I can't complain.

'This okay for you?'

'It's fine, thank you.'

Helena's hand trembles as she places a menu in front of me, and I can't help but feel glee that my presence is causing her discomfort. She hesitates as though waiting for me to explain why the hell I'm in her café, but before I have a chance to say anything, a toddler throws a plastic cup onto the floor. It sends streams of orange juice up the legs of nearby tables and customers.

'Damn it,' Helena whispers and then rushes off to mop it up.

I grab the menu and study the front cover. Once again, the theme is pink and the words The Lovely Café are embossed with silver sparkles that glint in the sun. Underneath, the proprietor has written a corny welcome message in a Comic Sans font, and finished it with a gigantic, looped signature.

I manage to control my distaste by flicking straight to the desserts page. Today calls for chocolate cake.

A bloody huge slab of chocolate cake.

'So, do you know anything at all about Craig's new woman?' I ask. 'Do you even know who she is?'

Helena is perched at the table next to mine, trying to reattach a *No Smoking* sticker onto the window. The café is closed, the families have dispersed and my cup of tea went cold hours ago... and yet I continue to sit here. Why? I'm yet to work that out.

Helena considers my question, abandons the sticker and then proceeds to tear a napkin into dozens of pieces. I hate it when people do that.

'I have no idea.' She sighs. 'Okay, that's a lie – I do know that her name is Anna Wilson.' There is drawn-out silence and then, 'I'm also positive that he's living with her in the Hill View estate. You know that new development next to the butterfly farm?'

I nod.

'Yes, Kate mentioned that.'

'Ha!' Helena smirks. 'Kate's been gossiping about me, has she?'

Yes.

'No, not at all. She came around to tell me that Craig had left, but that was it.' Helena gives me a look that says she doesn't believe a word I'm saying.

'How long did it take her?'

'What?'

'To tell you. How long did it take for Kate to tell you he'd gone?'

The atmosphere changes from one of mild awkwardness, to bitter resentment – on her side, not mine.

'I don't know,' I say. 'A day maybe? Two?'

Helena makes a harrumph noise through her nostrils. I couldn't be happier that this revelation has made her uncomfortable. It's the very least she deserves after what she's done to me. I use my spoon to tap a little tune onto the side of my cup, and Helena visibly prickles.

'Anyway,' I say, 'I'm surprised Craig has moved to that side of town. He wouldn't even get a beach hut up that end, because he said it was too far from the action. Though what action he was talking about is debatable. Cromwey isn't renowned for its high life.'

Helena rubs a crumb off her chin and my eyes are drawn to her blue polished nails. How old does this woman think she is? Sixteen?

'I was surprised he'd go there,' she says, 'but I followed him, so I know he lives there.'

'You followed him?'

Helena shrugs and sweeps some abandoned sugar into the palm of her hand, before scattering it all over the floor. I hope she's inundated with ants in the morning.

'Too right I followed him,' she says. 'How else could I find out what he's up to?' Helena's phone rings to the sound of 'Kiss' by Tom Jones. She takes one look at the screen, presses a button to silence the tune and then places it face down on the table.

'Anyway, after he'd told me we were over, Craig said he'd be back to pick up the rest of his stuff later in the day. I told him I'd be out, but instead I waited in a neighbour's house. When he came out of our – my – house with all his boxes, I jumped into my car and went after him.'

'Didn't he see you?'

I brush some imaginary fluff from my trousers in an effort to seem unconcerned.

'No. I was three cars behind him and he had no idea. I was able to keep up with him pretty well, but when he turned into the new estate, an old woman with a yappy Yorkshire terrier stepped right out in front of me. I had to do an emergency stop, and then I lost him.'

'So, where do I fit into all this?' I'm feigning impatience but inside I'm enthralled.

'I... I just wondered... I just wondered if you knew anything about this new relationship. I need to know who the woman is and why my husband left me for her.'

She emphasises the word *my*, and the word grates against my teeth. I resist the urge to tell her that Craig was mine first, because that would be childish, but he was and that will never change, regardless of how many wives he ends up with.

'Helena, I'm not being funny but Craig works about thirty feet away – if that. He's there right now and I've seen him stare over here at least a dozen times since I arrived! Why don't you ask him yourself?'

Helena pulls the elastic from her hair and her curls tumble down to her shoulders. She offers a bemused smile.

'You think he'd tell me the truth? Doubtful! I only got her name out of him because I threatened to slash his tyres, and believe me I would have done it, too!'

I chuckle. Craig has been a tyre snob for as long as I've known him and always buys the most expensive ones he can find. Threatening to destroy them would have pushed him over the edge, and I can't help but be happy that Helena did that – if only because it would have made Craig dislike her even more than he did already. Helena straightens up, and rubs her shoulders as though she's fought an epic battle. Poor, misguided soul.

'Well, you've got more spunk than me,' I exclaim. 'I wouldn't even dare touch his clothes, never mind his car. So, do you think he's telling the truth? About her name, I mean.'

Helena shrugs and her arms collapse onto the table, defeated again.

'I'm not sure. If someone was holding a knife to my tyres, I'd make up a name too. But that's where you come in. That's the favour I wanted to ask you about the other day.'

I tilt my body towards Helena and lean my head in my hands.

'That's why I'm here,' I say. 'But to be honest, I'm not sure what I can do to help you. I don't know anything about his relationship with this new woman, but I can tell you this – if you're hoping he might come back to you, forget it. I've known Craig for over half my life and if there's one thing I've learned, it's that he never, ever looks back. *Keep moving forward* is his motto and I've never known him to break it.'

Helena is crushed, and tears spring to her eyes. I'm thrilled that I've made her feel this way. I've given enough of my own tears in the past, and now I'm passing the baton. Helena leans forward, places her hand on mine and peers at me. I grimace. This woman – the one who shared a bed with my husband while he still belonged to me – is clinging onto my hand. It's clammy and cold and if my tea was still hot, I'd pour the liquid all over it. I yank away and Helena's body jerks. This motion does not, however, stop her from whining.

'I'd like you to find out everything you can about Anna Wilson. I'll even pay you for your trouble!' Helena reaches into the front of her tabard, and brings out a wad of notes. 'Here! I have 200 pounds. Is that enough? How much do others pay you for a family tree? I'll pay the going rate, I promise!'

She thrusts the notes into my hand and I recoil as if they're on fire. I don't understand what's going on.

'You want... You want me to compile Anna's family tree?'

'No! I want to know what kind of person she is. What she does for a living, who her friends are, and all that stuff. I tried stalking her on Facebook but I couldn't find a damn thing. Since you're a professional researcher, I thought maybe you'd have more luck than me.'

Helena glowers at me through wounded eyes. I know that look. I've studied it in my own mirror, and it fucking sucks. No woman should have to go through it. Well, unless that woman is the skank who stole your husband. Then maybe she could do with a bit of grief in her life.

And for the rest of her life.

'I'm not sure if it's appropriate for me to research that stuff, if I'm honest.'

Helena's face hardens and she bites her lip.

'Please,' she begs, 'I need your help. When I close my eyes, all I can see are their naked, contorted bodies. I have no idea what this woman looks like, and yet I can see every part of her. The vision keeps me awake for the whole night.'

I nod my head.

'Welcome to the club,' I say. 'You're going to love it here.'

The house is silent. I'm in my study, putting the finishing touches to a client's family tree. Despite claims to the contrary, there are no royal ancestors once again. However, there is a shop girl who was once arrested for trying to scramble over the railings of Buckingham Palace. Maybe that's kind of the same thing.

Tomorrow, the completed tree will be ready to send, but for now I save the file, switch off the laptop and head to the living room. Outside my front window there's a woman feeding a gull from a paper bag, while standing next to a signpost that tells tourists not to do that. I ponder knocking on the window, but I decide against it. Last time I told someone off for feeding the wildlife, she gave me a right mouthful.

The tourist empties the crumbs out of the bag, and the wind sends them into the harbour. The bird squawks in frustrated rage and flies away, causing the woman to cover her head from its flapping wings.

My phone pings, and I'm surprised to discover that it's Helena.

> Thanks a million for meeting me this afternoon. I know it must have been hard for you and I appreciate you taking the time. If you can find out anything at all about the new woman, I'd be grateful. I'll let you know if I find out anything myself. Helena.

My stomach flips. How does she know how hard it must have been for me to meet her? Is she being patronising, or sarcastic? It's hard to know at this point.

I read the message twice and beg myself to ignore it, but it's just not in my nature. So, in the end I hit reply.

> I'm not sure I'll be able to find out anything, but if I do, I'll let you know.

I hate myself for being cordial, but before I regret hitting the send button, another text arrives.

> I'm so happy we met up. Let's do it again and next time you must try some of my home-made strawberry cake. It's baked by a fabulous old lady who lives in the harbour. Mrs Jenkins. Do you know her? :) Helena. Xx

No, I do not know Mrs Jenkins, and if she has anything to do with Helena, I hope I never do. Also, what's with the kisses? In fact, two kisses and a smiley face? This woman is an infuriating twat. What the hell did Craig ever see in her?

I guess it's best I don't know.

6

It's the day after my café meeting with Helena, and Kate and I are having breakfast at a new American diner on the seafront. It's had terrible write-ups in the *Cromwey Chronicle*, because paranoid locals fear it's trying to steal business from our classic seaside eateries. However, the pancakes here are wonderful, and as long as the local fish and chip shop doesn't serve them, I see nothing wrong with giving the diner my business.

As we ponder a plate of waffles to go with our pancakes, I decide to mention my conversations with Helena. I do it in such a matter-of-fact way that even I believe it's nothing to be concerned about, but Kate doesn't fall for it. She lowers her menu, moves her reading glasses down onto the tip of her nose, and peers at me over the top of them.

'I must need my ears tested.' She frowns. 'I could swear you just said you'd met Helena.'

'Actually, if you want to be accurate, I said that we'd met twice.'

I avoid eye contact, though I am aware of Kate staring at me. I pretend to study the drinks menu but I can still feel her gaze. I throw the paper onto the table.

'What?'

Kate takes off her glasses and balances them on top of her head.

'Jenny, the last time I saw you, you were weeping into your tablecloth and blowing snot all over the kitchen! You were a fucking wreck and all because of that woman!'

I waggle my finger at her.

'And Craig! Don't forget his part in all this! But yes, I agree that I was upset.'

'Distraught.'

'Okay, I know I was distraught, but for good reason! You'd just shared some bloody shocking news, and it brought back hurtful memories. But I'm okay now. I'm back to living in the present, like all those self-help books taught me to do.'

I smile, but Kate doesn't return the gesture. Instead, she leans back into her chair and doesn't utter a word. For the next four minutes I read the menu and admire the framed photos of Elvis on the wall, but in the end the atmosphere becomes unbearable and I end up telling her the entire story, just to break the silence.

'She threw money at me, Kate! That's how much she wants my help.'

My friend hugs herself and scowls. She seems to do this whenever I say anything she disapproves of, and it drives me nuts.

'She doesn't need your help,' Kate says. 'She needs your attention. She's the master of attention-seeking.'

'Well you certainly gave her enough, when she was with Craig.'

The fact that my best friend stayed close to my husband and his new woman has always been a bone of contention. Kate ignores my sarcasm and lets out a long breath.

'And are you going to help?'

I shrug and swat at a fly on my elbow.

'I haven't thought about it.'

Kate raises her overly-plucked eyebrows. It makes her look like a disgruntled owl.

'Let it be known that I think you're playing with fire! This woman helped break up your marriage and sent you into a spiralling depression for months – maybe even years! You need to step away from the situation now, Jenny. There's no way you could help her and keep your sanity intact. I'm telling you, no good can come from any of this.'

'Thank you, *Mother*,' I reply. 'I'll be sure to keep that in mind.'

For the past two days, I've replayed Kate's words like a record on repeat and I agree with at least some of what she said. But here's the thing. I research people for a living, it's what I do. Any of my clients could be husband-stealing whores and I'd never know it (well, except if I did some research into their private business, which I don't). Maybe – just maybe – there is no difference between a regular client and Helena.

Maybe I could help her.

Maybe I *should* help her.

What could go wrong with a tiny bit of research? Whoever died from that?

Questions, dilemmas and answers swarm through my head while I'm washing up, and when my phone vibrates on the counter, I get such a fright that I drop the teapot into the sink. Bubbles and drops of water shoot all over my blouse and I grab the tea towel to mop up the mess. The phone continues to buzz and when I pick it up, I discover that the caller is Helena.

'Hi, Jenny, it's me.' Her voice is urgent, as though if she

doesn't say the words right now, they'll never come at all. 'Listen, I know you're busy and I'm the last person you'd want to meet up with again, but I was wondering if you'd like to come over for a cup of tea sometime...'

Tea? She wants me to go to her house – their house – for a cup of tea? Why would she want that? I hold onto the sink for support.

'Jenny? Are you still there?'

I force myself back into the room.

'Yes, sorry I got distracted for a second.'

'That's okay. Look, I thought maybe you might like to come over, firstly to discuss the research job but also because there are some things over here that belong to Rebecca. I know she often comes into town to see you, so wanted to pass them along. I'd hate her to think she's lost her stuff.'

I'm floored. My mouth feels numb and when I open it, I wonder if I'm still capable of speech. I'm relieved when the words tumble out.

'You have things that belong to Rebecca?'

'Yes, just overnight things. Y'know, like toiletry bag, pyjamas, etc. She keeps them here for when she stays the night, only I doubt that she'll be coming back now that her dad is gone, so...'

'Rebecca has stayed at your house?'

A pause.

'Yes, many times. She did tell you, didn't she?'

'No, she didn't.'

Another pause, and then a long sigh. My hand won't stop shaking, which is ludicrous because I know Rebecca used to visit her dad. But I didn't imagine that she'd stayed over, so that's kind of a big deal to me.

'Shit.' Helena coughs and I hold the phone away from my ear. 'Well, when I say that she stayed many times, I mean occasionally. She'd bunk here if she'd had a drink, or missed the last train home or whatever. She didn't visit a lot, but she always kept a few things here so that she didn't have to worry about bringing stuff with her.'

'I see.' It's funny that on questioning her, my daughter's visits went from many times to occasionally, and then not a lot. I'm confused. Rebecca always told me she didn't know Helena well, and that she just popped over for dinner every now and then. According to her, any 'friendship' they shared was to keep the peace between herself and her father, but now I find that she's stayed in their house while I am alone, not a mile away. I don't even know if this is something I'm allowed to be bothered by, since it's none of my business what my adult daughter does. But still, this knowledge hurts me in a deep, unexpected way. I try to sound casual, but it's difficult.

'I'll come over and pick up her belongings tomorrow,' I say through a forced smile.

Helena lets out a breath. She's relieved by my tone, but I wish she wasn't.

'That's great. Look, I'm sorry that you didn't know Rebecca stayed here. If I'd known she was keeping the information from you, I'd have made sure she told you.'

I nod into the phone; wish my caller a good afternoon, and then hang up.

I am certain that as soon as I finish my call with Helena, she'll contact my daughter. I pour myself a cup of coffee and then watch my phone for Rebecca's number. Sure enough, nine minutes and twenty-three seconds later, my handset buzzes and I swipe to answer.

'Mum, it's me! How are you?'

'I'm doing okay, thanks. You?'

I can sense my daughter squirming on the other end of the phone. She knows I've been told.

'Mum, I...'

I'll make it easy for her.

'Why didn't you tell me you've slept at Helena's house? Why did I have to find out from her of all people?'

Rebecca sniffs and then blows her nose. I run my finger over a flower embossed on a table mat, while she gets herself back together.

'I was going to tell you, but in the beginning, you were always upset about Dad. I mean, you were heartbroken, weren't you? And it felt awful to bring him up when there was no need to. Then as time went on, I just kind of decided that it would be best for you if I kept quiet.'

My finger comes to a standstill, and I feel guilty for causing my daughter to feel that way.

'Look,' I say, 'whatever I think about him, your dad will always be your dad. You're entitled to go and visit whenever you like. It hurts that you lied to me, that's all.'

'When did I lie to you?'

There's a trembling in Rebecca's voice that indicates a genuine aura of confusion.

'You told me on numerous occasions that you had never stayed over there. In fact, I believe you said that you couldn't think of anywhere worse, that their house was a dump and Helena never cleaned.'

'I might have exaggerated a little,' Rebecca says, 'but she doesn't do much housework, I promise. And I did hate staying there. I only ever went to see Dad.'

I can't be angry at Rebecca for long. No matter how old she is, she'll always be that little tot who sat on my knee and read *Goodnight Moon* at the top of her voice.

'It's okay,' I say. 'Don't worry about it. I'm going over to collect your things from there tomorrow, and I'll return them when I next see you.'

'Great, thanks a million. And that reminds me, I was going to come over the weekend after next, if that's okay with you?'

I gaze over at a photo of Rebecca aged six, clutching a *Superstar of the Week* certificate that she earned at infant school.

'It's more than okay – it's lovely. I'll see you then. That's if you aren't holidaying with your dad and his new woman.'

I'm joking, but there's a slight hint of truth in my words.

'Mum! I don't even know where they live for one thing, and for another... for another, I wouldn't want to share a house with him and his... his... whatever she is. I'm too pissed off with him right now.'

I grunt. 'I can't argue with that. I'm sure everyone feels the same way.'

7

Helena Love's house is not so dirty that it needs a visit from environmental health, but no one can deny it's messy and in need of a good clear-out. The pastel-blue sofa is deep and comfortable-looking, but on one end there is a crumpled pile of magazines and books, of various shapes and sizes. I take a closer look and see at least three self-help books piled on top of the magazines, while a copy of *The Complete Works of Shakespeare* balances on the arm. I'm sure it's the same as the one I've got at home; I recognise the gold edging on the pages. The pile of stuff makes the room look even grubbier than it is already.

On the mantelpiece there are smiling photos of Craig and Helena in gold frames, and scattered around there are at least three pictures of Rebecca. I pick one up. There's my daughter, posing in front of a Christmas tree in this very living room. The tree is silver with pink-and-white baubles hanging from the branches. I always wanted a silver tree, but Craig assured me they were tacky – common even – and would never want one in the house. Another photo shows Craig, Helena and Rebecca standing at the gates to Cromwey Castle. The picture makes them seem like the perfect family, and I'm surprised that it – and others like it – are still on display. As soon as Craig moved out, our photos were thrown into the deepest trunk and forgotten about. Kind of.

'I'm glad you could come,' Helena gushes, as she carries through a tray of tea and Battenberg cake. 'I made yours with a little milk but no sugar, because I remembered that's how you took it in my café.'

How observant of her.

Helena lays the tray onto her coffee table and hands me a mug with an elephant on the side. I hope that's not a dig.

'I see you've been looking at the photos. No doubt you think I'm crazy for still having them out, but I haven't had time to put them away yet. Besides, I like to see pictures of Rebecca around the place. It reminds me of happy days. Please, sit down.'

I place the photo back where I found it and then find a space to sit, as far away from the book pile as I can. Helena notices me swerve, and her face flushes.

'Just ignore the books. I've been reading to take my mind off that bastard. Maybe it will inspire me to write my own novel, one of these days.'

She plonks herself down onto the armchair opposite me, and grabs a slice of cake. For someone with such a slim figure, she has a sweet tooth.

As I contemplate a sip of tea, a thought enters my mind that it could be poisoned. Maybe that's what she'll write a book about: how to murder the first wife in five easy steps.

Helena stares at me while I pretend to admire the surroundings.

'Y'know, I hope I didn't get Rebecca into trouble yesterday. I was sure she had told you about her visits.'

'No, we're fine. Rebecca and I rarely fall out to be honest.'

I gulp my tea, but it's far too bitter and strong for my liking. I hide my distaste with a mouthful of Battenberg.

'That's good. I'd hate you to argue because of me.' I nod and then my attention is drawn to the pattern of the wallpaper. It is peppermint-coloured, with tiny birds and butterflies all over it. Craig would have hated this paper; it's not to his taste at all.

'Have you heard from him?' Helena gawps at me through enquiring eyes and for a second, I wonder who she's talking about.

'Sorry?'

'Have you heard from Craig? Or as I like to call him, that miserable, waste-of-space prick!' A flicker of rage flashes across Helena's face, though she disguises it as a joke. 'I call him that on good days.'

'I can imagine. It's nothing compared to what I call him, but then I've had a lot more time to practice.' I smile and Helena grins back, though it's half-hearted and awkward. 'To be honest, I haven't heard a word since I saw him in the garage, and I don't expect to. If anyone hears from Craig, it'll be Rebecca. Or you – since you work right next to him.'

'That counts for nothing, believe me.' Helena runs her fingers through her hair, and her curls fall back into place. If I did that, my scraggy mane would do nothing but stick up in the air. 'I see him hovering at the door of the garage and even though I've waved over a few times, not once has he ever acknowledged me. Not once! I shared his bed for five years, but now he can't even spare me a second look!'

Helena wipes a tear from her eye with the back of her hand. I place my cup on the table, then search in my bag for a tissue. My hand falls on a scrunched-up napkin that I used to mop up some random liquid from a dirty café table, and I offer it to my new 'friend'.

'Here, it's a new one I promise.'

'That's very kind. Thank you.' She grabs the tissue and dabs her eyes. 'Please excuse me, I just need to use the toilet. I'll be right back.'

I nod and Helena disappears into the hall, and then up to the first floor. I use the time to imagine what it must have been like when Craig lived here, such a short time ago. Did he sit on this sofa and read his car magazines, like he used to do in our house? Did he make her cups of tea and massage her feet? This room is full of memories of him, and yet I can't imagine him living here. The décor, the furniture, the artwork – even the thick smell of blossom air freshener – none of them say Craig to me. I bet he never felt comfortable in this house – or maybe that's just wishful thinking on my part.

I gaze into the hall and my eyes fall onto an item that transports me straight back to 2014. It's a yellow hooded jacket; the same one Helena wore when she turned up on my doorstep, and persuaded my husband to leave me on our twentieth anniversary. My chest contracts and all the past agony hits me once again. How could she do that to a human being? To another woman? I've been through it in my head, time after time and I'm still no closer to knowing how she could be so cruel.

I tiptoe over to the coat hook and feel the material. It is cheap and itchy. There are huge blue buttons running down the front, and a zipped pocket on either side. It's weird to imagine that this coat was witness to such a catastrophic occasion in my life. I wonder what else it was witness to.

Before I can stop myself, I reach for the top button, and yank it as hard as I can. It comes off and leaves a thick, yellow thread behind. I shove the button into my pocket and dart back to the living room. I doubt Helena will ever be able to find an exact replacement. What a shame. What a bloody shame.

As I sit on the sofa, fingering the button and waiting for Helena to come back downstairs, I make the decision to help investigate Craig and Anna's relationship. Not out of sympathy, not out of helpfulness, and not in any kind of caring capacity. No. I decide to help Helena Love because I want to, and because by keeping her close to me, I can play with her life in ways she can't even begin to imagine.

This will be fun.

8

'Can I help you with anything?'

A young lad wearing a badge with Sarrington's Stationers emblazoned on the front, smiles at me from behind the counter. It's quiet in here today, and I suspect he's only asking because he has nothing better to do. Normally I could be in here for a good thirty minutes before anyone speaks to me.

'It's okay, thanks,' I say. 'I'm just looking for a new notebook.'

'We've certainly got a lot to choose from.' He grins. 'I'm Andrew, by the way. If you need any help at all, just give me a shout.'

'Thanks, Andrew.' I nod, and then I return to staring at the display in front of me.

The lad is right – there are loads of notebooks in here, ranging from tiny paperbacks for your back pocket, right through to A4, spiral-bound hardbacks. I need something between the two – small enough to hide on my bookshelf, but big enough that I can write down whatever comes into my mind.

I pick up a blue, A5-sized book, with tiny owls embroidered on the front. It's pretty, but with a twenty-pound price tag, I can live without it. An old woman appears next to me, and chooses a thick yellow journal with a daffodil printed on the cover.

'Whenever I start one of these, I always wonder if I'll live to get to the end of it.' She laughs. 'I'll be eighty-six in June, and I've gone through four of these books in the past three years! They're perfect for keeping track of all my birthdays and shopping lists!'

I nod and make noises suitable for a random stationery shop encounter. The elderly lady trundles off to the counter, and I take her lead and pick up a journal of my own. It's turquoise in colour, with white bluebells that snake their way up the cover. I open it up and see pages of blank columns, lines and boxes. The old lady is right, it is perfect... perfect for jotting down the many different ways I can create havoc in Helena Love's life!

On my way home from the stationery shop, I head to the supermarket for some bread. I normally try to give my business to my local bakery, but since I'm at this side of town, one loaf of bread won't do any harm.

The breeze is warm against my face, and only adds to my good mood. Since Helena's heart has been broken into pieces, my own seems to have mended somewhat. Oh, of course it had been on the right trajectory for the past two – maybe three – years, but it wasn't until Helena's crumpled soul arrived on my doorstep that I noticed just how much I had recovered. It feels good to recognise my recuperation, especially in the face of Helena's utter turmoil. My stomach tingles at the thought of her current misery. I guess that's what you get when you steal another woman's husband. No good can ever come from it, and I'm ecstatic about that.

I push past the dozens of trolleys piled into the plastic enclosure, and just as I'm wondering what I'll write in my notebook this evening; there she is.

Helena Love.

My husband's ex locks the door of her electric-blue Audi, and then strolls towards Tesco carrying two gigantic shopping bags. She must be stocking up on comfort food or something. I know that feeling only too well.

I stop walking and pretend to fiddle with the buttons on my coat, so that I don't catch up with her. She walks so slowly that I wonder if I'm going to stand here for the duration, but finally I see her flouncy brown hair disappearing into the store. A smile plays on my lips. There's no doubt about it, I'll have to body-swerve her in the supermarket, but that doesn't mean I'll have to avoid her brand-new car. I head straight for the vehicle, and make sure the buckle on my handbag is at a perfect thigh-high position. Gosh, she's parked so near to the next car that I have no option but to pass as close as I can, and as my bag makes contact with the paintwork, it makes a satisfying zipping sound, from the back straight through to the front.

Oh dear, it'll cost a fortune to sort out the paintwork for that scratch, especially as she can hardly ask Craig to fix it for her. Poor Helena. Luck just doesn't seem to be on her side recently.

While playing with Helena's feelings is my ultimate concern, I did promise I'd look into Anna Wilson's life, so I start in the usual way – by attempting to stalk her Facebook page. I find dozens of women with her name, but none living in Cromwey or even nearby. Instagram and Twitter are no good either, and Pinterest has so many I lose count.

With such a common name, and with no idea about age or appearance, I have no choice but to accept that social media is a losing game. I therefore decide to turn my attention to newspaper reports, but that just flags up hundreds of articles about everything from netball results, to car adverts. I need more information, and that means another meeting with Helena.

For that I'll need reinforcements. I grab my makeup bag, down a cup of espresso and ready myself to face her.

~

'Just so we're on the same page... You're sure that you know nothing whatsoever about Anna Wilson, apart from her name?'

Helena's café is closed, and we're huddled in the corner, tea in hand; comparing notes – or lack thereof – in an attempt to move forward with the research. So far all I've discovered is that Helena serves an outstanding chocolate gateau, but I keep that information to myself.

'That's it! That's all I know about the woman who stole my husband. I don't think that's fair, do you? I was with him for five years. I deserve an explanation at the very least!'

I gawp at her through narrowed eyes and try not to rip her hair out, right here in the café.

'I'm not being funny, Helena, but I'm pretty sure you weren't lecturing Craig about fairness when he left me for you!'

She shuffles in her seat, bites the skin around her thumbnail, but doesn't answer my comment. I can't help but notice that her usually perfect nails are chipped and ragged. I hope that's on account of all the stress she's faced this past week.

'Anyway,' I continue, 'given Craig's reputation, I can tell you that whoever the woman is, you can guarantee she's younger than you. So be prepared!'

Helena touches her neck. There is a trail of unblended foundation around her jawline, and I wonder if she has any idea it's there.

'If that's true,' she says, 'he'll soon be dating women young enough to be his daughter.'

'That's a disgusting thought.' I help myself to another slice of cake. No wonder Craig goes for younger women – they've had less time to pile on the pounds. 'Look, I'll do my best to find out anything I can about Anna Wilson, but with nothing concrete to go on, it's going to be an uphill struggle. Unless...'

'Unless what?'

'Look, I know this is going to be an unpopular choice, but maybe I could just go straight to Craig and ask him.'

Helena's torso clenches, and her head rocks from side to side in tiny, rapid movements. Good, I've hit a nerve!

'No! Then he'll say I put you up to it – which I did, but that's not the point. If you have to consider asking him, keep him as a last resort. Please?'

'Okay, but listen, I need to know something before we start. Are you sure you want to find out more about this Anna woman? And if so, why is it important to you?'

Helena inhales through flared, aggravated nostrils and her back is as straight as an ironing board.

'Yes, I'm sure! And why? Because my husband has moved in with her, that's why! I need to know what she has that I don't... what she looks like, what she weighs, what her hobbies are, what her favourite sexual position is! I need to know *everything*!'

I gaze at the ceiling and notice that the lights are in the shape of teeny white roses. I'm interested to know where you'd buy such items, but now isn't the time to ask.

'That sounds macabre,' I say. 'When Craig moved out, I wanted to know nothing about you at all. You could have been a wrinkled troll, living in a dead tree for all I cared!'

A lump forms in the back of my throat, and I fight to keep it there. I scratch my head and then cross my arms; protecting myself from Helena's intense stare.

'I'm not like you then.'

'No, you're certainly not.'

Helena pushes herself as far back in her chair as she can.

'If this woman is better than me, then I want to know why!'

My face flushes and I can feel the warmth spreading down into my neck and behind my ears. I adjust my blouse and stare down my nose at the pathetic woman in front of me.

'Look, just because he deserted you for someone else, doesn't mean she's better,' I snap. 'Often, the other woman is a down-graded version of the original wife. Look at all those celebrities who leave their model wives for the nanny, for instance. The nannies are always a poor man's version, and real life is no different.'

'You mean me.' The bedraggled expression on Helena's face is perfect, and despite the awkwardness of the moment, I make sure my eyes remain trained on hers.

'Now, I didn't say that, did I?'

'You didn't have to.' She sniffs. 'I know that it was implied.'

Although the harbour makes up a small part of Cromwey, we have far more going on than people first realise. Aside from the obvious fishing boats and yachts, we're proud to house six restaurants, several pubs, a greengrocer, gift shops, museum, hairdresser and even a gym. If not for the fact that I have to go to the supermarket once a week, I would never leave my beautiful space; just lock out the world and potter around my little blue house forever.

Today, there is a craft fair going on at the harbourside and the place is full of holidaymakers fighting their way to buy raffle tickets, hand-knitted teddy bears and patchwork handbags. The road is closed off and there is a large gazebo standing at the entrance, filled with members of the Harbour Committee. Next to this, a car horn beeps and the owner demands to know when the road will reopen.

'I've got a meeting at the pub,' he says. 'I can't miss it.'

Nobody takes the slightest interest in his dilemma, so the man slams his car into reverse and screeches backwards towards the bridge. He misses a lorry by inches and then speeds away.

As much as I hate an angry man, I can't help but feel a little empathy. I know these harbour events are essential for our tourist industry, but sometimes I wish I could get to my front door without being crushed or pawed by a bunch of curious strangers.

'Have you paid your entrance fee?' An enthusiastic pensioner rattles his tin in my face. It's Stan, chief treasurer from the Harbour Committee. He gives me a wide smile, revealing brown, nicotine-stained teeth, complete with several absent incisors.

'For goodness' sake, Stan, it's me, Jenny. I live here, remember?'

He gives a little bow, and removes his cap. His bald patch stares at me for a moment, before he comes back to an upright position.

'I know that, my dear, but every penny helps as they say. One pound from every visitor will ensure we can run these events in the future.'

Stan's breath is rancid, and I hold a tissue to my nostrils to pretend I'm wiping my nose.

'I'm not a visitor, I'm a resident, and what if I don't want them to run in the future?'

Stan rattles his tin at a young couple with a pram, and they stick in two shiny pound coins without hesitation.

'You know you'd miss these days if they were cancelled. Besides, there are all kinds of interesting stalls to visit.' He studies my yellow, seen-better-days T-shirt and grins. 'Maybe you might like to pick up a new cardigan from the stall over there? They're pretty, you know. Very fashionable.'

I stare at Stan, wearing his brown high-waist slacks and his mustard anorak, and wonder what he could know about fashion.

'Okay, if I give you a pound, will you stop criticising my clothes and let me get to my front door?'

'Absolutely, my love.'

'Great.'

I slide a pound out of my pocket and pop it into the tin. It makes a dull, clanging sound as it finds the other coins inside.

'Thank you, Jenny. You'll be rewarded in heaven!'

'I better be!'

I wander through the gazebo, but before I make it to the other side, Stan taps me on the shoulder.

'I almost forgot to say. I saw that poor woman yesterday. Awful business, it is!'

'What poor woman?'

Stan thrusts his tin at a tourist, and waits for her to find a pound in the bottom of her pocket.

'That lady your Craig ran off with. Helen, wasn't it? I heard he's chucked her and gone off with another one! What a cad! She's in bits about it! She was telling me and Bill, the window cleaner, all about how he packed up and left, just like he did with you! I don't know how these men live with themselves, I really don't. Terrible business. Unsavoury as my Doris would have said!'

The wind stings my cheeks and prickles my ears. Why the hell is Helena whinging to Stan and Bill about her tormented love life? She has no pride whatsoever. A crowd of Girl Guides gather around Stan, waving coins in the air. I take the opportunity to leave, because the idea of talking about how awful it is that Craig broke Helena's heart is too much to bear.

I fight my way through the impulse shoppers arguing over brooches and cheap necklaces, and then I reach my gate. I am frustrated to see that somebody has abandoned a beer can on my wall. As I pick it up and scan around for the perpetrator, I'm even more concerned to see my ninety-year-old neighbour – Mrs Moore – down on her hands and knees, retrieving litter from her own garden, and throwing it nonchalantly into mine. I cough and she glances up, chip wrapper in hand.

'Good afternoon, Jenny. I didn't see you there.'

'Evidently. Would you like me to take that rubbish and pop it into my flower bed for you? It'll save you the bother.'

Mrs Moore sighs, places one hand on the wall and heaves herself up with a series of groans and yelps. She's wearing a navy sweater that is frayed around the bottom, and a pair of ski pants that are baggy at the knees. She must have owned both since the 1990s. Her hair is so greasy that it sticks to the top of her head, but her face is made up with crimson lipstick and a slick of blue eye shadow.

'Could you get rid of this, dear? My bin is all the way round the back and by the time I get around there, it'll be dark.'

She thrusts the chip paper into my hand. The woman has a lot of nerve, I'll give her that. I bend down to pick up the mess she's thrown into my tiny garden, but even the sight of that doesn't make her embarrassed. Instead, she retrieves a broom that's leaning against her front door, and then motions towards the harbour.

'It was nice to see Craig today,' she mutters.

I stop my litter-picking and give her my full attention.

'You saw my ex-husband?'

'Yes. He was buying a handbag from that stall over there.' Mrs

Moore points towards a red-headed woman wearing a patchwork jacket and crumpled velvet hat. 'He was a little paunchier than how I remember him, but he still looked the same. He was with a young woman. She wasn't old enough to be the one he left you for, and I thought it must be your daughter. But then she turned and I saw she had a totally different face, so he must have got himself another new woman! Strange girl, she was. Kind of wispy and drippy. She reminded me of a little anaemic sparrow. Yes, that's what she was like... an anaemic sparrow. Do you know what I mean?'

I have no idea, but I nod anyway, relieved that Mrs Moore has finally stopped yapping. So, Craig was here with Anna Wilson, was he? And on my turf of all places! I'm about to inform Mrs Moore that I'm not interested in my ex-husband's love life, but then it occurs to me that her nosiness might be of some use.

'Did he speak to you?' I ask, pretending not to care.

'No, he just bought the bag and then they went up towards the church, hand in hand. I couldn't see them after that because of all the crowds. He did gaze over here when he left the stall, but he didn't wave or say hello. I thought that was rather rude to be honest with you, and I hope you'll tell him so.'

'I try to keep out of his way nowadays. I'm afraid you'll have to tell him yourself.'

Mrs Moore flashes me a phoney, sympathetic grin and pats my arm with her gnarled and veiny hand.

'Now you mustn't worry, dear. You'll find someone else one of these days. If serial killers in prison can find partners, I'm sure there's hope for you, too.'

9

The flamboyant owner of the Itsy-Bitsy Seaside Stall scowls at me. She has a thick, bleached moustache on her top lip, and I try my hardest not to stare at it.

She sniffs, and her nostrils flare. 'I'm sorry, miss, but I simply cannot share details of my customers with you. Besides, I sold fourteen handbags this afternoon. I'm not sure I can even remember the couple you're referring to.' She dismisses me with a shake of her head; unhooks three purses from the top of the stall and stuffs them into a clear, plastic bag. It's 4.45pm and most of the tourists have gone, but still a few mingle around, grasping for that elusive, last-minute bargain.

'How much for the iPad cover?'

Mrs Itsy-Bitsy glances over at a spiky-haired teenage boy rummaging through the box of assorted covers.

'Full size is fifteen pounds. Mini is ten pounds.' The young-ster turns it over, holds it up, and inspects a tiny random thread.

'I'll leave it,' he says, and wanders off. The stallholder whisks the box away before the lad can change his mind. I realise that I'm not going to get any information from this woman, but I have to try. I pick up a cream purse that is in the shape of an envelope. It's thirty pounds, which is pretty extortionate, but if it helps my cause it'll be worth it.

'I'll take this, please.'

Mrs Itsy-Bitsy's stern face breaks into a smile.

'Good choice. They're from a London designer. I order them special.' She reaches for the purse, turns over the ticket and writes the stock number into a notebook. I hand over the money and she drops my purchase into a paper bag. I reach over to retrieve it but the woman holds it to her chest in ransom.

'Before you go, would you like to go on my mailing list? You'll receive lots of special offers and event dates.'

'No thanks, I'm not... I'm not... Oh hang on, maybe that's where you can help. Perhaps the woman I'm looking for signed onto the list. Could you check that for me?'

Mrs Itsy-Bitsy gasps and a nearby woman twists round to see what the fuss is about. I imagine I'd have caused less of a stir if I'd demanded she hand over her entire stall.

'Absolutely not! First of all, it would be against the law to divulge such information, not to mention that it is unethical and morally wrong! No! Your request is against everything I've been taught as a stallholder.'

I'm shocked that there is such a thing as being taught morals for a market stall, but as she glowers at me in disgust, I know I'll never get anything from her. I'm about to cower away, but then an unexpected miracle occurs, when the spiky-haired teenager appears again.

'Hey, I'd like that iPad cover. The one I was looking at a minute ago.'

Mrs Itsy-Bitsy groans, throws my new purse at me, picks up a box from behind the stall and shoves it under the young lad's nose.

'First of all, my name isn't Hey. And didn't your mother ever teach you to say please?'

The boy nods.

'Sorry... I mean, thank you... I mean... Can I have it please?'

Mrs Itsy-Bitsy rummages through the iPad box and meanwhile her order book resides on her chair like a gigantic button that says *Do Not Press! Do NOT Press!!* I've never been one for abiding by the rules, so I pick up the book and thumb through the pages... May 24... May 25... Here it is, May 26... My finger glides down the page but there's no sign of Anna Wilson's name. Instead, I'm faced with a handful of random monikers. Laura Hamilton, Joanne Smith, Lorraine Tuft, John Stewart, Annabelle Wilson-Price.

Annabelle Wilson-Price?

The name sounds familiar, and not just because it's similar to the one I've been searching for. I feel as though I should know who that person is, but I can't pinpoint it. Still, because I can't find any trace of Anna Wilson, my brain goes into overdrive and I wonder if Annabelle may be her full name. Perhaps Craig told Helena it was Anna Wilson to fool her or something.

I memorise her email address; throw the book back onto the chair and saunter away before Mrs Itsy-Bitsy can arrest me for breaking the Human Rights Act, or whatever it was.

As soon as I get home, I switch on my laptop. I do have Facebook on my phone, but over the years my eyesight has become terrible and it takes me all my time to focus on the text. Today, I need serious concentration, and that means using my seen-better-days computer, with its crumb-infested keyboard and worn-away keys.

I type in the name – Annabelle Wilson-Price – and a handful of possibilities pop up. The first is a graphic designer in Los Angeles, and the second is an artist in Cromwey.

Bingo!

I've found the woman mentioned in Mrs Itsy-Bitsy's note-book, but is she the same woman who shares Craig's bed? As soon as I click on the profile, I receive my answer in the shape of a selfie. My ex-husband and Annabelle hug each other twenty yards from my house, with the glistening water of the harbour and the bobbing boats behind them. Annabelle has hair the colour of gold, and it cascades down past her shoulders in mermaid-type waves. She looks to be in her early twenties and has a glowing complexion, straight from the pages of a beauty magazine. She's wearing minimal makeup and even her freckles are symmetrical along her nose and cheeks. It sounds crazy, but I'm sure I've seen those beauty marks in the past. But where?

I can't see past her chest but I'm sure Annabelle has a beau-tiful figure to go with her face, and although she's stolen someone else's husband, I imagine that this woman has a personality that nobody can resist. While she looks different to either Helena or I, I can understand how Craig was charmed by her. Let's face it, if he could lose his mind over Helena, then his standards can't be high, but this woman! He's raised the bar with this one. She looks decades younger than him, and is one hundred per cent out of his league.

Annabelle's Facebook page is locked down to everyone except friends, but her Instagram is wide open, with a staggering 2,145 posts. I pour myself a glass of apple juice, grab my reading glasses and spend several hours gawping at everything she's done for the past three years.

Annabelle Wilson-Price was born in Cromwey, but later moved to Bournemouth. She studied art in London, and has now returned to her home town to work as an assistant and resident artist in a gallery. She spends her free time making sculptures out of crap washed up on the beach, and her pieces are often displayed in the space where she works. She has a bichon frise called Bruce, is crazy about some band called Hollywood Undead and her favourite food is gammon with pineapple. It's fascinating what these young people upload onto their social media. Her entire life is here for anyone to trawl through, and I can't think of anything more distasteful – and helpful – than that.

I scroll through post after post of flowers, driftwood, memes and pets, until something peculiar catches my attention. I enlarge the picture and I'm faced with a snap of an eleven-year-old freckle-faced girl and a cute friend, wearing scruffy denim shorts and pigtails. The children are posing in a paddling pool, while a Yorkshire terrier stands to attention, waiting for a treat. The girl with the freckles is Annabelle, the pool is in our back garden, the dog is our old pooch, Sam, and the little pigtailed friend is Rebecca.

My daughter has her arm around the shoulder of her father's future lover.

What the fuck?

All the air vanishes from my lungs and I'm unsure as to whether I'll ever breathe again.

10

The photograph floors me. Is this some kind of joke? According to the data, it was uploaded a year ago but it isn't until I read the description that I understand what's going on.

Throwback Thursday! Me and my friend Becca, summer 2007. We went to primary school together, and this was taken in her back garden, during a get-together with friends. I left Cromwey for Bournemouth (and then boarding school) shortly after. I wonder what Becca's doing nowadays? Girl, if you're out there, get in touch! Would love to see you again!!

There then follows a row of smiley-faced emojis, interspersed with flowers, suns, hearts and cocktails.

It's been over a decade since the photo was taken, but after reading the description, everything becomes clear, and I know why Annabelle looks familiar to me. Rebecca and her friends were about to leave primary and would be scattered around various different secondary schools. All the girls made a pact that before they parted, they'd host a garden party for each other. That way they'd create new memories, despite their impending new schools, friends and lives. Rebecca's was the second event – the first being a friend called Erika who had a hot tub in her garden. My daughter begged Craig and I to buy a tub so that her party would be just as great as Erika's, and wasn't impressed when faced with her dad blowing up the old paddling pool instead!

Annabelle was a member of Rebecca's group of school friends, but wasn't close enough to hang out in our house. In fact, I'm pretty sure the garden party was the one time I met her outside of the playground, though I do remember the hoopla it caused when she announced her plans for boarding school. Rebecca was into reading my old copies of Enid Blyton's *Malory Towers* books at the time, and begged us to let her go, too. There wasn't a hope in hell that we'd ever have the money (or inclination) to send our daughter away, and the reality of the local comprehensive came as a blow to her.

And now, twelve years later, here we are. Annabelle has grown into a mermaid goddess, is back in town and has somehow hooked up with Rebecca's father! Does Annabelle know who Craig is? Does he? It makes no sense, and the fact that there is a twenty-seven-year age gap confirms that my ex-husband has all the makings of a dirty old man.

My hands tremble, but I somehow manage to send a text to Helena.

I've found out who Anna is. You better come over.

Nineteen minutes later, she's at my front door.

❧

'Why would Craig move in with someone who has a dog? He hates dogs!'

I stare at Helena through the corner of my eye. Her husband has left her for a woman almost three decades younger and that's all she has to say? Shock comes to everyone in different ways I guess, but still it's bizarre that's the first thing that comes to her mind. I'm sitting at my desk while Helena paces up and down, rubbing her cheeks so hard there are red streaks emblazoned across them.

'Did he hate dogs when he was with you? Or did he make that up?'

I shrug.

'We had a dog called Sam, and he seemed to love him, but I do know he wasn't a huge fan of cats. Maybe you're getting them mixed up.'

Helena shoots me a look that would freeze molten lava and then moves over to my desk. She swings the laptop around to take a better look, and I resist the urge to tell her to get her grubby hands off my belongings.

'No, I'm not getting mixed up. He always said...'

Helena's voice trails off and I twist up to glance at her. Her mouth hangs open in horror.

'What's wrong?' I follow her gaze to the screen.

'Look where she works! Angelic Galleries. That's the art place on Grosvenor Street. You know, the one with the angel-shaped sculptures hanging outside.'

'Yes, I've been past it plenty of times, but I've never been in there.'

Helena leans her elbows onto my desk and rests her chin on her hands.

'Throughout our marriage, Craig was always going into that gallery. He said he enjoyed the seaside paintings and the sculptures. Ha! Paintings my ass! He was going in there to see her.'

Helena straightens up, stomps to my study door, opens it, slams it and then storms back to my desk.

'That's not possible.' I move my laptop towards me. 'Look, according to this, Annabelle didn't come back to Cromwey until last year. See? She started in October 2018.'

'Yeah, that's what she wants us to think! There's no way Craig was going in there to admire the paintings. He's the most uncultured bloke I know! He must have been going in to see her! He was cheating on me for years!'

Helena slams the heel of her hand onto the desk, inches from my vintage George Michael mug. I move it to the other side of the table as I ponder the idea that allowing her into my study wasn't my brightest moment.

'Look, I know you're upset but it's not possible that he was seeing this woman for years. Although, granted, I'd say that going into the gallery is how they met.'

'No! Every weekend Craig went into that place! He's been carrying on with her all that time, I know he has!'

On and on Helena goes, but the words don't reach my ears. It's all background noise at this point and I have an overwhelming desire to get rid of her; get her out of my house before she fills it with all her negative energy. However, while I'm wondering how to do that, Helena grabs my laptop again, leans over and starts tapping away at the keys.

'What are you doing now?' I signal to the clock, ticking above my door. 'It's getting a bit late, you know.'

Helena doesn't say anything, so I peer at the computer to see for myself. I can make out the Google home screen, and I watch as Helena's fingers enter and re-enter different strings of words.

'Craig Collins, Annabelle Wilson-Price, Cromwey,' she mumbles to herself. 'Art gallery, Craig Collins, Cromwey.' Each sentence brings up a stream of possible results, but nothing is to her satisfaction. 'It's no good; I can't find anything that brings the two together.'

'Well, you're not likely to. Not unless the company publishes information on each and every visitor.' I try to pull the laptop away, but she grabs it back. 'Come on, why don't you go home and get yourself back together? Craig wasn't cheating on you with Annabelle for years. It's not possible. She's far too young for one thing, and for another, I think maybe you're being a bit... a bit... neurotic.'

Helena bites down on her lip and her nostrils flare in response.

'Oh my God! Y'know what? Craig could have been seeing this Annabelle bitch while he was with you!' I grunt and my cheeks deflate like punctured tyres.

'That's absurd. We split up five years ago, and even if Annabelle was in town at that point, she'd have been eighteen years old!'

'That may be, but...'

'But what?'

Helena's eyes cloud over, and she rubs her jaw as though trying to work out a complicated equation.

'Look, don't freak out, but I know for a fact that Craig cheated on you, way before he met me. He told me that himself.'

Her words hang heavy in the room, and I almost choke on them.

'What do you mean?'

Helena coughs; picks up a pen and starts twirling it in her fingers.

'I probably shouldn't tell you this, but Craig said that he used to pretend he'd fallen asleep on his friend's couch, when he was with other women. He was pretty amused that you believed him.'

I gasp and my throat dries to dust.

'I think you should go now.' I sniff. And then I slam the laptop screen onto her fingers.

11

After Helena leaves, I run a bath filled with lemon-scented bubbles, and then I lounge in it for a good hour. The whole time I'm in there, angry tears stream down my face. How could Craig discuss his dalliances with Helena of all people? Bastard!! I feel angry and disappointed, because if I'm truthful with myself, I kind of suspected that he'd played around and yet I did nothing about it.

From the beginning, Craig was what you'd describe as a lad. He was the guy that every fourteen-year-old girl wanted to date; the one who had long hair and a motorbike when he was still in sixth form and then passed his test and bought a car before everyone else had saved up for lessons. Even though we went to different schools, I knew from the moment I met him that he was 'that guy'. I'd known a dozen just like him, but I'd never been lucky enough to date one of them.

I wasn't an ugly girl, but I wasn't what you'd call beautiful, either. I was – and maybe still am – more 'cute' than anything else. I'm maybe a young Felicity Kendal, rather than an Angelina Jolie. But from the moment we met in the pub in 1992, Craig and I just gelled. We bonded over his Freddie Mercury T-shirt, because my brother was a huge Queen fan and I used that to break the ice. The next thing I knew, I was standing in line at an obscure Bournemouth venue, fighting for front-row seats at a Queen lookalike concert. The band couldn't sing a note, but the date was hilarious and from then on, we were together almost every evening. I felt lucky that out of everyone he could have had, Craig chose me.

In retrospect, he was the lucky one.

As the bubbles gather and explode around my shoulders, I sink further and further into the water, and then repressed events from many years ago start popping into my brain. I have many memories that I had decided were figments of my imagination, because the idea that they could be true would have made our entire marriage into a lie. So, each time something happened during our relationship, I swallowed my worries down like the nasty pills they were.

Once, during the early days of our marriage – when I worked as a library assistant – I came home for lunch because I wanted to see if a parcel had arrived. Craig's BMW was parked on the road, which was not that unusual because he did sometimes pop home for a sandwich instead of eating in his garage. However, while seeing his car caused no alarm, my first thought as I parked next to him was that when I left for work that morning, the curtains had been open. Now they were closed tight. Why would you close the curtains in the middle of the day, when you were eating your lunch? It made no sense at all.

I let myself in and placed my coat in the middle of the hall. I was terrified and I had to push my feet into the ground to stop my legs knocking against the living room door. I held my ear up against the rough wood, but could hear nothing – not even the sound of Craig eating or rustling papers. In the end I had no choice but to hold my breath and barge into the room, where I expected to see him with another woman. Instead, however, he was on his own and the curtains were now open. My husband was grey with shock and looked guilty as hell, but still – he was alone.

He muttered something about being home for lunch, but there was no food to be seen. His stutters and gasps for air were unsettling, and instead of listening to him, I sped around the house searching for another woman. I flung open each and every door, wardrobe and cupboard, but there was no one to be found. When I returned to the living room, Craig laughed the incident off and said he had closed the curtains because the sun was shining on the television. This would have perhaps made sense if not for the fact that it was the middle of winter, there were raindrops all over the window and the television was switched off.

I was too scared to press my husband about it, so I ignored what I hoped was my crazy paranoia, and never uttered a word – not even to Kate. We got on with our lives, had a beautiful baby girl and moved to our dream harbour home. The lunchtime drama has been a distant memory for decades, but now I can't help thinking that I should have opened the back door. I imagine that whoever Craig had in the house was by then hiding in the garden, waiting for me to leave. Instead, I turned my back on the situation and believed him, because I didn't want to cause any trouble. Damn, I bet they both had a right old snigger at my expense when I'd gone.

I must have been senseless.

Or maybe he was.

I get out of the bath, dress in my unsexy – but comfy – flannel pyjamas and step into my flowered bedroom, with my beloved 1950s dressing table and matching, polished wardrobe. As I wonder if I should read a book or watch a film, my phone pings.

I'm sorry I upset you, but I really thought you should know. I guess we've both found out things we didn't want to know this evening. Gutting, isn't it? H. xx

I ignore the attention-seeking text, and instead reach for my notebook and pen. Whether Helena intended to upset me or not is irrelevant. I scribble down the date, time and description of how Helena has pissed me off, and the ways I intend to repay the favour. Some people may say that this is rather an odd habit to get into, but it makes perfect sense to me.

I finish my concise report of Helena's behaviour, and then I turn on the television. *Fatal Attraction* has just started. The irony of it all!

I curl up to watch.

12

'I can't believe this. Have you told Rebecca?'

Kate glowers at me from behind a stack of books. It's Tuesday afternoon, and I'm leaning on the front counter of the library where we worked together for a mammoth twenty-four years. Thank goodness I somehow managed to escape into the genealogy world.

'Shush, don't shout! Someone could hear us.'

My friend rolls her eyes and we both glance around. Sturdy wooden bookshelves cover three walls, while a dozen metal shelving units line up on one side of the library, and create the perfect place to gossip, hide and even read. On the other side of the counter there are study booths, a carpet area and a young person's section, but there are no children to be seen today. When I worked here, the place was always bustling with researchers, tapping away at the resident computers, and flicking through newspapers. Today, however, the library is silent; a result of e-books, the internet and plain old laziness, I guess.

'Can you see anyone in here?' Kate asks. 'Nobody uses

libraries anymore! That's why I'm hanging onto my job by a thread.'

'Is it always like this? I know I haven't been in for a while, but I'm pretty sure it wasn't dead the last time I visited.'

Kate grabs the pile of books from the counter.

'It's not this quiet when we run the OAP coffee mornings or the mums and tots' yoga classes, but when nothing is organised, it's like a place where people come to die. Myself included! Here, you know what to do – help me re-shelve these.'

I sigh and heave half a dozen books from Kate's arms. No matter how long it's been since I stopped working here, I still understand every digit of the Dewey Decimal System, which at this point is a curse, not a benefit. We make our way to the biography section and I shove the first book – a self-published life story of a local plumber – into the appropriate space. No wonder the library's going downhill if they're buying crap like this.

'Anyway,' Kate shouts from the top of the ladder. 'You didn't answer my question.'

'For God's sake, watch what you're doing up there. Driving you to A & E is not how I want to spend my afternoon, but in answer to your question, no I haven't told Rebecca. She's coming home soon. I'll break the news to her then.'

Kate stomps down from the ladder and peers through a gap in the shelf, wary that her boss may appear at any moment.

'So, how do you think she'll react?'

'To be honest, I think she'll lose her mind. She's already upset that her dad has found yet another woman. Christ knows what she'll say when she finds out who it is!'

My friend nods and dumps the remaining books on the foot-stool beside her.

'Let me look at the photo again.' She holds out her hand and I give her my phone, open at Annabelle's Instagram page.

'Y'know, I'm sure I remember that Annabelle girl from when I helped out at Guides.'

Kate enlarges the photo and stares even harder.

'You helped at Guides?'

'Yes, for a little while. Don't you remember? I did it as a favour to my aunt after she did her back in, because she couldn't face a room full of pre-pubescent girls on her own. Was Annabelle in the Girl Guides? Her face is familiar.'

I rub my eyes. I had four hours sleep last night, and it's catching up with me.

'I have no idea. But on another note, Helena went crazy when I presented her with my research! She decided that Craig and Annabelle must have been seeing each other for years, even going back to when he was married to me!'

'What? That's crazy. We all know Craig likes women, but going after a teenager is too much even for him.' She studies the spine of a Frank Sinatra biography and groans. 'Ugh, this book has no bloody label.'

Kate trudges back to the counter with the errant volume. I follow her and dump the remainder of my books onto a nearby trolley.

'That reminds me of something I wanted to ask you.'

'Mmm?' Kate punches the book title into the computer, writes the number onto a sticker and throws it to one side. Then she gazes up at me. 'What is it?'

A white-haired old lady wanders into the library and waves over. She wears a floor-length purple raincoat and the strap of her leather satchel crosses over her body.

'Afternoon, Kate,' she shouts. 'Has my *People's Friend* arrived yet?'

'Yes, it's in the usual place. Help yourself.'

The lady thanks Kate and trundles off to the media section. I wait until she's twenty feet away, and then I lean closer to my friend and lower my voice.

'Helena said that Craig cheated on me with many women before we separated.'

Kate makes a noise that could be described as a cross between a snigger and a grunt. She pulls a tissue from her pocket and dabs her nose.

'What a pile of crap! Helena's saying that to make herself feel better. Everyone knows that Craig only had eyes for you until she came along. I don't know what she did to snare him – and I don't want to know – but I would bet my last pound that Craig never flirted with anyone while he was married to you.'

I pick up the date stamp and start branding a random Post-it note. The ink is blotchy and I can hardly make out what it's supposed to say. I rub my finger across the numbers until they smudge all over the paper.

'After she said it, all I could think about were times when Craig could have been playing around, and now I can't get it out of my head. You'd tell me, wouldn't you? If you thought he'd been with other women?'

Kate grabs the date stamp and places it out of my reach.

'What do you think?! Besides, Pete would have mentioned it. He and Craig share everything – well they did until Annabelle came along.'

'I hope you're right,' I say. 'Otherwise my self-confidence has plummeted to rock bottom once again.'

'I'm always right. Now just forget about it.'

Kate swoops down to retrieve some envelopes that have fallen onto the floor. I want to believe her, but I can't help but notice that during the whole time she was assuring me of Craig's innocence, not once did she look me in the eye.

Rebecca has taken the news of Craig's new woman as I expected – in alternate waves of anger, tears and complete denial. We're at the kitchen table, where we've been for the past ninety-three minutes. Steam rises from the hot chocolate my daughter requested ten minutes ago, but so far it remains untouched.

'Do you remember after Dad left, you and me used to sit at this table and play Uno?' Rebecca smiles, and a stray tear tumbles down her cheek. I dry it with a tissue, and motion to her cup.

'Don't forget your drink... And yes, I do remember our Uno marathons. I used to look forward to you coming home from university, so that we could play.' I get up and grab a glass from the drainer and take my overdue vitamin tablet. 'You want one of these? They're evening primrose oil – good for your hormones apparently.'

She nods and I pop one into Rebecca's hand. Before I have a chance to pass her a glass of water, my daughter has already swallowed the capsule with a gulp of hot chocolate.

She sighs. 'I have such mixed emotions about all this Dad crap. On the one hand, I'm kind of glad that he's left Helena, just because she didn't deserve him in the first place, but on the other hand, I just... I just can't get my head around why he can't stay in one place for more than five minutes. And why would he ever want to date someone the same age as me? Somebody who knew me as well!'

I sit down and rub the top of her arm. The material of her hoodie reminds me of the soft outfits she used to wear as a toddler.

'It's okay to feel mixed up. I feel that way every day!'

'But I worry that all this will mean the end of my relationship with him. What if I never get used to his new situation? At this point I don't even want to go into his house! How can I see him if I can't visit?'

Rebecca picks at her black nail polish, until tiny pieces fall onto the table. She blows them onto the floor, and then drinks her chocolate.

'I don't think anyone will blame you for not wanting to visit,' I say. 'But your dad is still your dad. Granted, he does seem to think that his moral responsibility ended when you turned eighteen, but that doesn't mean he'll abandon your relationship.'

'You think?'

'Yes, I do. Look, if he stays with this Annabelle girl – and I can't imagine he will to be honest – then I'm sure he'll find ways of spending time with you as well. It'll all work out, I promise.'

Rebecca pushes away her mug, dries her eyes and then throws her arms around my shoulders.

'Thanks for looking after me, Mum,' she says.

I kiss her hair. It smells of almonds and vanilla.

'I'll always look after you,' I reply.

Helena, Rebecca and I, sit in the window seat of The Lovely Café. I must say that for someone who hadn't entered the café even once since it opened, I've made up for it in the past few weeks. Spending this morning with my ex-husband's wife was not how I wanted this day to go, but after breaking the news to Rebecca, she insisted we march over to the garage so that she could speak to her father. When we arrived, the shutters were down, and a large notice informed us that he'd gone on a breakdown. Before I had time to turn Rebecca towards home, Helena was waving us into the café, and that's where we've been ever since.

Helena spoons a massive blob of jam onto a warm scone, and then dollops some clotted cream onto the top. I raise my eyebrows because as far as I'm concerned, everyone should put the cream on first. She catches me staring and misconstrues my snobbery for concern about her dietary habits.

'I didn't have breakfast.' She shrugs, as half the scone disappears into her mouth.

Rebecca studies her reflection in a pocket mirror.

'I had a cold strawberry Pop Tart on the train. It was okay, actually.'

'They still make those?' I ask.

'Well, they were selling them in a shop next to the station, but they may have been there since 2002, for all I know.'

Rebecca smiles at her little joke, and Helena scowls.

'You're taking the news of your father's new woman remarkably well, I must say.' Helena bites the scone and surveys my daughter through hooded eyes.

'I'm just a good actress.' Rebecca glares at her stepmother, shoves the mirror back into her handbag and then slurps on her Coke. 'This has fucked me up – sorry, Mum – and I know I haven't seen Annabelle in twelve years, but the news that she's now screwing my dad is not something I expected to hear this morning. It's sickening!'

I pat my daughter's hand. She shakes beneath my touch.

'I was trying to remember more details about her,' I say, 'but it's hard after all these years.'

'Do you remember her pretentious dad?' Rebecca slaps her hands against the table, as though she's realised something life-changing, but I shrug.

'Vaguely,' I say. 'I'd maybe know him if I saw him.'

Rebecca laughs and snorts at the same time.

'I'll always remember the time he came in for the "Bring your parent to school" assembly. The teacher introduced him as Stuart Wilson-Price, and he leapt up out of his chair and boomed, "My name is *Mr* Wilson-Price! Mr!!" We all nearly jumped out of our skins, and Melissa Tivey started crying!'

I laugh and Helena's mouth trembles, obviously uncomfortable with the sharing of age-old stories. I'm happy that this woman only has five years of memories with Craig. Rebecca and I have a lifetime, and that will never change. I pick up my cup and take a sip of tea. The scalding liquid burns my tongue, hurls itself at the back of my throat and then sizzles all the way down to my stomach.

'So, what do we do now?' Helena asks. 'Do you think we should confront Annabelle? Or do we confront Craig?'

She gazes at me as though I should have all the answers. I study my tongue in the reflection of a knife. My poor mouth is bright red.

'To be honest, I'm not sure that I can have any say in this at all. I mean, Craig and I have been separated for almost five years and divorced for three. Anything between us is long over by now.'

'That's not true.' Helena gulps her tea and coughs. 'Jesus, what is this made from? Lava?' She turns to confront her waitress, but the wise girl has disappeared into the kitchen.

Helena dabs her tongue with a napkin. When she stops, a sliver of tissue remains in her mouth and she spits it out with a series of raspberry sounds.

'I disagree that everything between you is over,' she chides.

'Erm, I think you'll find it is.'

'I don't mean romance-wise!' She collapses into peals of laughter.

Bitch!

'Excuse me?'

Helena waves me off, blows on her tea and then takes another mouthful. I hope it chokes her.

'Now you know that Craig was cheating on you for all those years, don't you want to ask him about it? Aren't you dying to take some measure of revenge?'

Helena grins, while Rebecca scowls at me from behind her glass of Coke.

'What do you mean, "cheating on you for all those years"?'

I glower at Helena. I cannot believe she said that! She seems oblivious, however. She's too busy inspecting a stain on her flowery tablecloth.

'Mum?'

I pretend to be interested in a couple arguing on the street outside, but I know I'm going to have to offer some kind of explanation.

'It's nothing for you to worry about. Helena believes that Dad might have had a few... dalliances... before we broke up. But even if it did happen – and that's a big if – it's ancient history and not something I intend to dwell on.'

Rebecca's eyes start to water again, and she dabs at the tears with her napkin.

Helena exhales. 'Anyway, back to my original point. Regardless of whether or not you want to bring up the infidelities, you and Craig have a daughter together. Don't you owe it to Rebecca to find out what's going on? Annabelle was her friend!'

'Huh! Some friend,' Rebecca growls. 'I could slap her for what she's done.'

Helena slams her hand against the table and several diners twist to see what's going on.

'Yes!' Helena gasps. 'And with good cause! Listen, I am convinced that in order to get any measure of revenge we all need to stick together and work out a plan. We need to do this for Rebecca!'

Helena grabs my daughter's hand. Rebecca whips it away and moves closer to me.

'We need to do what exactly?' I ask.

The waitress hovers nearby, pretending to sweep crumbs out

of the door, with a broom covered in hot pink flamingos. Where does one buy such a thing? Helena leans in and whispers.

'I don't have a long-term plan yet, but the first thing we'll do is finish our tea, and then after that we'll go over the bridge and visit precious Annabelle Wilson-Price in her angelic little gallery.' Helena makes her arms into the shape of wings and then brings her hands into a prayer position. 'See, I can be an angel too.' She sighs.

'Only if that angel is Lucifer.' I wink, but Helena doesn't return the gesture.

13

The lily-white façade of Angelic Galleries rises up in front of us. Outside, decorations in the shape of cherubs sway in the breeze and the window is awash with framed, seaside-themed photographs and paintings. We press our noses against the window, like three little girls eyeing dolls in a toy shop.

'Ugh! Why do seaside galleries always carry pictures of the ocean and beach huts?' Rebecca screws up her face. 'I haven't seen a single beach photo in a London gallery. Thank goodness!'

'Well, maybe that's because London doesn't have a beach,' I say. 'Maybe you'd prefer a display of Jack the Ripper crime-scene photos?'

I laugh and Rebecca tuts. We both look at Helena; she stands as still as one of the sandcastles depicted in the window display.

'Are you okay?'

Helena places her hands on the gallery window, and when she removes them, two sticky patches remain.

'No.'

'You want to go home?'

Please say yes! Please say yes!

'I don't think so.'

My shoulders droop in disappointment. Rebecca mumbles something under her breath and then glares at her stepmother.

'Helena! You wanted to come, and now we're here. So, let's go!'

My daughter shoves the door and the gold bell above our heads rattles its call. This gallery must have been open for at least twenty years that I know of, but never once have I been inside it. I'm not sure what that reveals about me, but nothing positive, I imagine.

A lady of about sixty-five is seated behind a desk, but as soon as she sees us, she jumps up and beams. She's dressed in dungarees and a yellow T-shirt, which makes her look more like a Minion than a gallery owner. I stifle a chuckle.

'What are you laughing at?' Rebecca asks.

'I'll tell you later.' I smile at the woman and she nods her head.

'Good morning!'

We all wish her the same and she beams. Her joyful expression leads me to believe that we're the first people she's seen all day, though it's doubtful we'll end up buying anything.

'Feel free to look around, ladies, and please do return for our upcoming exhibitions.' She shuffles some paperwork on her desk and hands us each a leaflet. The paper shows off an array of multicoloured driftwood sculptures. They look beautiful to my non-artistic eye, but Rebecca doesn't look impressed, and drops the handout onto a nearby table.

'If you need help with anything – anything at all – give me a shout. I'll be right here.' The gallery lady's eyes flit from me to Helena to Rebecca, and then she lowers herself into a grass-green easy chair and picks up a fancy photography magazine. It looks like one of those highbrow publications that costs more than a hardback book.

'Look at this place,' Helena whispers. 'It's so... so... angelic.'

'Hence the name, most likely.'

Having never been in here before, I'm mesmerised by my surroundings. The room is immaculate, with a flawless, ivory carpet and pastel-coloured chairs scattered all around. Rebecca has already made herself at home on one and is staring at her phone. Anyone would think she doesn't want to be here, which is true, let's face it.

All around us are pieces of art in a variety of shapes and colours. Painted wooden sandcastles reside in glass cabinets; beside them delicate glass seahorses, starfish and squid. Photos of the harbour – some featuring my own little blue house – hang on the wall, while bright paintings of the pier are displayed beneath stark spotlights. I wonder if I'm owed some kind of royalty for having my house in the pictures. I could certainly do with some spare cash! I make a mental note to look into that when I get home.

The main theme of the gallery interior is white – I imagine that's to give full attention to the works – and the whole place smells of fresh paint. In the corner there is a lilac surfboard decorated with daffodils and next to it a sign declares that *Surfers are the Flowers of the Sea*. What on earth does that mean? I doubt even the artist knows the answer to that one.

Helena stops to admire a tiny wooden replica of a typical seaside house.

'Craig bought me an ornament like this once,' she whispers. 'It came from the gift shop on the beach and was a snip of the price it is here.'

As she turns away, I give her oversized handbag a nudge. It rocks back onto a pile of glossy catalogues and sends them clattering to the floor.

The gallery lady jumps up from her easy chair and marches over.

'Please be careful! We only have a handful of those catalogues left!'

Helena stares at the books and I swoop down to retrieve them. A few of the volumes are bent at the corners, and I straighten them before I stand back up.

'It's okay, they're all in one piece.' I pop them back onto the shelf. Helena stares at me and I notice a bulging vein, right in the middle of her left temple. 'You caught them with your bag. No harm done, but you should think about investing in something smaller for everyday use.'

Helena glares down at the handbag, while I pretend to be fixated on the archway that leads into the back room. There's another decorated surfboard hanging above it and adjacent is a flight of stairs with the words *Private, Staff Only* printed onto a wooden, wall-mounted plaque. The gallery lady returns to the main desk and lights one of those incense sticks that you find in hippy stores. Thick wafts of smoke spiral into the air, and the stink sets itself up at the back of my nose. I cough and then a gigantic sneeze comes out of nowhere.

'Bless you!'

I turn to thank my companions, and then realise they weren't the ones who spoke. Instead, the words have come from a figure floating down the stairs in a haze of turquoise and lemon. My eyes take a while to adjust, but I realise that the person coming into view is Annabelle. Her sun-kissed hair is piled on top of her head and she wears a 1950s style dress, with a white chiffon scarf around her neck. She doesn't seem real and must be the only person who looks better in real life than she does on her Instagram profile. I don't want her to see me stare, so I avert my eyes to Helena and Rebecca. Both wear a glazed expression, and their mouths sag open. They appear somewhat unhinged and I pray that Annabelle doesn't notice – or doesn't realise – that we're all together.

'Can I help you at all?'

I glance back at my ex-husband's new flame and grimace.

'No, it's okay thank you. We're just browsing.'

We make eye contact and for a second, confusion flickers across her face.

'I'm sorry, but you look familiar. Have you been in here before?'

Helena and Rebecca are still in a robotic trance. I ignore them and shake my head.

'No,' I reply, 'I never have.'

'Well, enjoy your first visit.' She smiles, showing perfect white teeth, and then glides towards the back room. The relief almost knocks me off my feet. I turn to Rebecca and Helena, and nod my head towards the door.

'Let's go!'

Rebecca lurches up from the seat and I touch Helena's forearm, encouraging her towards the exit.

Thank God Annabelle didn't recognise who we were. Thank God for...

'Why are you screwing my dad?!'

The boom of Rebecca's voice comes out of nowhere, and I'm sure even the driftwood sculptures tremble with fear. The gallery lady's head jolts up from the safety of her desk and I'm shocked when Helena grabs my daughter and begs her to shush. She shrugs her stepmother off and lurches past us towards the back room.

Shit.

I spin round to see my daughter and Annabelle glowering at each other through a suspicious haze.

'Rebecca,' Annabelle gasps. 'Wow, it really is you.'

'Yes, it's me. Surprised?'

'Yes. No. What are you doing here?'

'She came with me.' Helena steps forward with her arms folded in front of her chest.

'And you are?'

'Don't pretend you don't know. I'm Craig's wife, which is something you will never be!'

From behind me, the welcome bell jingles its little tune once again, only this time it sounds like the chimes of doom.

'What's going on?' enquires a familiar voice.

I turn to the door and there is Craig in all his faded jeans and Gap T-shirt glory. If he were to ever star in his own real-life horror movie, this would be it.

The energy in the room shifts from static to ice cold, and just like that, we're in the midst of a family reunion... a noisy, unwelcome, stressful reunion.

When Annabelle bursts into tears, she turns towards the lady at the desk and throws her hands into a prayer position.

'I'm sorry, Sheila,' she cries, and then bounds up the stairs and away from the fury of Helena and Rebecca.

'Well done!! Are you happy now?' Craig glares at Helena through cold eyes.

Helena gasps. 'Am I happy? Am I happy?! No, I'm not fucking happy!! You've broken up our marriage, abandoned our home and for what? Someone who looks like she's still at school! You're scraping the bottom of the barrel this time, that's for sure!'

Although this is the worst possible situation for me to be involved with, I can't help but stifle a snigger when the words jump from Helena's mouth. Scraping the bottom of the barrel? That happened during the last break-up, love, not this one.

The doorbell rattles again, and a man in a blue tailored suit wanders in. Until now, the gallery owner has remained quiet, but on seeing a potential customer, she comes out from behind the desk. In a voice that's little more than a whisper, she demands that everyone leave her precious establishment.

So, we do.

~

Outside, the sun is bright in the cloudless sky, and I hide my eyes from the glare and the reality of what has happened.

'I'm going back to work,' Helena says, and before anyone can reply, she disappears into the crowd of tourists and morning shoppers. The rest of us hover outside the door as though we don't have a clue what to do next.

Because we really *don't* have a clue what to do next.

'What the hell just happened?' The bottom of Craig's T-shirt blows in the wind, exposing his still-toned stomach. I avert my eyes – and the question – until he exhales far longer than normal and slumps against the wall. He's defeated, which stirs up combined feelings of joy and unexpected sympathy for the man I once loved.

'Dad, how could you do this to me?' Rebecca shouts above the chattering tourists. 'Annabelle was my friend at junior school! Your new girlfriend is the same age as me!!'

Craig nods.

'Rebecca, believe me I had no idea about that when we met. Junior school was years ago, and all you girls looked the same back then! It wasn't until after we started... after we started dating... that I realised who she was, and by then it was too late.'

'And how *did* you meet? Well, apart from the school run, of course.' I'm shocked by how easily the words fly out of my mouth. It's really none of my business, but I'm intrigued to know. Craig smiles through tight lips but his voice is calm, soothing almost.

'Not that I need to explain myself, but we met two-and-a-half months ago. Annabelle's car broke down by the bridge. She didn't have any breakdown cover, so she rang the first garage she could find on Google. Luckily, it was mine. I went out, picked her up and somehow or other we hit it off. We've been together ever since.'

As simple as that.

'But, Dad, she's twenty-seven years younger than you,' cries Rebecca. 'You're making a fool out of yourself. And out of me, too!!'

'That may be, but you can't control who you fall in love with.' Craig steps back into the gallery and as the door closes, he spins round and catches my eye.

'You said the same thing after you left me,' I yell, and Craig nods.

14

After kissing her goodbye and then drying her tears for the second time today, Rebecca heads back to the station. I offer to pay for a taxi, but she insists that the walk will do her good, so I go with her as far as the beach and then watch until my daughter disappears out of sight.

A row of pretty, colourful huts runs almost the entire length of the beach and today most of them are occupied. Excited families and older couples spill out onto the path with their tables, picnics, buckets and spades, and one lady even uses her hut to sell crocheted dolls and teddies for a local charity. Above the small cabins there is Driftwood Hill; a raised patch of greenery and flowers, which leads up to another row of shelters and a tennis court. The path then twists and eventually reaches a garden, coffee shop and small outdoor stage.

Tour brochures describe Driftwood Hill as 'a hidden delight' because it is only accessible from a stone staircase that ascends between two rows of beach huts. It's often busy with tourists, but today there is nobody on it at all. Determined to find some peace on this peculiar day, I head up the steps and follow the twisted path towards the café. However, as I turn the corner, I'm disturbed by an urgent voice.

'Please! Please! Can you help me?'

I turn back towards the staircase and there is a scrawny man of about thirty years old, with greasy hair and dirty stubble, wearing jeans and a pea-green anorak. The path is deserted and I regret my decision to come this way.

'What do you want?'

'My girlfriend has collapsed! She's around this corner, please help me!'

As soon as he mentions his girlfriend, alarm bells go off in my head. Last week there was an article in the newspaper, warning residents and tourists about a new scam – that of an unwell friend or partner, who happens to be lying somewhere she can't be seen. Anyone compassionate enough to lend assistance is robbed the moment they set foot off the main path.

'No, I can't help. I'm sorry.'

I descend the steps back the way I came, but the scruffy guy doesn't give up.

'Please, miss, come this way! She's right over here!'

'Phone an ambulance then,' I shout, but the man is still right behind me. He reaches forward to grab my arm, and as I ready myself to scream, a miracle happens.

'Tyson!!'

We both look up to see an out-of-control German shepherd, bounding towards us. I'm even more terrified of huge dogs than I am of strange men, but at this moment I'd sooner take my chances with the former. My body tightens in preparation for the dog to leap onto me, but instead, he races straight past and chases the would-be mugger up the stairs and into the hedges.

'I'm sorry!' the male owner says, as the dog comes back to heel.

'It's okay. He did me a favour.'

'Was that guy trying to rob you or something? He looked pretty intense.' The dog owner gawps at the bushes, but the man is long gone.

'I think so. He said his partner was in distress, but...'

'A distraction mugging. Bastard.'

I nod and try to control my breathing. Anxiety bubbles all over my body and I feel as though I might cry.

'Well, thanks again.' I turn to leave, but my rescuer isn't too keen to let me go.

'You seem a little too stressed to be left alone right now. Do you fancy a cup of tea from the little snack shack over there? I'm sure it will help calm your nerves.'

I shake my head and hold onto my handbag in case this is another scam.

'No, I have to go, but thank you anyway.'

I take about four steps and trip over a loose paving slab. My rescuer darts forward and steadies me before I face-plant into the ground.

'Bloody hell,' I stutter. 'I'm a walking disaster.'

He points at the broken concrete.

'No, you're the victim of Cromwey Council's incompetence. So, what about that cup of tea then? It might delay any more catastrophes.'

He gives me a broad, dazzling smile. Minutes later, I'm perched on the beach wall, with a cup of tea in one hand and a serviette in the other.

'You know, I don't normally have cups of tea with men I've just met,' I say.

'Well, I'm glad you were willing to make an exception today. You seemed pretty shook up. I'm Stuart by the way.'

He reaches out and I balance my tea on the wall and take his hand. He has a firm shake, which hurts far more than I expected it to.

'I'm Jenny. It's nice to meet you.'

'Likewise.'

Stuart and I sip our teas in silence for the next few minutes. I'm grateful to this man for stepping in during what could have been two hellish experiences, but even so, I feel a little absurd and wonder how long it's acceptable to stay here. Today hasn't been the best, and I have an overwhelming desire to forget all that's happened, and sink into a bath with a good book.

Stuart is in his early fifties, tall, broad with greying hair and a dark mole on his left cheek. There's something about him that's familiar, but then that could be because there are many men of his ilk in Cromwey. Distinguished, you'd perhaps call him. He smells of minty shower gel and expensive cologne and I imagine he's the type to be on the town council or maybe even run for mayor. He's dressed a little too smart for a day on the promenade, in a short-sleeved white shirt, tie and blue summer trousers. He has a little designer stubble and his face has those laughter lines that make a man look handsome and a woman seem haggard. As Stuart drinks his tea, Tyson the dog sits upright in the hope of catching a treat or two. He's out of luck, however. My rescuer didn't think to buy any biscuits from the snack stall.

'So, are you from around here?' As pleasant as Stuart may be, I'm wary of giving too many personal details to a stranger. I nod and offer a few words to satisfy his curiosity.

'Yes, I'm a Cromwey girl. Lived here all my life. You?'

He swallows his tea and coughs.

'I lived here until twelve years ago, but then I moved to Bournemouth with my wife and daughter. I still live there, but separated from my wife last year.'

'I'm sorry to hear that.'

He chews his thumbnail and clears his throat.

'These things happen. It hadn't been working out for a

while, and then after she left, I discovered she'd been having a year-long affair with one of my colleagues!'

This conversation is getting a little too personal, but I am not the kind of woman who doesn't show concern, so I offer him an empathetic nod.

'I've been there myself,' I say. 'Except with my husband it wasn't a colleague – it was some woman who owned a business, next to where he works.'

Tyson jumps up to sniff a passing poodle, and the smaller dog yaps at him. Stuart drags the dog back and pats his head.

'Infidelity is pretty common.' He sighs. 'More common that you'd think, but that doesn't make it any easier. In the end I had to leave my job for fear of doing something stupid to the bastard she shacked up with.'

'I know that feeling. I could have killed my husband. And her!'

Stuart gives a lopsided grin.

'Don't worry, I imagine we've all fantasised about killing someone at one time or another.' Stuart stares straight into my eyes and my toes curl up inside my shoes.

'Well, I was just being dramatic.'

'Of course.'

An awkward silence descends between us. I occupy myself by watching a man trudging along the beach swinging a metal detector from side to side. The contraption beeps and he bends down to dig in the sand with a tiny spade; picks up a bottle top, swears and tosses it aside. Yards away from the detectorist, a young boy wearing a dinosaur T-shirt begs his mother for one last splodge in the sea. His mum throws a gigantic, flowery beach bag over her shoulder.

'No, Christopher, you've already had five more minutes. Come on, it's bath time now.'

'But I don't want to be clean!' The boy grunts. 'I love being dirty!!'

Stuart laughs and nods his head towards the family.

'I remember when my daughter was that age. Funny little thing she was. Always wanting five minutes more, no matter where we were, but especially the beach. She'd have stayed forever if I'd let her.'

Memories of Rebecca flood into my mind, and a tinge of happiness stirs inside me.

'Mine was the same,' I say. 'Except with her it was always crab fishing. She'd spend all day with her bucket and line, complaining that she couldn't catch anything. Then when she did get a crab, she'd cry because she was worried it wouldn't be able to find its way home again. We couldn't win.'

Tyson stands up to inspect a neglected crisp packet, and Stuart brushes it away with his foot. It whirls itself towards my shoe, and I pick it up and stick it in the bin, along with my empty cup.

'How old's your daughter?' he asks.

'Twenty-three. Yours?'

'Same.'

I look at my watch. It's 2.35pm. The harbour is a good twenty-minute walk away and I need to get going.

'Does she live nearby?' he asks.

I nod, and then ask him the same question. Maybe he's comfortable answering queries about his child, but I feel a little odd about it. I've shared enough about my life as it is.

'She moved back about six months ago,' he says. 'She was living in Bournemouth with her mother, but then she got a job in Cromwey. As a matter of fact, that's why I'm here. According to the ex-wife, my daughter has got herself involved with someone I don't approve of. I've come to talk some sense into her and drag her home again!'

Drag her home? What a strange thing to say about your adult daughter. The conversation makes me uneasy. I don't want to know all this gossip about a stranger's grown-up child.

'It sounds complicated,' I say, while Stuart rolls his shoulders and stretches his neck as though he's preparing for a Mr Universe contest.

'Yeah, you could say that. She moved out of her flat-share and into a house with this bloke, but she left no forwarding address. Presumably because she knows we don't approve of the relationship. She's also taken to refusing my calls, and now I'm forced to visit her at work, but as soon as she sees me, she locks the gallery door before I've even had a chance to get into the place.'

Did I hear that right? The *gallery* door? Surely he can't mean...? No, there must be more than one art place in Cromwey. Isn't there?

'She works at a gallery?' I ask the question, though in truth I'm not sure I want to hear the answer.

'Yes, the one on Grosvenor Street. Angelic Galleries. You know it?'

I nod, and every tiny detail falls into place. That's why Stuart looked familiar – he's Annabelle's father and I must have seen him on the school run about a thousand times. He was younger and skinnier then and he had black hair, but I still should have known who he was. Damn it, why didn't I know who he was?

I stare down at my feet and try to concentrate on the chipped, violet polish on my nails. It's no good – my heels bop on the paving slabs like an overactive tap dancer. A young mother walks past with a chubby baby in a buggy and I want to grab her and beg to walk home with her.

'To be honest, I'm pretty concerned about her.' Stuart's voice breaks into my thoughts like a pneumatic drill. 'My daughter – Annabelle – has always been a vulnerable girl. A real crybaby you could say. She leads from her heart and doesn't think about the consequences of her actions. She's just like her mother in that regard.'

I squint at my watch and then leap down from the wall.

'I'm sorry but I need to get back. My friend's visiting me soon and she'll be concerned if I'm not home.'

Stuart gets up, and Tyson grunts and pulls himself to his feet. Stuart offers me his hand and I shake it, hoping that he won't feel the tremors shooting up and down my arm.

'Okay. It was great to meet you, Jenny. Maybe we'll see each other again sometime. Somewhere more glamorous than the sea wall.'

He grins and swaggers over to the dustbin, where he disposes of his cup. His manner is so super-confident that if you stuck a Stetson on his head he could pass for a main character in *Dallas*.

I return his smile through pursed lips.

And then I stroll away.

As fast as I can.

15

During the walk back to the harbour, I feel disconcerted and alarmed. Did Stuart Wilson-Price know who I was? Did he seek me out? It seems impossible and yet if I went into a bookmaker right now, what odds would they give me for bumping into the father of my ex-husband's new girlfriend? Maybe not a million to one, but it would have to be high.

As I reach the tiny jetty at the bottom of the cliffs, a dozen kids dart out of the old wooden canoe station. They're all wearing wetsuits and bright orange life jackets, while the woman instructor is dressed in a thick bomber jacket and bobble hat. It may not be tropical this afternoon, but that's going a bit overboard.

'Don't rush! Don't rush!' she shouts at the children, though none of them pay her any attention. 'And whatever you do, do not get into the boats until I say so. Do you hear me, Jonathan Wells? Until *I* say so. Not you, not your friend, but *me*. Understand?'

A blond-haired boy nods his head and his mate sniggers and elbows him in the ribs. As I watch them, a wave of nostalgia hits me like a tsunami. Gosh, it seems only five minutes ago that

Rebecca was in the canoe club. How has so much time passed? It makes no sense to me. No sense at all.

I lean against the cliff face and feel the cold, uneven surface against my back. The children clamber into the canoes and as painful as it is, I can't tear my eyes away from them. Twelve years ago, I would have been standing here, watching Rebecca. Twelve years ago we would have walked back to our happy little home, where we'd be greeted by my loving husband and steaming cups of hot chocolate with cream. But now here I am, watching children I don't know have the same kind of fun that Rebecca once did. Soon, I'll walk back to my lonely house and there'll be no hot chocolate in the cupboard and nobody to make it for me. No cream, no marshmallows, just a teabag in a mug and a television screen filled with other people's stories. Life marches on and all we can do is hold tight and hope that we can reach somewhere safe and warm and welcoming. Maybe one day I will, but for now I'm still hanging on.

~

'That story is insane.'

Kate scowls at me from behind the library counter. I lean my head in my hands and lower my voice. There are only three people in the room, but still, I'd like to keep this news between my friend and I.

'I know,' I whisper. 'What are the chances of bumping into him like that?'

Kate guffaws and grabs a copy of *The Great Gatsby*. It's dog-eared and the cover is ripped at the top, but she deems it good enough to be returned to the book trolley. In my day I'd have taken great delight in repairing it with the special tape I acquired from an antiquarian book dealer. I used to love repairing books, but Kate never shared my passion.

'Come on, Jenny! You don't believe that was a chance meeting, do you? He must have planned it for sure!'

Kate's voice goes up an octave whenever she's trying to make a point. I squirm and an old lady reading *The Times* shushes us with a finger to the lips.

'I think he must have planned it as well,' I whisper, while the old lady scowls and tuts before getting back to the newspaper. 'But I was hoping you'd say otherwise.'

'No one in their right mind would say otherwise.' Kate licks her finger and rubs at an ink blot on her thumb. 'But you know that already.'

'Maybe, but then what would be the purpose of it? Why would Stuart Wilson-Price want to meet me? And how would he even know who I was after all these years? It's all too absurd. Don't you think?'

Kate shrugs, opens a copy of the new Marian Keyes book and scores out the return date.

'Who knows with men? They've all got a bloody screw loose if you ask me.'

I'm taken aback because it's not like Kate to criticise the male species. In fact, out of everyone I know, my friend has always preferred the company of men rather than women. Men are drawn to her overconfidence and outspoken nature, while those aspects of her personality seem to turn women right off. Except me; I've always loved her in spite of those things.

'Is everything okay?'

She waves my question away and rubs her eyes. Her eyeliner smudges out towards her hairline, so I reach over and rub it away with my thumb.

'Yes. No. Oh, I don't know.' Kate sighs and then a young lad arrives at the desk to return a copy of the first *Harry Potter* book. She recovers enough to thank him for returning the book on time, and then bids him farewell.

'So? What's wrong?'

'Ugh, Pete and I had a falling out, that's all.'

'Want to talk about it?'

'Nope. It might be nothing anyway. He's just being a moany old git. Must be his age!'

'Is he going through the male menopause?' I say, half-joking. 'He hasn't bought a Porsche and a pair of leather trousers, has he?' I giggle but Kate doesn't raise a smile.

'Who knows what the fuck's wrong with him.' The old woman looks up and Kate apologises before the customer has the chance to shush us again. 'Anyway, let's change the subject and get on to more important matters. Like what are you going to do about your encounter with Annabelle's dad? Are you going to tell Rebecca?'

I play with a pen on the counter and it flips off and rolls under the desk.

'Definitely not! I'm just going to forget about him, and avoid strolling on the promenade for a while.'

'Good call,' Kate says. 'You've got enough drama in your life already.'

16

I seem to have experienced a curious turn of events. Since discovering who Craig's new lover is, Helena Love has decided that she, Rebecca and I are now somehow interlinked. According to her, we've all been cheated and humiliated, and therefore can empathise with each other's sorrow and lend some support. It's all bullshit. Where was this empathy five years ago, when Helena was screwing my husband in my own house? What sympathy and understanding did she have for me when she arrived on my doorstep on the evening of my twentieth wedding anniversary? I'm guessing zero.

Because of this supposed shared agony, we're now somehow bound together, marching through the battlefields. Crusaders! Down but not out, fighting on despite the world's cruel ways! I'm not being dramatic, that's the way Helena sees it. How do I know this? Because she told me. And then I wrote it all down in my notebook, like the good little researcher I am.

Being an over-sharer and general attention-seeker, Helena likes to disclose every insignificant thought, complaint and fantasy that comes darting into her brain. I have to admit that most of what she says is whinging bullshit, but occasionally a golden nugget will slip out that reveals something about me, my marriage or both. Like the time before, when she knew where my bathroom was, and her revelation – real or imagined – that she and Craig discussed his affairs during our years together.

To this day I'm sure she doesn't realise the bathroom slip-up. Me on the other hand... I forget nothing.

Nothing, nothing, nothing.

∼

'Root your right foot into the floor and raise your left foot, placing it gently onto the right. Raise your hands above your head and join them in prayer position. Perfect. Now then, can anyone tell me what posture this is? Anyone?'

Louise – the leopard-print, leotard-wearing yoga teacher – gazes around the room until her eyes fall upon me. She beams, but I shrug. How am I supposed to know what position this is? This is my first ever class and I'm just happy I haven't collapsed already.

'It's the tree!' Helena shouts. 'Which is also known as Vrik-shasana.' As soon as the words leave her lips, she loses concentration and her foot falls to the floor. She tuts and regains her balance, though I wish she'd fallen straight onto her face.

'Bravo,' the teacher replies. 'Give yourself an extra point for learning the Sanskrit. That's extremely impressive.' The teacher applauds and Helena's face breaks into the brightest fake smile I've ever seen. She must surely have been the teacher's pet at school. I can just see her now, demanding they do tests and handing in her homework, the morning after it's given out.

This is the first time I've been in the community centre for five years, but it doesn't look any different: wooden stage at one end, complete with moth-eaten, merlot-coloured velvet curtains; blue plastic chairs piled up around the front; long Formica tables playing host to handbags and jackets; mustard walls that look as though they last saw a paintbrush in 1987 and a thick, dusty floor made up of tiny, wooden interconnecting tiles. The air is musty and I'm not sure how inhaling any of it can be good for our chakras – or whatever Louise called them earlier.

As I try to hold the aforementioned tree pose, it occurs to me that if I stumble from my borrowed sticky mat, I'll fall straight into Helena and then the whole class will turn into a giant game of human dominoes. I giggle at the idea of it and the trendy yogi behind me makes an irritated noise. If there's one thing I've learned today, it's that yoga students are mega serious about their lessons. From wearing the best gear, to using the latest bands, blocks and other accessories, and let's not forget the constant struggles into outrageous poses in order to impress the women on the row behind. With all that to consider, there's no time for giggles, talking, or any other kind of fun in this class.

As we move into a position that resembles a gigantic human starfish (Warrior pose as it turns out), I can't help but wonder what Kate would say if she could see me now. She'd definitely ask why I'm here, and I suppose the easy answer is because Helena invited me. She's been attending this class for years and thought that somehow it might benefit my 'body, mind and spirit'. I don't know if that was said in a sarcastic 'you're a fat bitch and need to tone up' kind of way, or if Helena does believe that yoga is the answer to everyone's problems. Either way, I'm here because she asked me to be here, though that's not the reason I *wanted* to come.

The truth is that since Helena has decided she's somehow spiritually connected to me, she has integrated herself into my life in almost every way imaginable. Some days she's 'just popping past'. Other times she wants to find a suitable outfit for solicitor's meetings, and I'm the only one who can help her to choose. The sensible side of my personality did wonder if I should push her away; tell her I've had enough and that what she's going through is none of my business. For a moment I pondered closing my curtains and switching off my phone; maybe even going away for a few weeks until she forgets about me. But deep down I know that's something I could never do, because when Helena does come knocking on my door, the temptation to open it is too hard to resist. What is it they say? Keep your friends close and your enemies closer?

And believe me I intend to keep Ms Helena Love very close indeed.

~

Yoga class ends with something called Corpse pose, which means lying on your mat in the dark; trying to relax without falling into a coma. There's no chance of me doing that since my mind is always chattering away to itself, but the long-haired bloke next to me has taken things to extreme and is snoring as though he hasn't slept in a week.

As the class finishes, we all peel ourselves off our mats and roll them into tight little sausages. At the front of the hall, Louise runs her fingers along the panel of switches and with a series of pings and ticks, the dazzling fluorescent lights burst into action. The teacher then wanders over to the sleeping bloke, while the rest of us adjust our eyes to the blinding glare.

'Come along, Raymond.' She pats the guy's shoulder and he wakes with a start. 'You've done it again, I'm afraid. Next week, try to remember that we're aiming for deep relaxation, not full-blown sleep!' Raymond rubs his eyes, farts and heaves himself up.

'That's the trouble with yoga,' Helena whispers. 'No matter how much you try to hold it in, wind will always find its way out in the end.'

I hold my hand over my nose and move away. Helena slips a pair of pink ballet slippers onto her ever-so-small feet, and then throws her yoga bag over her shoulder.

'I'm sorry I have to rush off. I promised my neighbour I'd look after her dog this evening and I'm already five minutes late.'

Before I have a chance to reply, Helena is gone. The nerve of the woman; bringing me into a class I've never attended before, and then leaving me to walk out with a bunch of strangers. I push my feet into my trainers and notice that the fabric is coming away from the sole. Terrific. While I'm examining it, Louise the yoga teacher towers above me. Her leopard leotard has round sweat patches under the arms and at the top of her thighs, and her breath smells of coffee and cigarettes. For a yoga teacher, she doesn't seem to be too involved with her health.

'How was that then?' she asks.

'It wasn't too bad. Although it did show me how inflexible I am!'

Louise waves my comment away.

'Oh, don't worry about that. If you keep up your lessons, I can guarantee that you'll be touching your toes in two months or less.'

I nod because I don't want her to feel bad, though I know that what she's saying is bullshit. I've never been able to touch my toes – not even when I was a kid. In fact, when I was four, my mother had to remove me from gymnastics club because everyone laughed at my inability to do it. I was heartbroken at the time, but at this point in my life my tight hamstrings are the least of my worries.

I gather up my belongings and start towards the door, but Louise follows me.

'So how do you know Helena?' she asks.

I pick at the tassel on my handbag and wonder if I should lie, but decide against it. 'She's... She's the estranged wife of my ex-husband.'

Louise's eyes bulge. If she was a cartoon character, they'd be on stalks by now. Behind me, two women stop rolling up their mats, and then whisper to each other.

'So, you're Jenny?'

Louise points her finger at me, and her eyebrows almost knit together in the middle.

'Yes, I'm Jenny. How did you know that?'

The teacher grabs my hand and holds onto it for far too long.

'It's wonderful to meet you!' she gushes. 'Although I have to say, you are nothing like Helena described.' She runs her eyes up and down my body and then turns to the women on the row behind. 'Doesn't she look different, ladies? I didn't expect her to look like this at all!'

The nosey women both nod and agree that yes, I do look younger, thinner and prettier than Helena had led them to believe. My bottom lip quivers and I do my best to disguise it as a smile, but I'm not sure I succeed.

'Does Helena mention me often?' I ask, and Louise realises that she perhaps shouldn't have greeted me with such enthusiasm. She waves her arms around, revealing a bigger wet patch than she had already.

'Oh no.' She chortles. 'Well, not in recent times anyway. I think it was just one of those ex-wife versus new-wife type things, y'know?'

I don't bother to reply, so in the end, Louise pats my arm and then turns her attention to Raymond, the yogic farter. I twist round to face the women behind me, but they avoid my gaze, gather up their mats and push past me.

After yoga, I head straight for Harbour Rise, and Helena's house. It's dark and miserable, and that drizzly rain envelopes me and attaches itself to my too-thin coat. The weather matches my mood perfectly, and my hands curl into fists as I reach Helena's driveway.

Now what?

The voice in my head demands to know what I'm doing here, but I don't have an answer. The moment Louise revealed that Helena spoke about me in class, I knew I was going to come up here, but what comes next is anybody's guess. In one aspect, I fully appreciate that Helena was bound to gossip about me to her friends and associates – it's human nature after all – but the fact that she then dragged me into the class, knowing what she'd done, is unforgivable. The invitation may have been innocent, but haven't I suffered at her hands enough?

Yes, I have. And now it's her turn.

Helena's driveway is concrete, with a border of flowers covered in tiny pebbles. Some of the stones have been knocked onto the drive itself, and I tread carefully past them, for fear that they'll give away my arrival. I wander past the Audi, and run my finger along the scratch that leads from the back end to the driver's door. It seems like forever since I vandalised Helena's car, and yet she hasn't even mentioned let alone fixed it. Perhaps she hasn't noticed. She's so wrapped up in her pitiful little world that it wouldn't surprise me.

I take a cautionary look into the living room window, but there is no sign of life. Helena must have been telling the truth when she said she was going to look after her neighbour's dog. A surge of dread lands in my chest. I don't know what neighbour Helena was talking about, but if it's nearby, she may well have seen me walking towards her house. I gaze around, but in the dark it's impossible to see if anyone is peeping out of their curtains.

I pull my hood up over my head, and once again wonder what the hell I'm doing here. I could be home right now, watching old movies and having a cup of hot chocolate. But instead, I'm standing on the doorstep of my enemy's home, like something out of an old gangster movie. I turn to leave, but then visions of Helena and Craig come flooding into my brain... the two of them carrying on for God knows how long. Her in my house, fucking my husband in our bed, and him loving the fact that he had two women on the go at once... And then that night – that bloody awful night when he finally told me it was over, and went scuttling over to Helena's house.

This house!

This horrendous, soul-destroying, husband-stealing house!!

The rage burns right through my chest as I look around for something – anything – that can relieve this pain. There's a small walled rockery underneath the front window, and the bricks are old and crumbling – crumbly enough that when I push the top one with my trainer, two conjoined blocks come away together. I look around to make sure that there are no dog walkers nearby, and before the rational side of my brain can kick into gear, I stick on some gloves that I found in the bottom of my pockets, pick the bricks up and heave them through a pane of glass in the old front door. The glass explodes in front of me, and the sound shatters through the night. Seconds later, I hear the high-pitched sound of Helena's alarm, and next-door's hall light flashes on.

My breath catches in the back of my throat, and I sprint as quickly as I can; away from Helena's house, away from this street, and away from the memories that still gnaw like rats in my brain.

By the time I get home I'm covered in sweat and the night air has numbed my chest. I throw my sports clothes in the washing machine and jump into the shower. Only then do I finally let myself relax and think about poor Helena's face when she sees the broken windowpane.

And then I laugh.

And I laugh.

And I laugh.

17

It's the morning after yoga and I'm wandering towards the stone pier with Helena. She came to see me early this morning, in a state because somebody had attempted to break into her home last night. Luckily, they only got so far as breaking the glass in her front door, but the incident has cost her eighty pounds to fix. Eighty pounds she doesn't have, since she also has to fix a gigantic scratch running the length of her car...

'So do the police have any idea who it was?' I'm surprised by my ability to act so calm. Maybe I should attempt a career in amateur dramatics. Helena sighs and rubs her face. Her eyes are red-rimmed; the result of only two hours sleep, or so she tells me.

'They said there have been a few break-ins in the area over the past month, but no definite leads. They've given me an incident number, but since the burglar ran off before he actually got into the house, there's not much they can do. I guess I should just be glad he was scared off.'

I enjoy Helena's conclusion that the 'intruder' must have been male. That gets me off the hook, though the likelihood of her ever suspecting me is minimal. I'm too good a friend to do anything so horrible.

At least I am in her eyes.

We approach the bottom of Smuggler's Steps and Helena freezes; her body rigid as a tree.

'Are you okay?'

'Yeah,' she says. 'I just hate those steps. They give me the creeps.'

I nod and stare up at the shady, grey stones. Smuggler's Steps are a series of narrow, steep stones located between the harbour and the stone pier, and they sweep up the cliffside to Harbour Rise – the estate where Helena lives. They have a brittle wooden banister to the left, and a whole heap of nettles and skin-tearing vegetation to the right. This means that anyone who dares use them runs the risk of plummeting to their death, being stung to pieces, or a mixture of both.

Legend has it that in years gone by, the stairs were used by smugglers coming into the harbour with their illegal wares. In fact, they also say that's how the Black Death was brought into Britain. I've done some research into this subject myself and can find nothing to confirm or deny the theories, but the legend keeps tourists coming into Cromwey year after year, so maybe it's best we never do find out for sure.

Thanks to a campaign hosted by Kate several years ago, there are now signs at the top and bottom, warning tourists that you enter the steps at your own risk. Still, a lot of locals refuse to use them because of the danger involved. This doesn't extend to teenagers, and on numerous occasions I've seen some little twat trying to get down them on his skateboard, bike or even rollerblades.

'They creep me out too,' I reply. 'I try to avoid them when-ever I can, even if the council does say that they're safe when used sensibly.'

'Yes, funny that they should say that and yet still feel the need to put *enter at your own risk* signs at the top and bottom.'

Helena reaches out to touch the banister, and then recoils when a sharp sliver of wood attacks her fingers.

'I slipped down them once. It was awful.' She examines her finger and I'm disappointed to discover that the wood left no splinter. 'Well, at least I'm pretty sure I slipped, but sometimes I wonder if maybe it was a mugging gone wrong or something like that.'

'What do you mean?'

'I don't have many memories of that day, so it's hard to tell. All I know is that I somehow ended up unconscious on the stairs and everyone said I must have slipped, but a lot of teenagers hang around those steps, and not all of them are friendly.'

There is a sound from above and as I look up, there is a family of five, heading towards us. The mother grips onto the banister and shouts at everyone to be careful, but the youngest of the group – a little red-headed kid of about six – throws his hands in the air and leaps up and down in protest.

'Can't tell me what to do!' he screams, before his ankle overturns and he grabs onto the handrail for support.

We wait for the group to pass, and then continue our conversation.

'I heard about your accident at the time,' I say. 'In fact, I even joined Kate's campaign to ensure that safety measures were put in place, after it happened. Not that it helped at all – except if you can call a sign a safety measure.'

Helena grabs my hand and the unexpected force of it causes me to jolt.

'I know you helped, and I'll never forget your kindness for doing that.'

I almost choke. Never forget my kindness? That's something to note down in my book later. The truth of the matter is that my actions had nothing to do with kindness and everything to do with a dictatorial friend who refused to take no for an answer.

On the day after the accident, Kate called at my house with a local reporter and photographer in tow. They made an odd threesome: my friend with her apple-green winter coat and striped pom-pom hat; the retirement-age photographer with a humungous camera held over his shoulder with a thick, black strap; and what looked to be a work experience lad with a bulging bag filled with pens and notebooks.

To be honest I was furious because it was a Sunday and I was still in my pyjamas, glued to an old Marilyn Monroe movie on BBC2, but Kate assured me that her quest was far more important, so I rushed to get dressed. My friend came upstairs with me and that was when she explained that 'a poor woman' had fallen at Smuggler's Steps. Kate, being the powerhouse that she is, had got it into her head that she'd make everyone aware of how dangerous the steps had become, and for that she needed me.

'We have to raise awareness,' she shouted, as we trotted back down the stairs. 'Let the councillors know that we will not tolerate the potential hazards of that crumbling monstrosity! We need plans in place to ensure this diabolical atrocity never happens again, and we need them now... not later... now!!'

I almost laughed out loud. My friend believed she was a Joan of Arc- or Evita-type character, and the reporter lapped up everything she had to say – right down to threatening a human wall at the steps if the authorities didn't take action.

Minutes later – and with no enthusiasm whatsoever – I was marched to the bottom of Smuggler's Steps for a photo shoot. Kate posed with one hand on her hip, the other raised to the sky in defiance. It would have looked far more powerful if she'd removed her bobble hat, but not even the photographer was brave enough to suggest it. As he clicked his camera and told her to move this way and that, I kind of hung around at the side, trying to smile in the freezing temperature and praying that the photos would never come out. They did though, and were plastered all over the newspaper the following day.

As we prepared to leave the steps, the reporter turned to Kate.

'I'll let you know if we hear anything from the council,' he said. 'But for now, let's hope that the young lady manages to pull through. I heard that it was quite a fall.'

'Thanks,' Kate said. 'Any news on who she is?'

The reporter flicked through his notes, and scowled as he tried to decipher his own handwriting.

'Helena,' he said. 'Helena Love.'

As you can imagine, this revelation caused a sensation, but it didn't quell Kate's determination to get the steps closed off. That is until somebody tried to grab her handbag on the pleasure pier, and then all her attention was given to placing extra security on the boardwalk. In fact, Kate was so obsessed with that particular campaign that when the council announced they'd be keeping Smuggler's Steps open with the addition of the safety sign, she declared it to be acceptable and then forgot about it.

Back to the present and Helena still grips onto my hand. Her palms are clammy, and I pretend to have an itch on my face so that I can free myself from her grasp.

'It was the loveliest thing to come from that tragedy,' she gushes. 'Knowing that despite everything that happened, you were *still* concerned for my safety. That meant the world to me and I'm grateful to you.'

There have been many times during our 'friendship' that I have just about managed to stifle my laughter, but today I fail.

'What's funny?'

'Helena, I had no idea that it was you who'd fallen. I found out that information after the photographs had been taken.'

'I see.' She's crestfallen, which makes this news all the sweeter.

'To be honest, if I had known it was you, there's no way I'd have ever been involved in the campaign. And I think that deep down, you kind of know that too.'

And with that remark hanging in the air, I leave my companion and stride back towards the harbour.

18

It's Sunday morning and I've been out for a run. I started the exercise about four years ago, in an attempt to quieten my mind. When I'm running, I don't have space in my head to think about anything other than breathing and avoiding potholes, so it's a healthy endeavour. Don't get me wrong, I'm no marathon sprinter and I'd be lying if I said I do it every day, but once in a while when the weather is pleasant and my legs are feeling up to it, off I go.

Today, there is a bracing breeze howling in from the sea and my hair is taking the brunt of it. As I cross the bridge and head back towards the harbour, I know that I'll be diving into the shower the moment I get indoors, but two minutes later, my plans evaporate into mist.

There, leaning against the front door of his former family home, is my ex-husband, Craig. He's wearing a Hawaiian shirt and khaki shorts, and his sunglasses are propped up on his head as he plays with this phone. He looks dressed for a trip to the Caribbean, not Cromwey. As I round into the garden, he gazes up and smiles.

'There you are. I was about to text you.'

'You'd have a hard job, since you don't have my number anymore.'

He waggles his phone at me.

'Rebecca gave it to me in case of emergencies.'

I rummage in my pocket for my key and slide it into the lock. We're so close that I can smell Craig's aftershave and feel his warm breath on my cheek. It is disconcerting, irritating and comforting, all at the same time.

'And this is an emergency because...?'

He ignores my comment and as soon as the door opens, he makes a move to enter. I cough and my ex realises that he has no right to wander in anymore.

'Oops, sorry. Force of habit.'

I push past and throw my keys onto the table. Craig hovers between the garden and the hall, running his fingers across the blue paint on the front door.

'Has the door always been blue,' he asks. 'I'm sure it was green when I lived here.'

'I'm surprised you can remember to be honest. You've lived in so many places since you moved out; it must all be a blur to you by now.'

'Ha, ha.'

I hate it when Craig speaks the words instead of expressing them. Why not laugh if he thinks something is funny, or do nothing at all if he doesn't?

'Can I come in?'

He stares at me through wide eyes, and I lean back and let him into my home for the first time in almost five years.

'Don't expect it to resemble Buckingham Palace,' I say. 'It's Sunday – day of rest and all that.'

'Was it ever like Buckingham Palace?' His lips turn up to feign a joke, but sarcasm oozes out of him.

I'm not biting.

I slip my trainers off and stare down at my *Winnie-the-Pooh* socks. Of all the days I decide to wear Disney socks, it had to be when my ex pays a visit. I step into the living room and Craig follows. His eyes scan the room and he pretends not to notice the new sofa, carpet and curtains that have moved in since he moved out. Another addition is the oak cabinet of antiquarian curiosities and a 1930s lampshade imported from California. Yes, my dear cheating husband, I did spend our divorce settlement on expensive treats. Thanks for asking.

I sink into my favourite armchair, while Craig paces around the room, his eyes flitting from one object to the other. It's strange. This man lived here for years and yet now it feels as though a stranger has infiltrated my safe space. What does he want? His silence is anything but comforting.

'So, are you here to wear a hole in my carpet, or is there an actual reason for your visit?'

He stops pacing, undoes the top button of his shirt and perches on the arm of the sofa. I've always hated it when he does that.

'Sorry. It's weird being back here again. Everything's so...'

'Different?'

'Yeah.'

His eyes dart around the room again and I wonder if he's a teeny bit pissed that I got to keep our dream harbour home. He'd never admit it, but it must aggravate him. Oh well, he could have had it too, if he'd stayed. If he'd been able to keep his dick under control.

'Listen, I came to talk to you about what happened the other day... at the gallery.'

His voice grates and I'm put on the defence.

'What about it?'

Craig moves from the arm onto the sofa itself and his back flumps into my John Lewis cushions. The cheek of this guy!

What does he think he's doing, acting as though he still lives here? His eyes are all over me, but I refuse to be intimidated and I stare straight back.

'Do I have to spell it out?'

'Evidently.'

'Okay then. Why were you, Rebecca and my ex-wife of all people, visiting Annabelle at her place of work? That was out of order. She could have been fired!'

I gasp and hiccup at the same time and it comes out of my mouth as an unattractive grunt. It's hilarious how fast Craig can move on. They're not even divorced yet and he's already referring to Helena in the past tense. I wonder how long it took him to do that with me. Thirty minutes? Twenty? Even less?

'First of all, Helena is not your ex-wife, unless you managed to get a divorce in the space of the past few weeks. Secondly, what business is it of yours what we were doing there? The gallery is a public space; we don't need your permission to visit.'

Anger flashes across his eyes and he wallops one of my cushions with the back of his hand.

'Come on, we both know you weren't browsing for paintings of beach huts! I'll ask again – what were you, Rebecca and my *estranged* wife, doing at the gallery?'

His accusatory tone is repulsive and the vein on his forehead stands out like a pale blue worm. He presses on it with his finger – another habit that has refused to die.

'What do you think we were doing there?' I loosen my pony-tail and my hair flops down onto my shoulders. Shit, I forgot that it's sweaty and frizzy from my run, but it's too late now. I smooth it as best I can and tuck it behind my ears. Craig still glowers at me, waiting for an answer.

'We went to the gallery because Helena was upset that you'd gone off with another woman. Then Rebecca was heartbroken that the woman was her former friend. They both wanted to see what she had to say for herself. That was it.'

'And you?'

'What do you mean?'

'What were you doing there?'

I pretend to be super-enthusiastic about a bobble in the material of my cushion. I have never noticed it before and as I start to pull, it turns into a thread and I realise that I'm about to unravel the fabric. I stop faffing with it and rub my eyes instead.

'I was there to make sure nobody got killed or maimed in the process.'

Craig huffs and heaves himself out of the sofa. His shirt is creased at the bottom and I wonder if he'll ask his new woman to iron it for him. Does a twenty-three-year-old even know how to iron? Does he?

'I'd be grateful if you could stay away from Annabelle from now on,' he says. 'If Rebecca has any questions about my new life, then she's free to come and see me. If Helena's got any – well, she's got the number of my solicitor.'

My ex-husband nods once, as though he's imparting some crucial information, and then he heads for the living room door.

'He's looking for you, y'know.'

Craig stops, groans and twists to face me.

'Who is?'

'Annabelle's dad. He bumped into me on the promenade the other day and told me all about it.'

Craig's face sags and he falls back onto the arm of the sofa.

'What do you mean, he bumped into you?'

'Just that! I don't know if it was on purpose or a coincidence, but since they say there are no coincidences, maybe it was the former. Either way, he's in Cromwey because he believes his daughter is involved with an undesirable bastard, and he wants to take her back home. He doesn't know where she lives but he's been to the gallery to see her and he's devastated that she's refusing to even see him. Also, he's pissed that you're the one who stole Daddy's little girl from under his nose.'

Craig cracks his knuckles and my shoulders tingle. I'd forgotten all about that disgusting habit. He used to do that whenever he was furious but trying to remain 'cool'.

'Well, Stuart Wilson-Price can be as upset as he likes. Annabelle's over the age of consent, she doesn't need his permission to do anything.'

He jumps up and marches towards the hall, but the front of his shirt catches on the living room door. He swears under his breath, and then examines his precious clothes for any damage.

'You know Annabelle's dad?'

'What?'

'You said his name – Stuart Wilson-Price. Do you remember him from the school playground?'

Craig reaches the front door and straightens a painting that's hanging at a slight angle. He leaves two greasy fingerprints behind, and I scratch the back of my neck to stop me saying how much he irritates me.

'No, I don't know him from the playground.' He sniggers. 'Stuart was a member of the Harbour Committee when I was, before he moved to Poole.'

'Bournemouth.'

'What?'

'He moved to Bournemouth, not Poole.'

'Jesus, same difference! Anyway, argumentative bastard he was; always trying to get the committee to fund his plans for a golf course up by the castle. Then when that failed, he wanted squash courts beside the beach. It never occurred to him that the only person interested in golf or squash was him. Twat.'

I roll my eyes. Typical Craig. He's sleeping with the guy's

daughter, but all he dwells on is how Stuart pissed him off over some sports facilities.

'So, what are you going to do about him?'

Craig unlatches the lock and the door pops open. A blast of cool air whooshes in and ruffles my already messy hair.

'Nothing at all. Stuart's problem with me and Annabelle is just that – his problem... and that goes for all of you, by the way.'

My ex-husband steps out into his former garden and takes a deep breath.

'What's going on with you, Craig?'

'What do you mean?'

He turns towards me, and I notice for the first time how old his eyes look. They're still his best feature, but deep lines have formed at the sides, and the skin below his eyebrows almost reaches his lids.

'I mean, you used to be one of the most together people I knew, and now – now you're all over the place. It's as though you've completely lost yourself.'

Craig bites on his lower lip and we make eye contact; it's soft and friendly and filled with something I can't quite grasp. Love? No, not that. Empathy maybe. I'm not sure, but it's definitely not hostile, I know that much.

'Don't you worry about me, I'm doing fine.' He smiles and then turns away. 'Listen, do me a favour and stay away from Stuart Wilson-Price. He's not the friendliest of blokes.'

I nod and close the door. The picture that Craig straightened hangs wonky again, and I have no desire to fix it.

19

Name-calling is a peculiar pastime, isn't it? You see, I'm comfortable labelling Helena with every derogatory term I can conjure up, but knowing that she spoke shit about me to strange women at a yoga class has been burning a hole in my stomach for the past few days.

But now I am happy to repay the favour. Again.

My fingers quiver and I have trouble steadying my breath as I dial the phone number I googled this morning. The line makes several ticking noises then connects to its destination, but rings for so long that I wonder if I should hang up. Finally, a woman breathes down the phone in an unexpected Geordie accent.

'Cromwey Council. Can I help you?'

'Yes,' I say. 'I'd like to report a rat sighting in a local café.'

'A rat? Okay, I'll put you through to the Department of Health. Hold the line please.'

Several cheek-chewing moments pass before there's a click and then a gruff male voice.

'Hello, I understand you've sighted a rat in a local establishment. Can you tell me where and when you saw it, please?'

'Yes, it was The Lovely Café. That pink restaurant on the promenade...'

I breathe and feel the air expanding my lungs to full capacity, and then I launch into my well-rehearsed speech. Name-calling is a terrible habit indeed, but sometimes it can be also be rewarding.

It's 8am and Cromwey is waking up. The fishermen have been up for hours, and many have arrived back with their nets full of cod, crabs and other delights. Gulls argue over scraps, while a local cat parades up and down, hoping that someone will take pity and throw a little something his way. The smell of the fishermen's wares made me gag when I was a kid. We'd all traipse past, making heaving noises and holding our noses in a dramatic fashion. But now I have no such problems. The sights and sounds of the harbour will always be home to me and I understand how privileged I am to live in this beautiful and coveted place.

I'm returning home from my run, and in the distance, I notice that Mrs Moore is talking to someone in the garden next door to mine. I imagine she must have collared the poor postwoman and it isn't until I get closer that I realise Mrs Moore's victim is Helena. As I approach, my neighbour gazes over Helena's shoulder and nods, then the woman herself twists round and gives an almighty wave.

'Hi!!' Helena Love's high-octane voice is too stressful for this time of the morning. I nod and she beams as though it's the most natural thing in the world to be loitering in my neighbour's garden.

'Good morning, dear,' Mrs Moore chirps. 'We were just talking about you.'

'Were you indeed? I'm sure that made for a riveting conversation.' My voice is light as though I'm joking, but I'm serious.

'Don't worry,' Helena says. 'It was all good.'

She gives me a dazzling smile and thrusts her thumbs in the air. She looks demented. My calves ache from the run, and I lean on the wall to rub them; all the time aware of my companions staring at me.

'Been for a run have you, dear?' Mrs Moore is nothing but observant.

I nod and pull my socks up.

'Yep, that's right.'

'It's always good to try and get in shape at your age,' she says. 'Good for you.'

Sarcastic old cow.

Mrs Moore rubs her knees, and grimaces.

'I'm not too good, I'm afraid. It's my old joints, you see. Playing up again, they are.'

'You'll have to go to the doctor if this keeps up.' Helena pats Mrs Moore on the shoulder.

'I agree, me duck, but I don't have any means of getting there.'

Both women gawp at me. I have no idea what's going on, and I have no wish to find out.

'You ladies will have to excuse me,' I say. 'I've got a lot to do this morning.' I turn towards the front door and rustle in my pocket for my keys. Helena hoists herself over the tiny wall, and then appears right behind me.

'Jenny, don't rush off. We need to talk!'

Do we though?

'Goodbye, Mrs Moore,' she says in a dainty voice. 'It was lovely to talk to you again.'

'You too, dear,' she replies. 'I'm sorry for what you're going through. But don't you be blaming yourself. It sounds as though you did everything you could to make Craig happy, but sometimes men don't appreciate what they have.'

Helena lowers her eyes in a perfect Princess Diana impersonation, and nods.

'Thank you, that means a lot to me.'

I open my front door and Helena strides into the hall without being asked. She's become a master of that. I pop the key into the dish at the front door and when I turn back, my unwanted guest grins at me.

'So, what was that all about?' I kick my trainers off and plod through the living room into the kitchen. Helena stays right behind me.

'What do you mean?'

'You and Mrs Moore. How do you know each other?'

I pour myself a cup of water. The coldness seeps through the glass and I hold it against my cheeks. Helena sits at my kitchen table, examines an apple and then throws it back into the fruit bowl.

'Craig introduced us years ago.' She chuckles. 'When we were... y'know... dating. It was during one of the rare times we came down to the harbour. Mrs Moore had driven her car into a bollard and was arguing with the policeman about it. Craig saw what was going on and managed to calm the situation down.'

'How nice.'

I pull out a chair and stare at Helena. I don't even care if she notices. Today, her scraggy hair is pinned up with a furry bobble and sparkly pink slides. They're the kind of accessories a twelve-year-old should find appealing, not a grown woman. Her mascara is blue and her nails are manicured with peach-coloured varnish. I've only ever had one manicure in my whole life and that was the day before my wedding. The beautician insisted on attaching tiny gems to the top of the varnish, and two of them had already fallen off by the time I got home. What a waste of money.

'I reintroduced myself last week, while I was waiting for you to come back from the hairdresser. Bless her heart, she remembered who I was. That quite surprised me.'

'Yeah, Mrs Moore always remembers an unusual face.'

Helena's eyes narrow. She has no idea if I'm being flattering or sarcastic, but it wouldn't take a brain surgeon to figure it out.

'Nice lady though. She was telling me all about her son and his ghastly wife. She sounds hideous.'

I notice there is a smear of red lipstick on Helena's teeth, which makes them look rotten. It gives me great joy not to tell her about it.

'Just be wary. Mrs Moore may come across as semi-pleasant, but to say she loves to gossip would be an understatement. Maybe best not to tell her too much about your new circumstances, or it'll be all over town.'

Helena adjusts her ridiculous hair slides.

'Oh, I don't know about that. She was really sympathetic to me, to be honest, and sympathy is exactly what I need right now.'

My mind goes back to Rebecca and Kate's comments about Helena being the queen of neediness and attention. If I'm going to keep her close, I guess I'll have to get used to that side of her. Will that be easy? No. Will it be worth it? Certainly.

'Hey, can I have a cup of tea? My mouth is dry as hell.'

Helena relaxes into the kitchen chair, picks the apple back up and takes a gigantic, crunching bite. She's got some balls on her, I'll give her that.

～

As I make her tea, Helena waffles on about the many new, understanding friends she's discovered over the past few weeks. I'd bet my CD collection that the only reason anyone is showing sympathy for her 'plight' is because they want to know all the juicy details. It's the reason we buy gossip magazines and watch reality shows, isn't it? We're not going out of our way to empathise with the forlorn Z-list celebrities – we're being bloody nosey! That's the absolute limit of our interest.

I pour boiling water over some teabags, and realise I've filled one cup far too high if I'm going to add milk. I throw some of it down the sink, steam rises up from the plughole and then I place the mugs down onto the table. I make sure to give Helena the one with a photo of Miss Piggy from *The Muppet Show*. This is a bit of a private joke. When I first saw a photo of the woman Craig had left me for, her hair reminded me of Miss Piggy's. Granted, it's a different colour, but the curls are the same. From then on that was my nickname for her, and Kate bought me a mug – this mug – so that we could laugh about it together.

Helena stares at the photo and scowls.

'Miss Piggy? My parents used to like her. Bit before my time though.'

Before her time? Who the hell is she kidding? Helena swallows her tea and then in true form, her eyes lower, her mouth turns down, and she makes a dramatic sigh.

'So, I'm having the week from hell.' She leans her chin on her hand and her throat makes a gurgling sound. She scratches her neck and then fiddles with her hair again.

'What's happened?'

I take a banana from the fruit bowl and unpeel it while Helena talks. She tilts her head to one side as though she's never encountered such a move.

'Did you know that you're really supposed to peel a banana

MICHELLE MORGAN

from the bottom up? I watched a segment about it on *Good Morning Britain*.'

I nod as though intrigued by this revelation, and then I stuff half of the banana into my mouth. If this nonsense keeps up, I'll be peeling *her* from the bottom up. She notices my lack of interest in her trivia and coughs.

'Anyway, first of all, the health inspector visited the café because some twat told them I've got a rat problem! It took many hours, and dozens of photos and forms before he was convinced that my café was clean! Can you believe that? The only rat around here is the one who phoned the inspector!'

The hairs on the top of my arms prickle and despite my joy, I try my hardest to appear sympathetic, and innocent.

'That's awful,' I say through a mouthful of banana. 'Any idea who it could be?'

'I don't know for sure, but I'm inclined to blame the guy who runs the tea stall across the road. Y'know, the one right on the beach? He pretends we're not rivals, but whenever I come to the door, there he is, glowering at me. I'm sure it was him who rang.'

I nod as though I know who she's talking about. In reality I don't have a clue, but I'm thrilled that there's someone else in the world who hates the sight of Helena Love.

'Yeah, that would make sense for it to be him. So, what else has gone wrong? Or is that it?'

'If only! I got a phone call from Craig's solicitor this morning. Apparently, he's pushing ahead with the divorce, and he needs me to find some legal counsel.'

She drops her head into her hands, and then regains her composure almost immediately. It's incredible.

'You sound surprised.'

'I am surprised! We've only been separated for a short while. I guess I thought... I thought...'

'That he'd change his mind and come back to you?'

Helena takes a gulp of tea and then wipes her mouth with the back of her hand.

'I suppose I did. I still do.'

I dunk a digestive into my tea and bring it to my mouth. The warm biscuit is comforting against my tongue. Comfort is the last thing Helena's feeling today, and that's fine by me.

'I hate to break it to you,' I say, 'but that's never going to happen. You knew Craig had hired a solicitor. Hell, he called one two days after he left *me*. He hadn't even cleared out all of his belongings before the letter came through the door.'

'I know,' Helena says. 'It was me who told him to get it sorted out.'

'You did what?'

Helena rises from her chair, picks up her abandoned apple core and throws it into the bin. She makes sure to keep her back to me as she speaks.

'I just recommended he get legal advice straight away, that's all,' she says. 'It was for your benefit too, after all.'

She turns to face me and her mouth quivers. She's embarrassed and so she should be. Tears sting the back of my eyes, and I try my hardest to keep them there.

'And how did you work out that it was better for me?'

Helena leans on the oven – in the exact spot where I dropped the lasagne dish after Craig announced he was leaving. I'm filled with rage and heartbreak all over again.

'Because I didn't think you'd want to be married to someone who was cheating on you!'

We make eye contact and I wonder if this woman has any concept of how her actions affect other people. Five minutes ago, she complained that Craig was desperate for a divorce, but now it's fine that she encouraged him to do the same to me. She's so wrapped up in her own little world, it's staggering. As she blinks, those bloody long eyelashes of hers whoosh up and down. She swoops back into the chair, picks up her mug as though nothing has occurred and swirls her tea in circles.

The strangeness of this situation is stifling. Why is this woman sitting in my kitchen? Why is she eating my fruit and trying to gain my sympathy?

Before I can say anything else, Helena is back on her feet, dancing from foot to foot.

'Do you mind if I use your bathroom? Tea goes straight through me.'

I have no words to share, so instead I nod and point in the general direction of the toilet.

But she already knows where that is.

Helena is gone just seconds when her phone rings. I stare at the device and then the door, but there is no sign of her. I swipe to answer.

'Hello?'

The line is static and then a male voice finds its way through.

'Hello? Is this Helena?'

I kick my leg out and knock the door. It doesn't shut all the way, but close enough.

'Speaking.'

'Hi, Helena, this is Tony from Parsons, Jones and Sons. It's about your coffee order. We wanted to confirm that you require the usual three containers this week.'

This phone call is so perfect that I almost screech with glee. I tap my finger on my lips. Dare I play a little game? Would it be terrible of me? I mean, it's not as if I've phoned these people myself. They came to me. Kind of. I can hear Helena walking around in the bathroom upstairs, so I take a breath and hold the phone close to my mouth.

'Erm... actually no. Unfortunately, I've had a decline in customers this past week... Between you and me, the café has had an infestation of rats!' There is an audible gasp on the other end of the phone.

'I'm sorry to hear that.'

'Yes, so am I! You've no idea how terrifying it is to see a rat perched on top of a freshly-cooked apple pie! Anyway, I've put poison down, and I'm sure we'll be rid of them soon enough, but it does mean that I've still got plenty of coffee left. So, can we leave it for now and I'll be in touch next week?'

Tony is confused. He stalls and I can hear him rustling papers on his desk. He'll be filing them all away under 'rodent-infested time-waster'.

'So, nothing,' he says. 'You want nothing at all?'

Helena runs the water in my bathroom, and I know she'll be out any second. I need to wrap this thing up.

'That's right. Goodbye for now.'

I press End Call, delete the call log and then replace the handset on the table. Seconds later, Helena appears at the door, and my heart races with a mixture of anxiety and excitement. I spring up from my chair, and the suddenness of it causes my visitor to jolt backwards, banging her shoulder on the door frame as she does so.

'Shit, Helena, I'm sorry but I just remembered I've got to phone a client. She's late paying her invoice and if I don't speak to her now, I'll forget later.'

Helena screws up her nose and rubs her shoulder.

'Is this the woman you were talking to when I came around the other day? Mrs Ewell, wasn't it? She lives down the road from me.'

My head throbs. I'd forgotten that Helena arrived as Mrs Ewell was leaving. It is true that I'm owed money from her, but she has thirty days to pay, so she's not late at all. Still, I decide to play along, if only to get Helena out of my house.

'Yes, that's the one,' I say. 'It's quite important for me to speak with her, so...' I motion towards the front door, but Helena stays rigid.

'Shall I stay here until you're done? Maybe you won't be too long.'

This woman will not take a hint. Maybe that's why Craig got sick of her.

'To be honest, it would be better if you go. I bought a load of house magazines this morning and when I've finished my meeting, I want to get stuck in. See what I can do to cheer my living room up a bit – it's a little dated.'

This is only half a lie. I do have some interior design magazines, but that's because Kate's recycling bin was full and she asked me to throw them in mine. Helena's phone buzzes and she switches it on and gazes at the screen. I hold my breath, wondering if it's her coffee supplier, but she then powers off and gives me a reassuring smile.

'Yeah, no problem. I know you're busy, and I should be too. I've got to get to the café. The waitresses will wonder where I am.'

I get up and follow her out of the kitchen and into the living room, where she stops and surveys the bookcase. My heart thumps, as I know my notebook is hidden on the third shelf, between a copy of *Hollywood Wives*, and the new Linwood Barclay novel. I normally keep the journal in my bedroom, but last night, Mrs Moore knocked at the door as I was filling it in, so I crammed it onto the shelf. I completely forgot about it until now, and sweat prickles my hairline as I wonder what the hell will happen should Helena find it.

'Hey, you have a copy of *The Complete Works of Shakespeare*!' she shouts. 'It's the same as the one I have. Do you read it often?'

My mind whirrs as my eyes fall to the volume, located just one shelf above my notebook. I pray that her eyes remain there, and not six inches below.

'I studied *Romeo and Juliet* at school, but that's as far as I got.'

Helena grabs the book from the shelf and hugs it to her.

'*Romeo and Juliet* is fantastic, but *A Midsummer Night's Dream* is my personal favourite.'

'That's a comedy, isn't it?' I ask. 'I'd have thought you'd enjoy the tragedies more. After all, you've had quite a few of those recently!'

I laugh at my own inappropriate joke, but Helena doesn't reciprocate. Instead, she unclasps the volume from her chest, slips it back into the bookcase and finally leaves my house.

'So, tell me again, why are you still letting Helena come over here?' My daughter's voice comes floating into the kitchen, on a wave of confusion and frustration. 'You should put a stop to it. Y'know, before it gets out of hand.'

I reach over to retrieve some mugs, and the steam from the kettle billows up my T-shirt sleeve and stings my arm. I wince and rub it, but that makes the pain worse.

'Mum? Did you hear what I said? You need to put a stop to her coming round here.'

I hold a piece of kitchen roll under the tap, and then place it on my arm. The cold compress soothes the pain from the steam, but does nothing for the anxiety caused by Rebecca questioning my 'friendship' with her stepmother.

'Yes, I heard you, and you're right, she shouldn't be in here, but it's a bit complicated at the moment.'

'Complicated?'

My daughter appears behind me, notices the wet kitchen paper and rolls her eyes.

'You burned yourself again? How many times do I have to tell you to keep the cups away from the kettle?' She unplugs the appliance, moves it to the other side of the counter and then proceeds to pour boiling water into the teapot. Sometimes it's easy to forget which one of us is the mother in this relationship. 'Anyway, as I was saying. How can it be complicated? Complicated is working out the bill during a night out with friends, it's not telling Helena Love to fuck off.'

'Hey, watch your language!'

Rebecca titters and swirls the teapot in circles. I get a little burst of joy seeing her make tea that way. When I'm on my own, I just sling a teabag into a mug and be done with it, but my daughter loves to do things properly. Well, if throwing a bag in a teapot can be considered doing things properly.

'In this instance I'm pretty sure that even you can agree that swearing is justified.' Rebecca pours the tea, but it's nowhere near as strong as I like it. However, I don't want to hurt her feelings, so I grab the milk from the fridge and pour it in.

'Here you go.' I lift Rebecca's cup and hand it to her. Her smile is the same as it was when she was a toddler. It hasn't changed at all.

'Okay, maybe don't swear at Helena,' she says. 'But do tell her to go away. She's your ex-husband's soon-to-be-divorced wife for goodness' sake! She has no reason to be in your house – or your life! It's ludicrous!'

I turn away on the pretext of putting the milk back into the fridge, but in reality, I'm stalling for time because I can't bring myself to answer my daughter's concerns. It's true, Craig's ex shouldn't spend time with me. The whole thing is wrong!

And yet it is oh-so right.

In all honesty, I can't describe my decision to have Helena in my life, because the reason is indescribable. At least out loud it is. In the confines of my mind, I know why she's there, and punishing her in small but significant ways is gratifying to say the least. But I can't tell Rebecca or Kate, or anyone else for that matter. Can you imagine? If I admitted that I keep a secret notebook loaded with information about my husband's mistress, as well as bullet points of ways in which to antagonise her, they'd haul me off to the nuthouse.

Or the police.

Or both.

So, for now I must keep quiet and carry on with my plan. After all, every girl needs a hobby, doesn't she?

20

Helena and I are in her café, nursing cups of hot chocolate. It's long past closing time, but my ex-husband's lover is still at work, trying to sort out the mix-up in her coffee order. She dabs at her eyes with her finger, and then wipes her nose on the back of her hand. I give her a packet of tissues, and she helps herself to four sheets.

Just as Helena is blowing her nose, an old lady taps on the window and points to the locked door.

'We're closed!' Helena shouts. The disgruntled woman stares in for a moment, then scowls, yells something unrecognisable and shuffles off down the road. Helena throws her head into her hands. Her curly hair plunges down onto the table and I can no longer see her face. She lets out a loud dramatic groan and when she lifts her head, I notice that her blue eyeliner has smudged down towards her cheeks.

'It's been a terrible week,' she whines. 'First of all, there was all that business with the health inspector and the solicitor, and then the bloody supplier didn't deliver my coffee order. When I asked about it, the salesman said I'd cancelled it for this week! Stupid bastard.' She throws herself back into the chair, finds a bobble and some grips in the pocket of her apron and then proceeds to tie her hair into a messy bun. She does it so effortlessly that it is remarkable to watch. 'And if all that isn't bad enough, yesterday I received another letter from Craig's solicitor. I feel like everyone's ganging up on me recently.'

There was another letter from Craig's solicitor? Now I'm invested in this wearisome conversation.

'What did they want this time?'

'Who?'

'The solicitor.'

'Oh.'

Helena inches her chair backwards and the legs grate against the tiles. Without offering a word of explanation, she gathers together various plates and used tissues, and flounces into the back room, her pink gingham dress swaying as she moves. I gaze over at Craig's garage and catch sight of him discussing car repairs with a smart gentleman in a trilby hat. It's almost 7pm and yet there's no sign of him leaving for the day. I wonder how Annabelle feels about that.

From the depths of the kitchen, I can hear Helena clattering around, loading the dishwasher and running a tap. She switches the radio on and an advert for PVC windows comes floating through. I wonder if I should leave, but as I gather together my phone, my purse and my handbag, she reappears.

'So, Craig is willing to leave the house without any claim to it, if I promise to give him all the possessions he came into the marriage with.' Helena dusts the Victorian cake cabinet with a canary yellow cloth, and then flicks the crumbs onto the floor. 'Well, that's okay with me, since most of what he brought was crap anyway. Family heirlooms he says, though why anyone would ever want to hand them down is beyond me.'

I scratch my head.

'But I thought the house was a rental?'

Helena waves her cloth in the air.

'Whatever made you think that?'

'I don't know. I just presumed.'

'No, I own that house! Or I will after ten more years of paying the mortgage on it. Craig used to give me money each month to help pay for it, so I guess his solicitor must have asked if he now wanted to lay claim to it or something. Christ knows, but I tell you what – he'd have had a bloody good fight on his hands if he'd tried!'

A strand of hair falls down from Helena's bun, and she tucks it behind her ear and then fans herself with the cloth. My mind zips from one thought to another, based on what she said about heirlooms being in her house. After Craig moved out of our family home, I was so busy trying to erase all trace of him that I didn't realise a number of my gran's hand-me-downs had disappeared. It wasn't until a year later that I was at an antiques fair with Rebecca and we stumbled upon a cream-and-brown ceramic dog.

'Hey, that's like the one my gran passed down to me,' I said. 'See the floppy ears? Gran's real dog had ears like those!'

Rebecca picked up the ornament and turned it this way and that.

'That's weird. Dad and Helena have one of these too. I suppose they must have been all the rage in the olden days.'

I didn't think much of it, but when we arrived home later that day, I hunted the house, but the ceramic dog was no longer there. It didn't need a genius to work out that Craig must have taken it with him when he left. It was an odd thing to steal, but then he was an odd kind of bloke – as it turned out.

The memory of the ornament, coupled with Helena's comments gives me an idea. If I can remove some of Craig's stuff from Helena's house, not only will I get my heirlooms back, but

I'll also create a whole heap of chaos for her at the same time. My ears itch and burn, but I can't help but smile.

'Are you ready?'

Helena switches off the lights and grabs her faded denim jacket. Just yards away, Craig throws down the shutters on the front door of his garage. He glances over at the café, and then slips into a crowd of tourists coming up from the pier.

'I'm ready,' I reply, and sling my handbag over my shoulder.

In fact, some may say that I've been ready for the past five years...

21

As I left Helena's café last night, I popped one of her flamingo-decorated coasters into my bag. Twelve hours later, and here I am ringing the doorbell of her Victorian detached home; early enough that Helena hasn't yet gone to work, but late enough that she'll be rushing around and unable to give me her full attention.

I ring the bell twice and then see Helena's shadow in the repaired, ribbed glass. After what appears to be a mini fight with the deadlock, the door opens and there she is – Helena Love in all her morning glory. She's wearing a blue, flowery dressing gown similar to one I wore aged eleven. Her curls are dishevelled, yesterday's mascara is smudged under her eyes and there is a toothbrush hanging out of her mouth. A blob of white frothy paste gathers at the corner of her lips, but Helena doesn't seem to notice it.

'Hey!' I say in the friendliest voice I can muster for this time in the morning. 'Listen, I'm sorry but when I opened my handbag this morning, one of your coasters was inside! I have no idea how it got there, but I wanted to return it before you open the café.'

I smile but it isn't reciprocated, so I rummage around in my bag and then drop the coaster into Helena's hand. She blinks, removes the toothbrush from her mouth and swallows. Didn't her dentist ever tell her that you shouldn't swallow toothpaste? The thought of it makes the back of my tongue tingle.

'Er, thanks,' she replies as more of a question than a statement. 'But there was no reason to return it now. You could have popped it into the café later on.'

Helena steps back long enough for me to pretend she's inviting me in (she isn't), and just seconds later, I'm installed in the living room. She follows me in, holding the damp toothbrush and trailing her hand through uncombed hair. She wants me to leave so that she can get on with her pre-work duties, but she's too polite to say anything. This is all working out as I hoped and affords me a perfect opportunity to be alone in her living room.

'Please don't let me stop you from getting ready,' I say. 'I'll sit here for a moment if you don't mind. I climbed all the way up Smuggler's Steps and it's even more of a bitch than I remember it to be. I'll just get my breath back and then I'll be off.'

Helena raises her eyebrows, but in spite of being pissed off with my presence, she offers a glass of water (I accept but don't drink it), says it is fine for me to stay a while (obvious lie), and then disappears upstairs. I perch on the overstuffed couch and give her enough time to get into the bathroom and lock the door. Then I plonk the glass of water onto the coffee table and dive out of my chair.

There is a long wooden unit that runs over the length of one wall; the kind that was popular in the eighties because of the mammoth array of drawers, shelves and cupboards. My gran had one with a pull-down section that housed her collection of sherry and the occasional spirit. Helena's isn't that different, except that instead of alcohol, hers is home to junk, paperwork

149

and phone cables. It's like an oversized version of a normal person's rubbish drawer, complete with the odd dud battery and a confusing array of shoelaces.

Despite the mess, it takes me one minute and twenty seconds to find my first liberated item: a small, pastel-blue candy dish with the words 'Gift from Bournemouth' emblazoned across the top. Craig bought this for me during a romantic getaway – well, to be honest it was more of a long weekend coach trip with a bunch of OAPs – but regardless, the dish is mine and it's coming home with me.

I drop it into my handbag.

I want to find the ceramic dog, but it's nowhere to be seen on the shelves or in the upper cupboards, so after ensuring that Helena is still in the bathroom, I bend down and open the lower drawers. These too are loaded with rubbish, but in one corner I discover a pink trinket box with a china stiletto shoe stuck to the top. That was given to us by my nana when we got engaged in 1993. We both hated it, so why the hell Craig felt the need to steal it is anyone's guess. I pick it up and discover that the lid has been broken and stuck together again. Who on earth would repair such a ghastly item?

There's no way I'm taking the trinket box back to the harbour house, but as I'm examining it, the two pieces of broken lid spring apart. Shit. I thrust the pieces back together and stick the box back where I found it. If I'm going to liberate Craig's belongings, I need them to be things he was fond of and is going to miss. This £2.99 trinket box does not qualify.

Luckily for me, the third item – a small silver box with a red clasp – more than makes up for it.

When Craig's mother, Patricia, passed away in 1999, the majority of her estate had been eaten up by care home costs and other expenses. All that was left was a handful of personal items she'd taken with her to the home, and a bin bag full of clothes.

Craig is an only child and had been close to his parents growing up. As a result, he didn't care about the lack of money or property willed to him. All he wanted was a reminder of his childhood, which came in the form of his mother's gold locket.

This sentimental piece of jewellery was in the shape of a heart, with a photograph of Craig on one side and his parents on the other. It wasn't worth a lot of money, but for Craig it meant the world. After his mother passed, my husband kept the locket – and box – in his bedside cabinet in our home. Needless to say, it went with him when he left, though why it is still in the bottom of Helena's 1980s unit is anybody's guess.

I open the box and the old springs squeak and groan. I skim my fingers over the glinting metal of the locket, close the box, and then pop it into my bag. If there is one belonging that Craig's going to want back, it's this one. My legs turn to string as I imagine the outcome of Helena's inability to return it to him. Not only will it create trouble between the former couple, but with solicitors involved, things could get even uglier than they are already.

But Helena need not worry. No matter how much Craig screams and the solicitor threatens, I will be there to lend a friendly ear to her.

Because that's the kind of person I am.

Two days later and Helena and I stroll along the stone pier together. To an untrained eye, we are old friends catching up: chatting about family; complaining about men and passing the time. It amuses and excites me that we look so innocent together. Not one passer-by has any knowledge of our history or the effort it takes to be this friendly to someone who stole your husband. They also don't know that at this moment, I'm half-expecting her to accuse me of stealing stuff from her house. I still haven't perfected my innocent look and I'm hoping the questions don't come, but to be honest there is such a lot of junk in her house that I'm pretty sure I could bluff my way through any tense conversation.

'How did you meet Craig?'

Helena has never asked me anything about my relationship, and her words take me by surprise. For a moment I don't reply and instead make a big deal of watching an old fisherman throwing a crab back into the sea. But no one can stay quiet forever, especially when the person asking the question is drilling a hole in your head with her eyes. How I met Craig is my own personal business, so I'm guarded and vague with my answer.

'We met in a pub when I was twenty,' I say. There's more to it than that, but the last person I'm going to reminisce with is Helena Fucking Love.

My ambiguous answer seems to satisfy my nosey companion, and we continue strolling in silence until we reach the end of the stone pier. As we lean against the old Victorian railings, the wind whooshes around my head, and I hold onto my sun hat for fear of it ending up in the Channel.

'We met in my café.' Helena sighs, and I bristle at the idea of learning more about their sordid courtship.

'I know. That was pretty obvious, since your café is two doors away from his garage.'

She nods, pulls her hair away from her face and reveals a high forehead. I hadn't noticed how big it was until now. Maybe she should consider a fringe, or a career as a dolphin impersonator.

'Yes,' she says. 'I suppose it is obvious really.'

I avoid her gaze and instead stare at the water below. There is a mass of jellyfish floating around the stone wall again, and I can't help but wonder why they're here and where they came from. Helena does not seem to share my joy of ocean life and instead gawps up at the sky. When I look up, I notice she has a pimple on the underside of her chin, though she's attempted to hide it with a blob of too-dark concealer.

As if reading my thoughts, she touches the spot and then pulls out a circular compact from her handbag. It has a yellow cupcake printed on the front, though part of the cherry has been rubbed away and there are grey streaks on the butter cream. Helena examines her reflection for a moment, snaps the mirror closed and throws it into her bag.

'Surprisingly, my café is turning out to be quite a place for meeting men.'

I crinkle my nose in disgust, but just about manage to disguise it as a sneeze.

'What do you mean?'

'Well, Cindy – she's a girl who worked as a waitress for a while – she met a guy who came into the café during a thunderstorm last summer. He ordered a double helping of apple pie and the next thing we knew, she was engaged and had moved to Tenby with him! Isn't that remarkable? The Lovely Café is a real-life love café!'

I nod in an effort to feign interest. Listening to tales of someone-who-knows-someone is almost as excruciating as hearing somebody else's dreams or political leanings.

'Lovely story, but let's hope Cindy's marriage is more successful than yours.' I smirk at my sarcasm and expect Helena to be furious, but instead, she giggles.

'That wouldn't take much, let's face it. But between you and me, I might have another chance at a future with my ideal man. Thanks once again to my café.'

Don't tell me she's still holding a torch for Craig. That would be unbearable.

'Don't worry.' She giggles. 'It's not my so-called husband. No, it's somebody else entirely. This guy came into the café the other day. We were quiet, so I plied him with chocolate cake and cappuccino and we got talking. Would you believe, we bonded over a shared love of Whitney Houston songs! After that, one thing led to another and...!'

Her voice trails off and she squeaks like a silly, excitable schoolgirl. I should leave it but I'm invested now. Helena Love's life is like a scab I can't stop picking.

'And what?'

She sniggers again and then covers her face with her hands.

'Don't think badly of me, but I ended up sleeping with him!'

'In the café?'

Helena's laugh booms and a random tourist turns around to see what's going on. She comes in close and lowers her voice.

'No! Have you any idea what the health inspector would say about sex in a café? No, no, he took me out for dinner and then we went back to my house. He ended up staying the night, but left early before the nosey neighbours could see him and report back to Craig. I enjoyed myself though. He was exactly what I needed to take my mind off my bastard ex.'

There are times in my life when I can't believe what I've just heard, and this is one of them. Call me naïve or innocent or whatever, but how is it possible to sleep with somebody a few weeks after a marriage break-up? For several years after I broke up with Craig, the idea of having sex with another man terrified me. What if I did it wrong? What if after twenty years of marriage, Craig and I had settled into some odd routine that nobody else would find erotic? It's only been the past year that I've thought about going out with somebody else, though apart from a disastrous one-night stand, the fantasy has so far outweighed the reality.

I'm aware that Helena is watching me, but I can't do

anything except try to avoid her gaze. She wants a reaction and maybe an enquiry as to all the gory details, but she'll be waiting a long time. I know other women who enjoy that sort of gossip, but it's not something I've ever been into. Kate could talk for hours about her sex life with Pete. When I worked with her, she often dragged me behind the ancient card catalogue to enlighten me on some new technique she'd discovered. I'm not that way inclined – especially with the woman who stole my husband. Still, I can't leave the conversation hanging in the air, so I search my head for something profound to say. In the end, I can only come up with one thing.

'Does this man have a name?'

'Not yet,' she says with a wink. 'But I'll be sure to ask if I see him again.'

Slut!

22

It's a beautiful late June day and the beach is full of early holidaymakers making the most of a sudden, unexpected heatwave. The place is full of families eating picnics behind striped fabric windbreaks; dogs chasing plastic Frisbees into the waves; and toddlers skipping around wearing fluorescent orange water wings. This is a noisy place, but this is a happy place.

Kate and I relax on my huge beach blanket emblazoned with the cast of *Friends*. I bought it for Rebecca when she went through a massive *Friends* phase in her teens, but after she left home the blanket became my full-time beach companion. Kate and I eat ice creams from an old-fashioned snack stall at the entrance to the beach. Creatures of habit, I have mint choc chip, while my friend – as always – has strawberry. Nearby, a young boy carries a bucket in the shape of a castle with what appears to be a dozen tiny crabs inside.

'Mum!! Mum!! Look what I caught! Can we keep them? I have names for all of them already!'

The boy plops the bucket onto the sand next to his mother and some of the water sploshes over the side. The woman closes her book, lifts her sunglasses, and then swears to herself. I watch for a while, and then turn my attention to Kate.

'Oh, I've just remembered! I bought you a present.' I dig through my oversized bag and bring out a vintage Madonna 7-inch. 'I found this in the antique shop, and thought you might like it.' I hand it to my friend, and she takes off her glasses for a better look.

'"Holiday".'

'Yes. I remembered that you didn't become a Madonna fan until the 'Like A Virgin' era, so thought you might not have this one.'

She turns it over and reads the back.

'That's great. Thanks. Now all I need is a turntable to play it on.'

Kate smiles, drops the record onto the towel and gets back to eating her ice cream. I'm disappointed. I thought she'd be much more excited about the gift. I hide my feelings of failure by zipping up my handbag.

'So, what's going on with you and Helena, anyway?'

The sternness of Kate's voice takes me by surprise. I shield my eyes from the sun, so that I can see her properly.

'What do you mean?'

Kate rolls her eyes in that infuriating way she has.

'Come on, Jenny, you know what I mean! You're round at her house; she's round at yours; you're out walking together. I even went past her café the other day and there you both were, drinking coffee in the window like long-lost buddies.'

'It wasn't coffee,' I say. 'Her supplier forgot to bring her any.'

'Jesus!' Kate gets up onto her knees and stuffs the remainder of her ice cream into her mouth. She chews and then wipes her lips on the back of her hand. 'It doesn't matter what you were drinking, Jenny. The point is that you were both there, looking more than a little cosy. It's just... It's just weird.'

I pick up some grains of sand between my fingers, and rub them together in an effort to avoid Kate's comments.

'Jenny!'

I flick the sand away and sigh. If I can say anything about Kate, it's that she rarely – if ever – lets anything go. She's always been that way, even when we were in our late teens. Then, when we had babies, her demanding temperament became ever more apparent. Kate's twin boys are five months older than Rebecca, so I had the pleasure – or otherwise – of seeing her grilling teachers and club leaders about all manner of subjects over the years. Once she gets it in her head that something needs sorting, there is no way she'll stop until it is.

'You know what's going on. I was helping Helena to find out who Craig moved in with. That's all!'

'Er, yeah, wasn't that weeks ago? Helena knows who the new woman is now and she's even spoken to her, hasn't she? Your part in this is over, so why are you still involved?'

That's a good question, but I'm not yet ready to share the answer. What on earth would Kate say if I told her I've been taking revenge on Helena at every opportunity? That I cancelled her coffee order, took items from her house, and phoned the health inspector? She'd think I was psychotic, or insane, or both.

And I'm none of those things.

Am I?

Instead of answering the question, I try to guide Kate into another – somewhat related – topic. Hopefully it will be enough to quench her thirst for answers, while deflecting her intrusive questions.

'Do you know what she told me yesterday?'

Kate sighs, rummages in her bag, picks out her phone and switches it on. Her fingers fly across the screen and I'm sure she can't possibly be reading anything.

'No, what did she tell you yesterday?'

'She's got a new bloke.'

Kate throws her phone back into her bag and cocks her head to one side like a flummoxed dog.

'She's got a new bloke?'

'Yep! I couldn't believe it either, but there you go. Apparently, she met him in the café, and they went out for dinner – or was it a drink? I can't remember. Anyway, she doesn't know his name, but get this – she screwed him anyway – in the same bed she was sharing with Craig! What do you think of that?'

Kate grips her wrist and rolls her arm back and forth. Then she opens her mouth, closes it and lets out a long breath through clenched teeth.

'To be honest, Jenny, I don't think anything about it. Helena Love can sleep with whoever she pleases. It's none of my business – and it's none of yours for that matter.'

Kate stands up and throws her huge flowery bag over her shoulder.

'I'm going home.'

She takes a step away from me, but I can't let her go. I spring up, grab the abandoned vinyl, heave the blanket from the sand and follow her.

'Wait!' I try my best to hurry, but my feet melt into the sand. 'What's wrong?'

'Nothing!' she shouts through the crowds of noisy sunseekers.

I manage to touch Kate's arm as we reach the ramp that leads back up to the promenade.

'It doesn't seem like nothing! Kate! Tell me what's wrong!' My friend turns and refuses to look at me, but I still notice the tears brimming in her eyes. 'You're crying. What's happened? Is it the twins? Or Pete? Are you still having problems?'

She glowers at me.

'Are you asking because you care, or because you want to

repeat my business to your new friend?'

'Don't be silly, I'd never gossip about you to her. And she's not my new friend! For goodness' sake, Kate, you're acting like a jealous schoolgirl.'

My friend yanks her arm away from my grasp.

'Jenny, in the past two weeks, you've seen me four times. Four times!' She holds four splaying fingers in the air. 'We normally see each other almost every day!'

I can't argue with that, and instead I hang my head like a teenager who has been caught shimmying down the drainpipe instead of doing her homework.

'I... I've been busy, that's all.'

An old couple approach to ask us the way to the bus station. Kate doesn't open her mouth, so it's left to me to impart my dreadful navigational knowledge. The couple thank me and once they've gone my friend points at me with an accusing finger.

'During the few occasions I have seen you, all you ever seem to talk about is Helena.'

'That's not true!'

'Ha!! Jenny, you're so wrapped up in her life that you can't even see how your own is unravelling. You seriously need to take a long look at yourself and then step away from all this drama. You're obsessed! And by the way, you sent that man and woman to the central bus station.'

'So?'

'So, they were looking for the tourist bus station! See! You can't even concentrate long enough to get that right!'

Kate storms off, and almost collides with a skateboarder in the process.

'Wait,' I shout. 'You forgot your record!'

'Give it to your friend!' she yells.

And then she disappears into the crowds.

23

Since my break-up with Craig, I've worked hard to keep my figure: UK size ten if anyone is interested. I walk and run for miles, I watch what I eat and I sometimes pick the clothes off the exercise bike long enough to use it for what it was intended for. However, I'm sure everyone will agree that some days – usually after something stressful or exciting has happened – I need to eat something naughty. Something that will pile on the pounds the moment I lay eyes on it.

Today is one of those days.

My conversation with Kate hurt my feelings. When I got home that day, I tried to call but it went straight to voicemail, and the messages I have left since then have gone unnoticed or unwanted. Now I'm fighting a depressive slump by filling up on fish and chips from my local takeaway. I live not even one hundred yards from the chippy, but if the weather is nice, I always get a kick out of eating my chips on the harbour wall. It makes me feel as though I'm on holiday – right down to fighting off the gulls and ignoring random toddlers with sticky fingers.

And it's the harbour wall where I'm sitting when I see him.

Stuart Wilson-Price.

He is the last person I want to see, so I lower my head on the pretence of finding a perfect chip. It's too late though. Within seconds of spotting him, the father of my ex-husband's new lover looms over me.

'Fancy seeing you here!'

His voice is bright and friendly, but it unnerves me nevertheless. I paste on a smile and forget about my dinner.

'Hi!' I say. 'No Tyson today?'

I gaze behind his legs, though I'm not sure why, since I know a huge German shepherd can't be hiding there.

'No, I've left him in Bournemouth this time. I had a day off, and thought I'd pop back on the off-chance of seeing Annabelle. No luck though.' He motions towards the wall. 'May I?'

God no.

'Sure.'

Stuart takes a seat next to me and his bare arm grazes my own. I feel sick and move a centimetre away, though I resist the urge to rub the feeling of his rough skin from my arm. The man who was dressed so smart a week ago is a little more casual this afternoon, though he still exudes an aura of superiority. He's wearing burgundy cords and a crisp white T-shirt with a tiny anchor embroidered on the pocket. On his feet he wears navy deck shoes, and I can't help but notice that his socks match the colour of his trousers. I look down at my own seen-better-days jeans and pink Betty Boop T-shirt and cringe. Next to Stuart Wilson-Price, I give off all the sophistication of a teenager attending a youth club disco.

My companion does not seem inclined to talk, so to break the silence I offer him a chip.

'No thanks!' He throws up his hand and pats his stomach. 'I've got to watch the cholesterol, and the waistline. We all need to think about what we eat at our age.'

He scowls as though he's some kind of health guru, and I

feel judged, fat and insulted that he thinks I'm anywhere near his age. He's at least five years older than me, but then again, maybe I've forgotten how middle-aged I am. I decide to ignore Stuart's comments and get back to eating.

'So,' he says, 'you've probably worked out that I know who you are.'

My appetite deteriorates and the chip that was heading for my mouth falls back onto the paper.

'What do you mean?'

Stuart chuckles to himself, and rubs his stubble with the tips of his fingers. It makes a harsh, scratching noise.

'You're Craig's wife.'

'Ex-wife. But yes I am.'

He nods and then despite his previous healthy disclaimer, he helps himself to a chip.

'Maybe I will have something after all. It's been a long time since breakfast.'

He stuffs the food into his mouth and then rubs his hands together as though they're covered in layers of salt. I'm freezing cold and I know it's because my body is reacting to the bizarre situation I find myself in. However, I refuse to be intimidated by any man, so I face the situation head-on.

'How did you know who I am?'

'I recognised you from my days at the Harbour Committee, and the school run.' He nudges my arm in what I'm sure he thinks is a playful manner, but it makes me cringe. 'You haven't changed at all. If anything, you look younger now than you did back then.'

His words send a cold chill down my back. I hold the chips to my belly in an effort to get warm, but I can still feel my flesh tremble beneath my clothes.

'So, the other day on the beachfront... you... you bumped into me deliberately?'

Stuart gives me a wide grin and the sun bounces off his top front teeth. I thought that only happened in the movies. My muscles tense and I feel at risk of hyperventilating any second now. Is Stuart stalking me? Does he know where I live? Why didn't I take my food home?

'No, believe it or not I didn't do it deliberately. I was just walking with Tyson when I heard that guy hassling you. At first, I stepped in because I saw a woman in trouble. It was when you turned around that I realised who you were. I couldn't believe it myself.'

I can't work out if Stuart's lying or not because I don't know him well enough to gauge it. But then again, longevity wouldn't help me. Craig lied often without me realising it, and I knew him for over twenty years. Stuart crosses his heart with his finger.

'Honest, that's true. Although I did wonder if you recognised me at first, but the way you reacted after I mentioned Annabelle made me realise you didn't have a clue.'

'I didn't. To me you were a vaguely familiar Samaritan who rescued me from becoming a crime statistic.'

Stuart licks the salt from his lips and sighs.

'I know it seems outlandish, but I promise I'm not trying to harass you or anything like that. However, I did wonder... Well, since I did you a favour, I wondered if you might be willing to do one for me.'

'What kind of favour?'

My voice quivers and my tongue feels too large for my mouth. What could this man want from me?

'Forgive me if I'm wrong, but I get the impression that you know Craig better than anybody.' I stifle a laugh and Stuart reaches over and takes two chips. 'I was hoping you could have a word with him, let him know that it's not acceptable to be in a relationship with my daughter.'

Not acceptable? That's the understatement of the century, but it's also not something I can control.

'You assume I have that much power over my ex-husband?'

'I'm hoping so.'

I jump up and ram the remains of my food into a nearby bin. It's already overflowing with papers and discarded drinks cans, causing the neighbourhood wasps to buzz in gratitude.

'I'm sorry to disappoint you,' I say, 'but I have never had any power over Craig. I didn't when we were married and I definitely don't now. I'm afraid your problem with him and Annabelle is just that – your problem – and I'd be grateful if we could leave it like that. Now, please don't come looking for me again.'

I deliver my mouthful and then walk towards home. I'm aware that Stuart will be watching every step I take, so at the last moment I head past my house and turn into the little lane that runs up to my backyard. Once there, I lean as close to the wall as I can, twist my head around the corner and squint back up to the chip shop. Stuart Wilson-Price is sauntering towards the bridge.

I dart into my garden, and make sure the gate and my back door are both locked up tight.

24

Helena gazes at me over the top of her bulging, ivory-coloured wedding album.

'I had the most beautiful dress in the world,' she laments. 'That's what Craig told me anyway.'

I have no idea why this woman has brought hundreds of wedding photos into my home, unless she's trying to play with me in some way. Perhaps she's realised that it was me who phoned the environmental health. Or even worse, maybe she's noticed the missing trinkets and wants some measure of revenge. My eyes dart around the room in an effort to make sure I've hidden them away. Thankfully I have.

'Look at Rebecca.' She sighs. 'Didn't she look divine as a bridesmaid?'

I stare down at the photo. It shows a disgruntled twenty-year-old, wearing a red, 1950s vintage dress and huge, flowery Dr Marten boots. Her shoulders are hunched, her back rounded and her mouth turned down at the corners. She's moping next to a gaggle of random young women, who all wear blue satin frocks and hold bulging bouquets of scarlet roses. What a short memory Helena has. My daughter was never a bridesmaid for her. In fact, Rebecca made a point of refusing the offer in a public Facebook post, and I still have the screenshot to prove it. All the photo shows is that she was somehow coerced into posing next to the actual bridesmaids. She isn't even holding any flowers.

'Helena, why are you parading around with your wedding album? And more to the point, why are you bringing it into my house? Don't you know how inappropriate that is?'

She gasps and raises her hand to her heart. If she were auditioning for the harbour amateur dramatics company, she'd be their star player.

'Shit! I'm sorry. Sometimes it's easy for me to forget that you were married to Craig as well.' My mouth curls into a tight ball and Helena senses my fury and waves it away. 'No, I don't mean that I forget about it, but after everything that's going on right now, it's easier for me not to remember. If that makes sense.'

It doesn't.

'Okay, but why are you carrying the album around with you? Even taking me out of the equation, fawning over your old wedding photos is not good for your mental health. He's not coming back, y'know!'

Helena closes the album with a bang and then snakes her hand over the cover photo. From this angle I can see a black-and-white picture of the happy couple, entwined in a dramatic embrace. It looks as though Helena is wearing white and Craig is dressed in top hat and tails. They are both laughing as though someone has told them the most hilarious joke they've ever heard. I guess now the joke is on them – or at least her.

'I don't carry it around with me all the time,' Helena snaps. 'I'm on my way to the garage, to give it to Craig.'

'He wants your old wedding album? He must be stranger than I thought.'

She shrugs and strums her nails down the edge of the book, as though it's some kind of instrument.

'He wants to keep the photographs of his family,' she says in a fake, posh accent. 'I've been instructed to take it over, so that he can remove the ones he wants, and then I can have it back. How kind of him!'

Helena shoves the album into a Tesco carrier bag and collapses back into the chair; bereft. I do the polite thing and pat her arm for a few seconds, all the time stifling the joy that's bubbling in my chest.

'Damn that bastard,' she says, and then her phone rings. She picks it up, groans at the number flashing on-screen, and answers. Craig's voice thunders out into the room.

'Helena, when you bring round the album, please drop off my mum's locket too. My solicitor says you haven't returned that yet and I need it.'

Helena screws up her eyes and pinches her lip.

'I can't bring the locket round today,' she squawks. 'It's at home and I'm already on my way to see you.'

'Fine,' Craig says through the handset. 'I'll be over this afternoon to pick it up myself.'

'Well, in that case you can pick up the wedding album while you're at it!' Helena finishes the call, drops the phone onto the arm of the chair and rubs her forehead. 'Shit! I can't bear to be on my own with Craig today – not the way I'm feeling.'

This is perfect! Imagining what will happen when Craig discovers the locket missing is exciting enough, but now I have the chance to witness the drama in person! I'm going to enjoy this.

'Don't worry.' I pat her arm again. 'I'll come over to your house and make sure he doesn't bother you.'

My companion beams as I look over towards the cupboard

that houses Craig's locket. It is three-and-a-half feet from where we sit, but it could be a thousand miles away.

~

Craig rummages through Helena's wall unit while she hovers behind him, skipping from foot to foot.

'Craig, please, you're going to break something. I have belongings in there too, y'know.'

He stops searching, stares at her and then continues.

'This is where I always kept it. It's a small silver box with a red clasp. It's been here ever since I moved in.' He turns to where I'm perched on the sofa and throws his hands out in bewilderment. 'Jenny, you know what it looks like. Small and silver.'

I rub my face in a way that I hope shows concern and empathy, and then I cross over to gaze into the unit.

'Yes, I know what the box looks like and I can tell you where it was kept in our house, but that doesn't mean I know where it is now!' Craig pouts and huffs in the same way chimpanzees do when they're communicating with newcomers.

'I know you don't know where it is now,' he says. 'I meant that you know what it looks like, so maybe you can help find it!'

My palms are sweaty and I can't stop swallowing. I don't want anyone to notice my glee (or my guilt for that matter), so I keep my eyes averted and my mouth turned down at the corners.

My cheating ex-husband's shoulders hunch and he takes a step back from the unit.

'I give up,' he says in a monotone voice. 'It's definitely not in here.'

Helena digs in her pocket for a tissue, blows her nose and then pokes her fingers through some of the clutter in the drawers.

'It was in here!' Her chin trembles. 'I could have sworn it was in here.'

Craig's features are blank and it's impossible to decipher what he's thinking. He tips his head back and stares at the ceiling for a moment, then releases a long breath.

'Helena.' He sighs. 'I know you're hurting. I know you hate me for what I've done and I don't blame you! I don't blame you at all. However, you have no right to keep my mother's locket. It's been in my family for a thousand times longer than our marriage lasted.'

From my position on the edge of the drama, I can see Helena's hands quiver as she pleads with Craig to believe that she hasn't done anything to his beloved memento. She gazes at the floor and her breath comes fast and frequent, struggling to maintain a regular rhythm. It's funny how karma works, isn't it? Five years ago, she stood on my doorstep, begging my husband to leave me, and now here I am, watching as her world implodes. Poor cow.

Craig rummages again, stops and produces a small pale-green box.

A ring box.

He opens it up and stares inside. I can just about make out some rings, glinting in the sun. Helena stops crying, sniffs and glowers first at the box and then at my ex-husband.

'It's your engagement and wedding rings,' Craig whispers.

'Yeah. So? Did you expect me to wear them now that you're gone?'

'No, I hadn't thought about it, that's all.'

Craig closes the box, and hands it to her. She rubs little circles over the top with her fingers and then clutches it in her hand. After that, the most peculiar thing happens. The former couple stare at each other, and I can almost see five years of memories pass between them. The room is silent except for the sound of Helena's rapid breathing, her ticking wall clock and a million broken promises scattering all over the floor.

And it is at that precise moment that I realise something I never knew before.

Helena and Craig did love each other.

All these years I imagined that the one thing they had in common was lust. After all, Craig and I had over twenty years of creating a family, building a business and being friends as well as partners. Helena shared none of these things with him, so I always believed that what they had was nothing more than an insatiable desire for sex. However, the way they contemplate each other now shows that to be untrue. There are hundreds of memories in this room, of two people planning a future together. They were a couple! An actual real couple!! The concept hits me like a brick and leaves me outraged.

What am I doing here? Why am I watching these adulterous bastards relive their former love, right in front of me? How dare they? It's disgusting and disrespectful.

Craig closes the drawer and lays his hand on Helena's shoulder. She doesn't squirm from his touch or shrug him away, which is what I would have done in that situation. Not that Craig ever came near me after he left. Once he was gone, that was the end of it.

'I didn't hide that locket,' Helena says. 'I have no idea where it's gone.'

'It's okay,' Craig replies. 'If you find it, let me know and I'll come over.'

Helena nods and something passes between them. Regret maybe? Sorrow? This is not going the way I hoped it would. Any loathing that may have bubbled up between them initially, has been replaced with a weird kind of empathy, and I hate it. I hate them! I have to get out of here, before I throw up – or punch them both.

I scratch my head and the movement breaks the spell between the couple.

'I've got to go.' I grab my handbag and try to sling it over my shoulder, but the strap falls and lands at the nook of my elbow. Craig and Helena gawp at me as though they had forgotten I was even there, and then my ex-husband gazes at his watch.

'Shit, I've got to go as well. I've got an MOT in twenty minutes.' He grabs his jacket from the back of the chair, and then turns back to Helena and I. 'If either of you see the locket, please let me know. It's the only thing I've got left of my mum and it would be nice to have it back.'

Craig pushes past me into the hall, and seconds later he is gone. My nemesis pretends to tidy the unit but I can see her studying me in the reflection of the glass door.

'That was the last thing I needed today.' Helena's hands stroke the bundles of memories scattered around the drawers.

I have nothing left to say, so instead I turn towards the front door. As I reach it, I notice that Craig and Helena's wedding album is resting on the little wooden table. Craig must have forgotten to take it with him. Without even checking to see if Helena's watching, I grab it, hold it upside down and let all the loose photos fall out. They spiral, scatter and skim over the shiny tiles, and then lay like abandoned pieces of a broken jigsaw puzzle. One of the photos – a pink-tinged monstrosity of Helena and Craig eating their wedding cake – lands on my foot. I scoop it up and stick it in my pocket.

I step over the remaining photographs and then turn back to dump the album on the floor. Only then do I see Helena in the doorway, her arms folded and mouth hanging open. I place the album back onto the table.

'I'm sorry,' I say. 'I knocked it over on the way past.'

I give an impersonation of a smile, while Helena's lips disappear into her mouth. I open the front door and the wind rollicks in and whooshes the loose photographs down the hall. Before I can even mull over whether to scoop them up, Helena throws out her hands.

'Just leave them,' she snaps.

And so, I do.

25

It's the morning after the locket incident, and Craig's garage is empty except for a blue Fiat Tipo and a ginger cat playing with some rope next to the entrance. I shoo it away, for fear that it will kill itself on the machinery, and then drift over to what we called the back office, but it's really a plasterboard partition. I stare inside, but there's no one around. The only clue that Craig is somewhere nearby is the vintage 1990s radio, tuned to BBC Radio Two. He gave up listening to Radio One the moment rave music became a thing.

The smell of old oil, engine fumes and petrol is rampant, and yet today I find it not altogether hideous. I spent many hours in this garage when Craig was setting up the business. I painted walls, helped install a desk where he could do paperwork, and made sure he had an abundant supply of notebooks, pens, paperclips and staples. We even had sex here once – right there next to the wall – but that was before the garage was opened. It wasn't like we were doing it in the middle of a breakdown or MOT situation.

There is a glamour-model calendar hanging on the wall,

covered in greasy fingerprints where the pages have been turned over. The sight of it makes me chuckle because giving Craig a saucy calendar was a Christmas tradition in our house. He didn't even like them (or so he said), but Rebecca bought him one as a joke after she found it in a bargain bucket, and it stuck after that. I wonder who is buying him those calendars now, since I can't imagine Helena ever agreeing to spend money on them.

It's now early July but the calendar is stuck on June. I wrench it from the wall and turn the page. A blonde bombshell stares back at me, wearing a pink bikini and a broad grin. I can't help but stare at her perky boobs.

'Developed a taste for glamour models, have you?'

I turn around and my ex-husband saunters towards me. He's wearing navy overalls and carrying an oil-stained mug that has a picture of a young Elvis on it. I shake my head.

'You hadn't turned the page over yet, so I was rectifying it.'

'A likely story.' He snickers in that flirty way he has. 'Tea? Coffee?'

'No, I'm fine thanks. I only came to give you something.'

Ever the comedian, Craig raises his eyebrows and purses his lips.

'Oh yeah?!'

'Don't flatter yourself,' I say, perhaps a little too brusque.

I slip my hand into my bag. The locket box is smooth beneath my fingers and I wonder if I'm brave enough to give it to him. What if Craig doesn't believe my story? What if he rings his solicitor or even worse – the police? I could get arrested for theft or be made to apologise to Helena. But there's only one way to find out my fate, so I take a deep, empowering breath, take out the box and offer it to him.

'What's this?'

'What does it look like? It's your mother's locket.'

Craig snatches the item from my hand and stares at it, mystified.

'Where did you...?'

'I took it. I took it from Helena's house.'

His eyebrows almost meet in the middle and his mouth draws into a thin line. He opens the box, studies the locket and then closes it again.

'I don't understand. Why would you do that?' Craig is so close that I can smell his Dior aftershave. 'What's going on, Jenny? Are you in league with Helena or something?'

The owner of the Tipo saunters into the garage and waves from the other end of the pit.

'It'll be about thirty minutes, mate,' Craig yells, and the customer gives him a thumbs up.

'No problem, I'll go and get a coffee.'

Craig watches him leave and then turns his attention back to me.

'So?'

He plonks his mug onto the counter and then stashes the locket box in the cupboard underneath. I know every hinge, every nail and every splinter that makes up that cubbyhole. Craig wanted somewhere he could stick customers' keys, and while I suggested a board with numbered hooks attached, my husband thought a locked cupboard would be better. A couple of weeks later, he was sick of bending down to retrieve the keys, so the board was installed. The abandoned locker ended up being a store for his lunch box and CDs.

And now his locket.

'Do you really think I'd be in cahoots with your estranged wife?' Craig makes a humph noise – similar to the ones Kate makes whenever I mention Helena to her. 'To be honest, Helena has been complaining about having to return your belongings, and I had a nasty suspicion she'd keep this one, knowing what it means to you. I was in her house about a week ago and heard her on the phone to her solicitor. I could have got it wrong, but I thought I heard him tell Helena that she shouldn't be in a hurry to return your stuff – not until the legalities have all been sorted out. I'd seen the locket box when she was rifling in the drawer earlier that week, so I dived in and retrieved it for you. I wanted to get it before it was too late.'

It's obvious I'm lying, but I pray Craig doesn't realise. Although to be honest, I might be telling the truth – in my own way. For all I know, Helena may have made it difficult for Craig to get his stuff back, though her insistence that she didn't want his crappy family heirlooms contradicts that idea. As if reading my thoughts, Craig's eyes widen and he presents me with a sarcastic grin.

'Okay, well, whatever the truth is, I'm glad to have it back. It means a lot to me.'

'I know it does.' I smile in the sweetest way I can. 'That's why I wanted to rescue it for you.' I give him a brief nod and then turn to leave.

'Thanks then,' he shouts, above the sound of Prince singing 'Purple Rain' on the radio.

'You're welcome,' I reply. 'Just do me a favour and don't tell Helena where you found it.' He nods and then I walk towards the door, making sure that my bottom swings from side to side, the way he always likes it. It's a cheap move, but I'm pretty sure Craig will be staring as I leave.

I get to the door and turn back to confirm my thoughts, but Craig isn't there. He's already disappeared into the back room.

After leaving the garage, I swerve Helena's café and head up the promenade towards the Royal Hotel. Craig and I used to visit 'the posh hotel' often during the early days of our relationship. Once Rebecca came along, we didn't have the opportunity (or the money) to go regularly, but it was always a delicious treat when it did happen. As I step through the revolving door and onto the thick, scarlet carpet of the foyer, I can't help but wonder if he ever brought Helena here. The idea of her going anywhere near 'our place' fills me with fury.

The uniformed doorman wishes me good morning, and I reciprocate and then saunter towards the restaurant. A cup of posh hot chocolate and a deep-filled strawberry tart are what this day needs, and as the waiter shows me to a table next to the window, a wave of joy floods over me. It's been a long time since I treated myself to something special, and I have no doubt that I'll enjoy this visit.

The restaurant – or The Tea Room as it is officially known – is how I imagine a 1930s Hollywood café to look. There are crisp white cloths on the tables, four sparkling chandeliers hanging from the ceiling and a vast mural based on the movie *Gone with the Wind*, covering one wall. Why they chose that film to decorate the restaurant has long since been a talking point. One theory is that the actor Clark Gable once dined here when stationed in England during the war. However, since I can find nothing in the newspaper archive to confirm this, I'd say the story was based more on hope than reality.

The hotel is situated opposite the pleasure pier, and from most windows you can see straight down towards the modern theatre at the end. Back in Edwardian times, there was a little pavilion at the end of the pier, but that was washed away during a storm in the 1940s. Since then we've had an amusement arcade, a restaurant and since the early 2000s, a theatre. While the original features of the pier have long departed, I still give thanks to those creative Edwardians for building it in line with the Royal Hotel. It makes for an interesting place to eat for a renowned people-watcher like myself.

I squint to get a decent view of the crowds on the pier and notice a couple in an animated conversation, next to the box office at the entrance to the boardwalk. There are several tourists mulling around them, which distorts my view somewhat, but as soon as they move on, I am surprised to discover that the warring couple is Kate and her husband, Pete.

My friend comes from a Scottish-Italian family and it is her habit to express emotion with her hands. I always thought it was the height of sophistication when I was young, but when I tried it myself, I swept my mum's favourite Lladró ornament off the coffee table, and never did it again. Today, Kate's hands fly about as though swatting a wasp, and she narrowly misses an old man with a walking stick and a startled young mother with a pram. Finally, Pete throws his own arms into the air and storms off up the pier. Kate watches him go, and then turns and crosses the path towards the Royal Hotel. When she's about fifteen feet away, she looks straight up at the restaurant and catches sight of me in the window. We both stare at each other for several seconds, and then exchange a wave.

Three minutes later, Kate is seated beside me.

'I'm sorry I shouted at you the other day.' My friend gapes at me through glassy eyes. She looks gaunt and exhausted and she's not wearing any makeup at all. That's not like Kate. Normally, she won't go out to the bin without slapping on her mascara.

'Just forget about it.'

'It wasn't about you, you know.'

I nod in empathy, though I imagine it was a bit about me really.

'It's okay. We all get pissed off sometimes. But I'm concerned about you, Kate. What's wrong? I saw you down there arguing with Pete. Are you two having problems?'

Kate looks down at the pier, and I notice that there are dark circles under her eyes.

'You could say that. We're going through some kind of crazy shit right now, that's for sure.'

'You want to talk about it?'

Her eyes leave the window; she shrugs and throws her hands up.

'I'm not sure there's anything to talk about. It's like we're strangers and I don't know what I can do to rectify that. If I'm honest, this could be the end for us.'

Kate's chin tremors and she leans into the chair. A moment later the waiter arrives with our hot chocolates, complete with whipped cream and marshmallows, and a strawberry tart for me.

'Can I get you anything else?' he asks.

'We're fine, thank you.' I smile and he nods and wanders away. Kate picks out a marshmallow from her cup, squishes it between her fingers and then tosses it onto the saucer.

'Surely it's not that bad,' I say, and I hope it isn't. Divorce isn't something I'd wish on my worst enemy. Well, maybe my worst enemy but not Kate.

My friend has known Pete since shortly after I met Craig. Pete and Craig were friends and Kate and I were friends, so it became a natural progression to all go out one evening as a foursome. Thankfully, the two friends hit it off, and from then on, we'd go everywhere together – pop concerts, day trips to London, even a camping holiday in Wales, though that was the first and last time we ever did that. It rained so much that Kate and Pete's tent started leaking and they had to spend the night in our tiny two-man. We called it our *Carry On Camping* moment and it's funny to reminisce about now, but then it was like a night in hell... if hell was cold, wet and overcrowded. We did go on holiday together after that, but to warm places like Majorca or Greece, holed up in a watertight hotel.

I spoon away some of the cream and sip my hot chocolate. The warm, soothing liquid trickles down my throat.

'This is delicious,' I say. 'You should try some.'

The cream on Kate's drink melts into the liquid, causing some of it to ooze down the side of her cup, like a chocolate volcano.

'Do you know where Pete slept last night?'

I swallow and shake my head.

'In his car.'

'His car?'

Kate nods and takes a sip of her drink. The foam leaves a trail across her lip, and she licks at it with her tongue and wipes the remains away with a napkin.

'He said he couldn't bear to be in the house with me any longer, and he stormed out. He's far too stingy to spend money on a hotel – and he can't stay with Craig for obvious reasons – so off he went to the car. I looked out at 4am and there he was, wrapped up in a sleeping bag on the back seat, with his head leaning against the window. I was bloody furious and opened the window to set off the security light. That soon woke him up!'

The waiter comes over to ask if we're okay, and I nod a bit too enthusiastically. He gives a gracious grin and then heads towards a table that does require his attention.

'This makes no sense.' I bite my tart, and some of the pastry falls onto the table. 'You and Pete are what Craig and I always wanted to be – or at least what *I* always wanted us to be. What's happened that could make him go and sleep in the car? That's mental!'

'It's a long story.' She sighs. 'And I'm not sure I have the strength to share it.'

I place my hand on hers and squeeze it.

'Well, when you are, let me know. I'm not going anywhere.'

26

Helena has been receiving odd text and voice messages from a local dating site called Cromwey and Dorset Singles. I know this because she turned up at my house this morning, with her mobile phone in one hand and a sparkly notebook in the other. This was accompanied by a sorrowful expression and jittery hands. I did the dutiful thing and asked what was wrong, and before she even made it past my front mat, Helena had shared the news that she had fourteen messages when she woke up this morning, all from men asking her for dates – and other perverted favours. Even as she trudged down my hallway, her phone pinged twice and she greeted each with an exasperated grunt.

And now she is propped on my sofa, jotting notes in her book. It is a similar design to the one I use to keep track of my grievances about her, and that fills me with displeasure.

'Why've you got a notebook?' I ask.

Helena stops jotting, drops her head to one side and sighs.

'Because I'm making a log of every message I've received, so that I can show the police,' she replies.

'You do know you can screenshot the messages, don't you?'

Helena's mouth drops open.

'Yes! I'm not stupid,' she hisses. 'But screenshots can get deleted. This...' she waggles the notebook at me, 'cannot.'

I nod and sit down next to her. She powers on her phone and heads straight to voicemail. 'Listen to this one message. You'll never believe it.'

I hear static on the line, heavy breathing and then, 'Hi babe. Saw your profile on Cromwey and Dorset Singles and wondered what you're up to tonight. If you want to come over, my mum's going out and we'll have the basement all to ourselves.'

The voice sounds as though it's coming from a teenage boy. This is confirmed when several other voices hoot in the background, and then the call ends.

'Well, that's obviously a fifteen-year-old boy and his mates, taking the piss!'

Helena runs her tongue along her top teeth, which gives her an unflattering profile.

'I know that,' she says. 'But it's still creepy. And listen to this text that came in about thirty minutes ago.' She clears her throat and then scowls. 'Ugh, I forgot to bring my reading glasses. Hang on.' She holds the phone about two feet away from her face, and looks down her nose at it.

'That's ridiculous. Let me look.' She throws the phone into my hand and I stare at the words. They swirl in front of me, but I'm not admitting to Helena that I need reading glasses too, so I screw up my eyes and read out loud. '"Dear Helena, I read your profile on Cromwey and Dorset Singles, and licked what I saw." Eww! Is that a spelling mistake or did he lick the screen?' I scowl at my companion, as she holds her head in her hands.

'I don't even want to think about it. Just carry on reading. You haven't reached the best bit yet.'

'Erm... Where was I? Okay, here we go: "I am looking for love, companionship and a good time. However, I hate time-wasters, so I'll be honest from the start. If you don't give head, there's no future for us. But if you do, I'll look forward to your call – Brian.'"

'Isn't that the most disgusting thing you've ever read? Ugh!'

Helena jumps up from the sofa and marches in a circle, rubbing her cheeks as she does so.

'It's definitely not the best,' I say. 'But seriously, what the hell are you doing on Cromwey and Dorset Singles anyway? You're not that desperate, are you?'

Helena's phone pings again and she stops stomping and grabs it from my hand.

'I don't need a dating site, thank you very much! I'm still kind of seeing that bloke I met in the café, but that's another story.'

As my husband's alienated wife dabs at her eyes with a tissue, joy ripples up from my stomach. Poor Helena Love certainly seems to be having more than her share of bad luck recently, and I couldn't be happier for her. But at the same time, I'm thankful that her mind is occupied by something other than the lost locket and me spilling her wedding album all over the floor. Hopefully this new scandal will keep her busy enough to forget all about both catastrophes.

At least that was my hope when I signed Helena up for Cromwey and Dorset Singles last night...

I comfort my companion by inviting her into my kitchen for a cup of apple juice and a cupcake I bought from one of her business rivals. Despite being distressed by the calls and messages, Helena's appetite is still fully functioning, and she devours the cake and slurps her drink as though she hasn't eaten in days.

She's dressed in a pair of ripped blue jeans with a #MeToo logo printed down one of the legs, and a black T-shirt with the word 'Feminist' emblazoned across her chest. Helena is making *Girl Power* a mantra for all middle-aged, whinging, scorned, almost-divorced women. Good for her! Or not as the case may be.

Her phone pings again and she picks it up from the table and sighs.

'Another one?'

'Yep. Ugh, this one wants to know if I enjoy masturbating! Do all single blokes talk this way?'

She flings the phone onto my flowery tablecloth, as if it's a used vibrator.

'It appears so. May I?'

Helena nods, so I pick up the handset and scroll through the messages. There are now seventeen requests, all from budding perverts and basement dwellers, and every one of them forwarded from the dating site. The first came in at 10.03pm, which is about five minutes after I signed Helena up for it. Either she's considered a great catch to the single men of Cromwey, or there are a lot of creeps in town. I imagine it's a combination of the two. I read a few of the funniest ones out loud and then hand it back. Helena accepts it with a quivering bottom lip.

'What shall I do?' She groans. 'I don't even know how I got signed up for this in the first place.'

'That's the problem nowadays. We give everyone our email addresses and God knows what else. Next thing you know, they've sold them on to a dozen companies and you end up on a sucker list. I imagine that's what's happened here.'

Helena nods and then picks at the crumbs left over on her cake case. I'm not sure if she believes me, but then she wouldn't have a reason to suspect that anyone would sign her up for some weird dating page. She licks her fingers. Her nails are bright green with glitter shimmering through them. How does this woman do the washing up? I guess she must have a dishwasher.

'How can I get off it?' she wails. 'I don't want my contact details on this kind of site. It's weird and disgusting! And besides, shouldn't they ask you to verify your account before you join? I never received any emails about it and that must be against the law!'

I have to admit that shocked me too. Even when I join a random mailing list, I have to verify my email to show that I'm not a robot or an imposter. But in the case of Cromwey and Dorset Singles, that wasn't even an issue. Maybe they're glad to find a woman for their books. From what Helena's shown me, it seems that horny, desperate men are their biggest clients.

I gather up the leftover cake cases, throw them in the bin, rinse the mugs and leave them upside down on the drainer. Helena has fallen silent and when I turn to see what she's doing I notice her head sagging towards her chest. Two fat tears run down her cheeks.

'Helena? Are you okay?'

She lets out such a groan that I wonder if she's in physical pain. I swear that I can see actual sobs billowing up the front of her neck. Tears plop onto the tablecloth and lie for a moment, before resigning themselves to their fate and sinking into the cotton. My poor, beautiful tablecloth. I'll have to put it on a high-temp wash later.

As Helena sobs, I put the next part of my plan into action. This dating dilemma is creating a solid distraction from the problems I've created for her recently, but it also presents me with an opportunity. If I can rid Helena's phone of unwanted texts and questions, it will disguise the fact that I'm the one who caused the distress in the first place, and maybe promote me to the role of hero in her eyes.

'Here, let me help.' I wrench the phone out of Helena's hand.

'You go to the bathroom and get yourself back together again. Wash your face and pop on some of my under-eye cream – it's in the cupboard under the sink. Meanwhile, I'll notify the site that you never signed up for it in the first place and demand they take your name off. It'll be fine, I promise.'

Helena sniffs, nods and lifts herself up from the chair.

'Thank you,' she says, and then disappears out of the kitchen.

As soon as I hear her feet on the stairs, I log onto the dating site, cancel the profile and then head over to delete Helena's internet history. The last thing I want is for her to see that I managed to log in to the account, and it wouldn't surprise me to find out that she'd checked.

As the bathroom water runs through the pipes above my head, I press a few buttons and I'm faced with everything Helena has looked at in the past few days. There are at least ten entries for Amazon, three for Debenhams, six for the *Daily Mail* website and one for the pleasure pier theatre box office. All your typical stuff, but then one particular search string catches my eye.

Smuggler's Steps, accident 2014.

Smuggler's Steps, woman falls 2014.

Smuggler's Steps, accident, witness 2014.

I'm stunned. Helena is searching for her own accident? Why would she do that after all these years? All the newspaper coverage is out there and I know she's seen at least some of it, since she knows I was part of the campaign. Maybe she enjoys googling herself. I guess we all do from time to time. Before I can research it further, I hear Helena's feet on the stairs. When she enters the room, I smile and hand over her phone.

'You look better,' I say, although in reality she looks worse than she did five minutes ago.

'Thank you.' She blows her nose into a wad of toilet paper and stares at the phone.

'I sorted out the weird emails for you. I turned off all notifications so you won't get anymore, and then I complained about you being signed up in the first place. I doubt they'll reply, but nevertheless, you shouldn't get any more messages.'

Helena shoves her phone back into her bag.

'Thank you! You're a life saver.'

And you know what? I really believe I am.

27

The events of yesterday prey on my mind as I take my morning run. I don't regret signing Helena up to the dating site, but when I phoned Rebecca afterwards, she was so full of joy and excitement for her life, that it made me question when was the last time I experienced that for myself? Yes, I feel delight every time Helena trips up or cries in my kitchen, but what about the happiness of just being me? Of waking up in the morning, full of hope for a new day, or going shopping for new shoes, or seeing a show on the pier? It seems that recently all I do is plan new ways to antagonise Helena, and it's exhausting.

As my feet pound the pavement, I make what I consider to be a bold decision – from now on I'll lay off playing with Helena's emotions in the way I've been doing. Don't get me wrong, I still loathe this woman after what she did to me, but at this moment in time, perhaps karma is destroying her life far more than I ever could. Maybe it's okay, therefore, to stand back a little and let the universe give her the bulk of what's coming.

I've been running for twenty minutes when I realise that I've reached the promenade, and I'm heading towards Helena's café and Craig's garage. I don't relish the thought of seeing either of them, so I stop running and walk over to the huge veranda outside the amusement arcade to take a breath. There is a group of tourists outside, and the manager is arguing with the tour rep about the amount of space they're taking up on the pavement. I unscrew the cap on my water bottle and take a long, cold swig. As I'm doing so, my eyes flick towards the promenade and there I encounter a familiar face.

Stuart Wilson-Price.

And he's heading towards the amusements.

What the hell is he doing back in Cromwey? He can't still be hoping to catch sight of Annabelle, can he?

I find a gap in the crowd where I'm sufficiently hidden, but I can still see a good portion of the promenade. From my space I observe Stuart striding down the street, hands in pockets, looking as though he owns the place. Was he always this arrogant? I suppose I had no reason to notice much about him at the school gates. I was always in and out as fast as I could be.

A thought occurs to me that perhaps Stuart is heading for Craig's garage, and that terrifies me more than anything. It's one thing to not care that they're embroiled in some weird, family love triangle, but another to witness Stuart confronting my ex-husband in his workplace. I decide to wait until he's gone past and then follow behind, but as soon as the thought enters my brain, my view is blocked by an old lady bemoaning the absence of the tour bus. When I'm able to break through, the promenade is quiet and Stuart is nowhere to be seen.

Several days ago, one of my clients – an older lady called Florence – told me that her grandmother moved to New York in

1883 to become a dancer. Used to researching servants, coal miners and farmers, the idea of delving into the life of a showgirl filled me with joy.

I started my search with a little apprehension, since the chances of finding someone out of the ordinary are pretty low. However, Florence's grandmother, Daisy, turned out to be something of a Victorian raver. Not only did she become a New York dancer, but she also wrote (and acted in) a play that was considered so shocking it was banned all over the East Coast. The poor woman was put on trial for indecency, before returning to London, where she suffered a full-blown nervous breakdown. Who the hell can blame her?

Florence lives in the same estate as Helena, and as soon as I've delivered the documents, I head straight to see her. Now, I know I said I wasn't messing with her life anymore, but honestly, if I didn't pop in to see her while passing, what would she think of me? It would be so rude! Besides, I won't stay long. Just a quick visit to see if there's any more Craig news, and then I'll be off. No big deal.

It's Helena's day off and as she's a creature of habit, the chances are high that she'll be pottering around her house. I knock at the front door for a while, but when she doesn't answer, I get a little nervous. What if the dating site trick was too much for her? I shake the thought from my head. No, it wasn't *that* bad. It was nothing but a stupid joke.

I crouch down and open the letterbox, but Helena's got one of those infuriating brushes over the gap, and I can't see through. I stand up and lean across to the bow window and stare inside, but the only evidence that Helena's been in there is a half-drunk cup of tea on the table, accompanied by a crossword book.

The gate into the back garden is always kept unlocked, so I

pop the latch with the intention of banging on the back door. However, in the end I don't have to, because there is Helena, sitting on a deckchair in the middle of the lawn, reading a book.

'Hey,' I shout. 'I've been knocking on your door for ages!'

Helena lifts her head and grins. From twenty feet away she appears somewhat attractive.

'I'm engrossed in a great book! Would you like a drink?'

Helena throws the paperback onto the picnic table beside her. From the cover it looks like a corny romance novel. So much for her love of Shakespeare.

'Something cold would be great,' I say. 'Orange if you have it. Thank you.'

'I'll bring some snacks!' Helena disappears up the path and into the house.

It feels like a hundred degrees out here, so I move the chair into the shade and take a look around me. Craig's personality shines in every corner of this garden. He wasn't what you'd call green-fingered when he loved me, but he did do his best and we always had pretty flower beds and hanging baskets out the front. I've given up with the baskets now – they need too much attention it seems to me – but the flower beds are still intact. Craig had a crazy obsession with gnomes during our marriage, and while I only allowed him a couple in our garden, I notice that in this one, there are at least a dozen – all gathered around the kidney-shaped pond, plotting world domination.

Helena's garden is made up of a large lawn with a thin line of raised flower borders on one side. Towards the back there's a small, bottle-green shed, a rockery with pansies, and the aforementioned pond, with a little bridge going across the middle. It reminds me of the garden my grandparents had when I was little, because it is surrounded by hedges that look as though they've been there since the 1960s. My grandparents' garden had little sprigs of mint growing in odd places, and sometimes I would rub the leaves between my fingers and breathe in the sweet, icy scent. I get down on my hands and knees and search under Helena's hedge, but there's no sign of any fragrant mint there. Just some nasty, stinging nettles instead.

Why doesn't that surprise me?

I make it back to my chair moments before Helena comes out of the back door, carrying a huge tray laden with a vintage jug filled with orange juice, tall glasses and a three-tiered, china cake stand. It's totally over the top – as one would expect from the owner of The Lovely Café. She places the tray onto the table and the ice rattles and clinks against the jug.

'Do you have any mint plants?' I ask, and Helena gazes around the garden.

'Mint plants, no. None of those I'm afraid. But we do have some minty biscuits if you care for one... and some French fancies.'

She thrusts the cake stand at me, and a yellow fancy slides off and lands on my lap.

'Looks like I'm having this one then.' I bite the corner and the frosting is smooth and sweet on my tongue.

Helena pours the drinks, drags another chair out of the shed and places it next to me.

'I'll have a custard cream,' she says. 'I used to buy these all the time for Craig. He loved them. I guess he still does, only I doubt Annabelle would know where to buy them.'

'I doubt Annabelle would have even heard of them. Unless her grandparents are fans.'

Helena pops the entire biscuit into her mouth, while I continue to nibble on my teeny cake.

'Is it me or are these things smaller than they were before?' I move the cake back and forth in my fingers.

'It's not you,' Helena says. 'We make huge ones for the café, but we sold out yesterday and I couldn't bring any home. Luckily, I had these shop-bought ones in the back of the cupboard.'

Helena leans back in her chair and drinks her orange juice. We fall into a relaxed silence and I feel happy and relieved that I've taken the decision to lay off with my revenge tactics. Now I can sit here and sip my juice and know that when I walk away from her house this afternoon, I'll be leaving behind the madness of the last month. It's time to break away from this situation and get on with my life. It feels good. But for now, I'm happy to partake in one more little dig.

Just for old times' sake.

'Did you hear that they're going to New York?'

Confusion flickers across Helena's eyes.

'Who?'

I wipe cake crumbs off my knees, and scrunch the wrapper into something that resembles a tiny untidy ball.

'Craig and Annabelle. Rebecca spoke to her dad on the phone the other day, and he said he was taking Annabelle for her birthday. Staying at the Plaza apparently, though I'm not sure when.'

Helena's face falls and she frowns. She's furious and gutted. I know that feeling, because while it's hard enough knowing your husband has left you for another woman, it's heartbreaking to discover that he's already splashed out thousands of pounds on a romantic holiday for his new love. Bless her, the pain must be unbearable.

I hope.

Helena slams her glass onto the table and some of the juice splashes over the edge.

'New York? That's not possible. Craig hates New York!'

'He does?'

Tears spring into Helena's eyes and she blinks them back. I avert my gaze and wonder how she came to that conclusion.

'When we were together, I was desperate to go to New York,' she says. 'I wanted to see all the places where they filmed *Sex and the City* and *Friends*, but Craig said he couldn't think of a worse place to go. I even offered to pay for it, but he said he had no intention of ever visiting the place and I should drop the idea. So, I did... begrudgingly.'

'Well, that's just bizarre. He didn't feel that way when we were there.'

Helena frowns on one side of her face and her nostrils flair. It's an expression that isn't the least bit attractive.

'I don't understand. Craig said he'd never been and never wanted to go.'

There is a ladybird wandering along the table edge. I offer it my finger; it strolls on and I blow it towards the hedge.

'In that case, I'm afraid he was lying.' I laugh. 'I know he's been to New York because I went with him! He took me for my fortieth birthday and we both loved it, and planned to go back before... well, you know.'

Helena grabs another custard cream.

'What a wanker.'

'Quite.'

A cat appears from under the hedge and heads straight for Helena's feet. She shoos it away and then scratches her ankle. Her demeanour is quiet and detached. She's probably wondering what else Craig lied to her about, but that's none of my concern, and I feel zero compassion for her.

I'm not that angelic.

'Do you think she googles us?'

The force of Helena's voice and the abrupt change of subject make my torso jerk, and I almost spill orange juice all over my new trousers. I place the glass back onto the table.

'Sorry? Who are we talking about?'

'Annabelle. His New York companion.'

She emphasises the words 'Annabelle' and 'companion' as though they're somehow distasteful. This amuses me a little, but her question baffles me. This is the first time I've ever thought about Annabelle being interested in anything going on in Helena's life. Or mine for that matter.

'I'm not exactly sure how to answer that,' I say. 'I don't know why she'd want to research the former wives of her new lover. Is that a thing now? I've never stolen someone's husband so I wouldn't know.'

I know I'm trying to behave myself now, but how could I resist that comment? It's the truth after all – there are two people sitting in this garden, and only one of them knows the protocol for when you've pinched another woman's fella. I smile and Helena stares at me over the top of her orange juice, swallows hard and then licks her top lip.

'It's human instinct,' she says. 'Before Craig and I got together, I stalked your Facebook page a lot. I searched for you so often that your name was on the top of my search page for months!'

She speaks in such a matter-of-fact way that I'm floored. Why reveal such a thing? Is this her way of punishing me for telling her about the New York trip?

'What do you mean you stalked me *before* you got together?'

A wasp buzzes around Helena's head and she swats at it with her book. She's wearing her wedding ring again I notice. How deluded this woman is.

'I wanted to see what I was up against,' she says. 'Craig was charming and friendly whenever he came into the café and I liked him a lot. However, I knew he was married – I'd seen his wedding ring – so I had to find out if he was happily married before I made my move.'

My body tenses and I beg myself to remain calm. This is not

five years ago and Helena did not win this war. I try to speak without my voice trembling, but it's difficult.

'And what did you find out?' I ask.

She picks at her cuticles and shrugs as though it's no big deal.

'To be honest – and I'm not saying this to be cruel – it appeared as though Craig was faking it.'

'What do you mean?'

I lean away and hold my glass to my chest as though it's some kind of shield. If Helena notices my discomfort, she sure as hell doesn't mention it.

'The photos on your social media, for instance,' she says. 'They didn't show a happy man. It all seemed a little too forced if you ask me.'

My mouth is dry and I have an intense thirst. My glass is empty of juice, so I grab a semi-melted ice cube instead. Maybe it will put out the fire of this intense conversation.

'So, let me get this straight.' I crunch the ice and it attacks my sensitive teeth. 'You decided to go after my husband because of a few Facebook photos that you figured were fake?'

Helena's shoulders hang loose and her gaze is everywhere except where I sit. There is a long, awkward pause.

'I guess I did,' she says. 'But if it makes you feel better, he didn't fall for me straight away. He took a lot of persuading and I had a serious amount of flirting to do before he eventually agreed to go for a drink with me. I was shocked if I'm honest.'

I clutch my head, as Helena's words cut right through me. All these years I believed that Craig glided into that café – and her bed – without a second thought for me at all. I might not have been giving him my full attention, but it was Helena who assured him that he could do better. Craig may have been more patient about my budding business had she not become involved, and he might have stayed in our marriage too.

I open my mouth, but no words come out. Helena must realise my grief because she reaches forward and grasps my arm.

'I'm sorry I did that to you,' she whispers. 'It wasn't especially nice.'

I release my arm from her grip and lean back into my chair. She's sorry? Who is she kidding? This whinging woman is not at all remorseful that she encouraged my husband to leave his family. She's just sorry that she's suffered as a result of it! The sun has moved from its previous position and shines down onto my cheeks. I rub them as though that's going to make a difference.

'Would you like some sunscreen?' Helena asks. 'I have a new bottle on the bathroom shelf. I'll get it for you.'

She goes to get up from the chair, but I throw up my hand.

'No, it's okay. I need the loo anyway. I can get some while I'm up there.'

I get to my feet and pray that my legs will carry me inside the house without collapsing. I can't believe what I've just heard. As I turn away from Helena, raging tears roll down my cheeks.

I don't bother to wipe them away.

Helena's bathroom is painted the most garish sky-blue colour I've ever seen, and the striped blue floor tiles have all the makings of a vicious migraine. The stark white contrast of the toilet, sink and shower are too much and I can't imagine that this is where Craig shaved and showered for five whole years. No wonder he decided to move out.

I grab a tissue and mop away my tears, and then I wipe the toilet seat in an effort to erase all trace of Helena Love before I sit down. I can't stop stewing over what she said in the garden. Even if these events had no bearing on my life at all, it was still distasteful – and disrespectful. I don't understand how a woman can pursue a man, knowing he belongs to another. And while I'm aware that it is nonsense to assume someone truly belongs to you, I can't help but wonder... whatever happened to sisterhood and solidarity?

They probably ran off with somebody's husband.

Helena's words fizz in my head and I hang onto the side of the toilet, in an effort to stay conscious. I place my fingers on the pulse in my neck and it is racing – as I expected it to be. I cannot believe that I had decided to stop torturing this woman! As much as I've been playing with her life over the past month, my actions have been innocent in comparison to what she's done to me. I must never forget that!

I get up from the toilet and wash my hands. I catch my reflection in the mirror and I'm pissed off to discover that my eyes are lined red and puffy to the touch, so I look around for some concealer or cream that I can dab on. My gaze wanders into the shower and I see a white, plastic contraption attached to the wall. Closer inspection reveals that it dispenses shower gel, shampoo and conditioner. I reach for a towel and as I do so, I notice a tube of hair removal cream, balanced on the shelf above the sink.

Helena's garden confession repeats in my head and all thoughts of stepping away from this insane situation are dismissed. There is no way I can leave her alone after what she said.

I was a fool to think this fight was over.

Before I know what I'm doing, the tube of hair removal cream is in my hands and I'm standing in the shower, tugging at the plastic dispenser.

She took my husband.

Let's see how she likes me taking her hair.

The front of the contraption pings open and I twist the top

off the cream. My hands quiver and the cap springs away from me and heads straight for the shower tray. Shit. I bend down to pick it up and it's only as I rise up again that I notice how light the tube is. I squeeze it and a pea-sized dollop of cream appears at the top. Damn it! That wouldn't even remove the hair off a mouse. I replace the cap and throw the tube back onto the shelf. My breathing is frantic and I bring my hand to my mouth in an effort to steady myself.

What the fuck am I doing? Was I really planning to make Helena go bald? At this point I have no answer to that question.

I pop the front of the dispenser back into place, and then I climb out of the shower. It's time to go home.

Rebecca and Kate stare at me from behind their bowls of spaghetti bolognaise. My daughter blinks; her blue eyes bright and inquiring. Kate dabs at her mouth with a napkin, leans forward and examines my face.

'You're joking. Please tell me you're joking!'

I twirl my fork around the spaghetti, and then I let it all fall off.

'Relax, I didn't actually do it.'

'But you would have,' Kate says. 'If the tube wasn't empty.'

My fork clatters onto the plate.

'For goodness' sake, Kate! I thought you'd laugh! It's funny!'

Rebecca lowers her fork and the handle falls into the tomato sauce. I grab a piece of kitchen roll and hand it to her. She ignores me and I drop it onto the table.

'Mum, it's not funny at all. You go into Helena's bathroom and contemplate putting hair removal cream into her conditioner? Are you hearing yourself? That's bloody insane.'

Kate wags her spoon in my direction.

'I have to agree. The fact that you even *thought* it might be a good idea is scary enough.'

I tut and pretend that they're taking me far too seriously. Inside, however, I wonder why the hell I had to open my mouth. Of course they think I'm insane! How could I ever doubt it?

'Mum, what would you have done if the bottle hadn't been empty?'

'What I just said,' Kate chirps. 'She'd have gone through with her plan!'

'I don't know.'

I pretend to look at my phone, but my eyes are swirling and I can't see any of my apps.

'I think you do,' Kate scoffs.

'Okay, I'd have probably filled up the dispenser.'

My daughter gasps and holds her hand to her throat.

'Told you.' Kate takes another forkful of pasta and rams it into her mouth.

'That's screwed up.' Rebecca pushes away her plate.

'You didn't let me finish,' I say. 'Yes, I'd have filled up the dispenser, *but* I would have regretted it and rinsed the whole thing out before Helena found it.'

'Exactly how long were you planning on being in the bathroom?' Rebecca asks, so I shrug and stop speaking.

'Jenny.' Kate finishes chewing, swallows and places her hands together.

'We love you and we know what you've been through over the past few years. But you need to step away from Helena.' I attempt to speak but she shushes me. 'I know you say you're being friendly, or whatever, but we all know that's not true. I'm not sure what your motivation is to be honest, but whatever it is, it's bringing out a side of you that's damaging. Your obsession with Helena wasn't healthy five years ago, and it is most certainly not healthy now.'

I get up from the table and clear the plates. Rebecca tries to grab hers back but it's too late. Dinner is over.

'I don't know what you mean.'

'Yes, you do,' Kate replies.

And she's absolutely right.

28

2014

It's Sunday morning, but there are no sweet dreams or breakfast in bed for me. Instead, I lie awake in the depressing October darkness because every time I close my eyes, all I can see are Craig and Helena's naked bodies. It's not something I conjure up myself, because believe me their sex life is something I never want to imagine. But like it or not, the vivid images appear right in front of me whenever I attempt to sleep, and the only thing that makes them go away is to open my eyes.

It's 6.24am. I know I'll never get back to sleep, so I admit defeat and head to the kitchen for some tea. My appetite has vanished over the past four weeks, and breakfast is not an option for me anymore. Even a bread roll seems like a three-course meal, and most of the time I'll nibble on a corner and then throw the rest in the bin. To be honest, that's the best thing about your husband leaving you for another woman. I can now wear slim-fit jeans for the first time in years, and it's all thanks to Craig not being able to keep his own jeans on. Who would have thought?

My laptop resides on the table and as the kettle boils, I fire it up and go straight onto Facebook. I scroll through the never-ending stream of self-important, boastful posts, and roll my eyes. Until a month ago I was one of those people. I posted updates on crap such as buying a new carpet, or decorating my hallway. I bolstered my ego with photos of Craig and I living a charmed life, in our little blue harbour home. 'Wow! Your house is like something out of a storybook,' my 'friends' would say, and I'd tap 'like' and comment with hearts and gratitude emojis.

It wasn't until Craig moved out that I realised the bullshit I posted about my life, and now Helena Love is doing the same thing – on her set-to-public profile. I'm not stupid; I know her Facebook is open because of me. It probably gives her the biggest kick to know that I research her, but does she know that I refresh her page at least four times an hour? Doubtful. Would that make her post even more corny photos and updates? I'm sure it would.

There are no new posts this morning, but there is one from late last night. Apparently, she and Craig went to see a Queen tribute band; the news of which tears my heart in half. That is what we did too, at the beginning of our relationship. There is an accompanying video of Craig wearing a backwards baseball cap and rocking out to 'We Are the Champions'. He looks like a bloody fool.

But he was my fool.

And now he's gone.

I know it's not healthy to spend hours scrolling through Helena Love's Facebook page, but I can't be the only scorned wife to do such a thing. Still, it's a habit I try to keep to myself, especially after Rebecca caught me snooping and acted as though I'd hacked into the MI5 headquarters.

I open the Cromwey Chats Back group and search for Helena's name. I've been a member of this community page for a couple of years now, but I'd never noticed Helena on there. Now that she's become a fixture in my life, I see her name constantly, asking crap about train times, traffic jams and the best place to buy carpets. Most of the people answer her civilly, but once there was a guy who told her to 'Fuck off with the questions and use Google like everyone else.' I sniggered when I read that comment – until Craig came on to defend her and then I cried. Again.

Yesterday I bought a small notebook, so that I can write down all of Helena's stupid Facebook questions and requests. This gives me a brilliant insight into the life she now leads with my husband. For instance, on Monday last week, she wanted to know if anyone had visited the Tower of London, and then enquired as to the price of two return train tickets. So, from that I could decipher that she and Craig were off to London pretty soon.

Cromwey isn't renowned for its supersonic travel, and we only have a couple of trains running to the capital per day – one in the early morning and one in the evening. The day after I saw Helena's post, I made it my mission to be at the station by 8am, in the hopes of seeing them. I had no luck that morning, but the next day I was back and within seven minutes of my arrival, there was the happy couple, strolling along the platform like something out of an old Hollywood movie. Helena was dressed in a vintage-style frock, black with huge red flowers all over the skirt. She was trailing a bright-pink suitcase behind her, and I could hear the click, click, click of the wheels against the platform cement. My husband wore smart black trousers with a navy-blue jacket; the likes of which I'd never seen him wear during our marriage. Even his shoes were shiny and polished. The mechanic scrubs up well – when he wants to.

I hid behind a grimy pillar and watched as the couple climbed into the first-class carriage. My husband stepped in and reached for Helena's luggage, before turning to offer his hand. Craig's new love accepted it and climbed into the carriage. He gave her a quick but happy kiss on the lips.

I felt as though I might die.

That evening, Helena's Facebook revealed that they were staying in a posh hotel in Russell Square, which was the exact location of where Craig and I celebrated our fifteenth wedding anniversary. I couldn't help but wonder if they were staying in the same room we shared, but the jobsworth receptionist refused to tell me when I called.

The new couple arrived back at the station two days later; armed with goodies housed in expensive paper bags with ribbon handles. I watched as Craig unburdened Helena of her luggage and carried everything down the platform himself. She patted his back and kissed his shoulder, while I hung onto a pillar and begged myself to stay upright.

Helena showed off her new purchases on social media, as soon as she was able. There was a bottle of scent from the Queen's favourite perfume store; several new dresses, blouses and skirts in vivid colours and patterns; chocolates from Liberty; a 1930s style hat; three silk scarves and something called a promise ring from Pandora. I had never owned one of those, but Google informed me that they are given between couples as a symbol of their forever love, when getting engaged is not an option.

That evening I busied myself by taking screenshots of everything Helena and Craig had bought, and then I checked out the prices online. I noted it all down in my journal on the pretext that my solicitor might be interested to see how much money Craig had spent. In reality it was so that I could suffer even more than I already was.

I guess I am a masochist at heart.

~

Sundays used to be my favourite day of the week and Craig and I rarely strayed from our routine. We'd sleep late, make love, do a little housework, cook a traditional roast lunch, and then curl up on the sofa together. My husband would be engrossed in his car magazines and I'd read my paperbacks or sometimes watch a good thriller on Netflix. Later we'd maybe go out for a stroll to the stone pier, or have a coffee at the old castle.

I had a blissful life, back in the day, and the saddest thing is that I didn't even realise it – until it was gone.

Nowadays my routine is the opposite of what Craig and I had. Housework is almost non-existent, lunch is a piece of chocolate or half a biscuit or whatever I can keep down, and my afternoon of reading has now turned into a real-life psychological drama.

You see, social media stalking is fine to an extent, but although she's a frequent poster, Helena Love doesn't spend every minute of every day online. That's a problem for me, so I need to use my imagination to find out more about her life, and the new life of my old husband. Now every Sunday afternoon, I throw on a winter coat, bobble hat and scarf, and head up to the estate where Helena and Craig live. The advantage of the autumnal weather is that I can dress like Bigfoot and nobody will notice. The disadvantage is the customary rain and wind, meaning that no matter how many layers I wear, I return to my house in utter disarray – in more ways than one.

Thankfully, today the weather is crisp and fine, but still cold enough to wear my disguise. Helena and Craig's house is on the estate at the top of Smuggler's Steps, but I don't go that way because if I do, I end up on the wrong side of their living room window – i.e. the side where they could notice me. I can't risk that happening, so instead I go around to the new harbour, past the bridge and then sweep up the hill until I come out onto their street and the correct side of their house.

By the time I've arrived, I'm out of breath and depleted due to lack of food. However, the huge tree and bushes at the bottom of their front garden provide an excellent shelter where I can hide, observe, and pretend to tie my shoelaces should a nosey neighbour appear. I probably shouldn't be concerned about that though, since Helena stalked my home long before I stalked hers – and she had the balls to stroll up our path and knock, just before our anniversary celebration. I'll never forget that she did that.

Craig and Helena have their Sunday dinner at 3pm precisely. This is later than he is used to, since we always sat down no later than 1.30. Their house is one of those large Victorian properties which once had both front and back rooms. Nowadays – in the era of Helena and Craig – both rooms have been knocked into one, so that it's a living room-diner kind of deal. The table is located in the large bow window, and from where I stand, I can see the side of Craig's face, and the back of his mistress's head. More precisely, I have a view of her 1990s-style curls. At first, I couldn't figure out if these were the result of a dodgy perm or unfortunate genes, but after studying photos of her grandparents on Ancestry.com I tend to swing towards the latter.

It takes Craig and Helena around thirty minutes to have their dinner, and I witness a lot of happiness in that half hour. Sometimes Helena will reach over to touch Craig's face and he'll put his hand on hers and smile – or worse, he'll lean in and kiss her. It's all very romantic. And sickening.

Afterwards, Helena clears the plates, while Craig folds down the sides of the table and pushes it over to the wall. He's only lived in that house for a matter of weeks, but from the routine they've established, it might as well be a lifetime.

I watch the happy couple until I can handle the pain no

more – or until they disappear from the window – whichever comes first, and then I give the house one last gaze and head home. I normally cry for the entire journey, but today I surprise myself and don't shed a tear until I am safely inside my front door.

I imagine a doctor would call that progress. Of sorts.

29

2014

I could normally take or leave my library job. It pays the bills and it isn't altogether horrendous, but being in such close proximity to the general public can often do severe damage to my mental health. You'd be surprised how crazy people get when a book they're after is already on loan, or if it's on the system but lost on the shelf. I couldn't believe it at first. They go bonkers about it, and don't get me started on having to issue a fine for a late book. I had one man throw a copy of a management text across the room, because I issued him with a twenty-pence fine. He was then invoiced for the entire cost of the battered book, which he didn't pay because he said it was my fault that he'd kicked off in the first place! It was the most bizarre occurrence.

The job would be pretty boring if not for the fact that my colleague is my best friend, Kate. Together we have made it through an unbelievable twenty-four years, filled with grumpy members, snappy stray dogs, crying lost children and an occasional laugh or two. I don't think either of us intended to stay for long, but somehow here we are – though if my genealogy plans come to fruition, I will be digging my escape tunnel pretty soon.

Here's the funny thing about this whole break-up crap. While I used to drag myself into work each day, now I can't wait to get there. The official reason for that is that it keeps my mind busy, so that I don't end up obsessing about Craig and Helena all day long. Liz (my boss) says she's proud that I've thrown myself into my work, and Kate is relieved that the library gives me at least an eight-hour respite from crying.

I smile and accept all the compliments and support I can get. However, the real reason I enjoy my work at the moment is far more complicated. I can't deny that it keeps my mind busy, but the real enjoyment comes in the constant (and free) access to old newspapers and genealogy websites. This means that whenever I have a few moments to spare (or when Kate and Liz have nipped out for lunch or a tea break) I can delve into Helena's past and find out more about the woman who stole my life.

Today is no exception. Finding myself on my own for the afternoon due to a staff IT course in the Bournemouth branch, I can't wait to delve into the newspaper websites. It's a rainy Wednesday afternoon, a time when most of our visitors are tucked up at home with a cup of tea. The only people that remain in the library are Joe, the local oddball, and Melanie, a lady researching a project about the history of Cromwey pleasure pier. Luckily at this moment both are happy to fend for themselves, so I find a private booth and go onto the internet. Seconds later, the words British Newspaper Archive stare up at me and I can't hit the advanced search button quick enough.

During last week's research, I discovered that Helena's paternal grandfather was a local councillor and the man responsible for bringing the yearly summer beauty contest to Cromwey in the 1950s. Always dressed in a three-piece suit and tie no matter what the weather, Mr Love was considered a local celebrity and loved nothing more than to pose for the newspaper, open shops and mingle with visiting entertainers. His star shone bright for many years... that is until he had a sordid affair with Dorothy MacMillan, aka Miss Cromwey 1958. When he returned to his wife, the beauty queen sold her story to the press and they printed it all over their front pages. Consequently, Councillor Love suffered the humiliation of the whole of the south coast knowing that he enjoyed trysts in a top floor bedroom of the Royal Hotel. His wife left him and instead of being known as a local hero, he then acquired the well-deserved title of dirty old man.

When I found the articles last week, I printed them off and then pasted them into a scrapbook when I got home. I doubt I'll ever drag them out again, but I'm glad to have them, in case I should ever need them. Today, I hope to find out more about Helena herself, and from the moment I log onto the library account of the newspaper archive, I'm not disappointed. First of all, I find a small photo of her dressed in a leotard aged twelve, having won a silver medal in a tap dance competition. Her hair is tied back in a huge ribbon and her smile reveals prominent front teeth. She must have had those fixed I imagine, but then I haven't been that close to know for sure.

She gains a small mention in a run-down of GCSE results, when she gained a handful of decent qualifications – one for childcare and development, one for cooking and the other for English. I'm ecstatic because while I'm not overburdened with terrific exam results myself, even I managed better than that. My joy is short-lived however, when I see a post in the *Family Announcements* section two years later, declaring that Miss Helena Love has been awarded a B and C in her English Literature and Language A-levels. She must have upped her game in sixth form – at least in those subjects anyway.

My next great find is a large article about the opening of The

Lovely Café in 2011. The piece is entertaining if only for the following quote: 'I'm very much looking forward to giving pleasure to the tourists and residents of Cromwey!' An ironic observation, given what's happened since. There is a photo accompanying the story, which shows Helena posing outside her café. Dressed in a rock 'n' roll-style dress, high ponytail and a flowery tabard, Helena Love seems every inch the perfect housewife.

I wonder if she is.

As usual, I print all the articles, ready to go into my scrapbook, but before I can grab them from the printer, Joe wanders over to my booth.

'Do you have any books about tinned goods?' he asks.

This is what Joe does – he comes into the library, stares at a directory for twenty minutes, and then comes to the counter to ask for some random piece of information. I will smile, point him towards another directory and then hide until he's left the building. Kate on the other hand, finds Joe fascinating and listens to his stories until Liz tells her to get on with her work. I don't have much patience for the man, and today I have even less than usual. I send him off to find the *Directory of Grocers and Supermarkets*, and hope not to see him again.

As Joe marches towards the shelves on the back wall, the telephone rings at the main counter. I leave all of my research in the booth and rush to answer. On the other end of the phone, a young mother gives me a 2,000 word explanation as to why she hasn't been able to return her books yet. Before she's finished speaking, I've already renewed them for another month, but it takes me five minutes to get her to that point. She thanks me and I manage to hang up, moments before Kate and Liz stroll back into the library.

'What are you two doing here?' I stammer.

Liz throws off her scarf and hat, and loosens her coat buttons.

'Bloody training was cancelled one minute before it was due to start,' she says. 'The trainer threw up in the conference room and the whole place was evacuated.'

Liz and Kate both shudder and I screw up my face in sympathy.

'Sorry to hear that, but nice to have you back.' That's a lie. Now that they've returned to the fold, it means I can't do any more research.

Shit!

In my attempts to lose Joe and help the telephone caller, I forgot about the wad of Helena-related paper that had spewed out of the library printer. The bright white pile now mocks me from twenty feet away, as Kate and Liz make their way towards the staffroom. My boss doesn't miss anything and she gives the paper an enquiring glance as she passes. The first headline is enough to make her stop walking, and she scoops the papers up and flicks through the first few stories.

'Someone printing out local history?' she asks. I nod but Liz doesn't see me. She stares at the pages again, reads some lines about Councillor Love and then waves the wad of paper above her head. 'These yours, Jenny?' Panic rips through me as Kate snatches the pages from Liz's grasp.

'Sorry, Liz, these are mine. One of our members is doing a school project about local scandals, so I said I'd help her out. I printed these off this morning but forgot to pick them up.'

She smiles at our boss, but Liz grimaces and doesn't notice.

'A student working on a project about local scandals? I've heard it all now! From now on, please be sure to take your research as soon as it's printed. I don't know how many times I have to tell you. And for goodness' sake, make sure you've logged out of the newspaper website. You know the patrons are supposed to ask before they access it!'

Kate nods, hugs the articles and apologises. Once Liz is gone, my friend marches to the counter and slams the pile of paper onto the desk.

'Jesus!! Are these what I think they are?' I don't know what to say, so I play with the stapler. Kate grabs an envelope from the tray and thrusts it in my direction. 'Put them in this and stick it in your handbag. If Liz finds out you've been researching your husband's mistress at work, she'll kill you.'

My face is itchy and my head prickles under the strain of the past few minutes. I do what Kate asks and the papers disappear out of sight.

'Thanks for taking the bullet for me,' I say, but Kate has already gone into the back room.

30

2014

Since the near miss at work, Kate is onto me and questions my movements every bloody day. I've been meagre with my answers, because according to my friend, while checking out Facebook is acceptable and 'just human nature', anything else is taboo. For instance, Kate believes that getting wrapped up in Helena's GCSE results and childhood competition medals is detrimental to my emotional well-being, and should be avoided at all costs. That's understandable I suppose, but it does make me wonder what Kate would say if she knew that in addition to paper research, I also spend every Sunday afternoon loitering at the bottom of Helena's garden. Hell, I'm like her unofficial biographer at this point, but Kate doesn't need to know that.

'You won't tell Pete, will you? He's the last person I'd want to know about this.'

Kate has come over to my house for lunch, though with my appetite the way it is, there's not much eating going on.

'I think you'll find that *Craig* is the last person you want to know about this.'

Kate sips a glass of wine, while I pick at a tiny, sticky blob of jam on my otherwise clean tablecloth.

'Yes! And that's why you can't tell Pete! Promise me!'

My friend draws a cross on her chest with her finger.

'I promise. But you have to make a promise too, you know! You need to stop snooping around. It's not healthy and will only upset you even more than you are already.'

My cheeks redden and I look down in an effort to hide it.

'You're right, I know you're right. I'll stop it straight away. I was going to anyway.'

Kate lifts her glass.

'Good! Cheers to the end of old lunatic tendencies!'

'I'll drink to that. Cheers!'

My words sound genuine, but my fingers are crossed.

For much of my life I've kept a diary, but for the most part it hasn't been one of those page-a-day volumes where you record every aspect of your life. I did attempt to do that when I was in my thirties, but then realised that time is precious and I couldn't justify writing 500 words a day on pathetic arguments with Craig, or Rebecca's reluctance to clean her room. So, my recent diaries have been those that give four or five lines to fill in the most important events, like parties or shopping excursions. Still, they're pretty interesting to look back at, which is the main reason I keep all of mine.

It's Saturday night – a time when Craig and I would have been watching silly programmes on TV, or playing a game of Scrabble. But tonight, I'm on my own and as always, my mind turns to what went wrong in my life. I'm not sure why, but since Craig said he no longer loves me I've had this overwhelming desire to inflict emotional pain on myself. To do this I will haul out old photo albums and gawp at the images of our once happy little family. Then I'll play sad songs from the 1980s and bawl my eyes out for hours on end. If I want to really torture myself, I get out my old diaries and see what we were doing on this day five years ago, ten years ago, even fifteen years ago. Tonight is one of those nights.

Time marches on and it's now 1 November. Already there are multicoloured fireworks banging in the skies above the harbour. I grab my diary to see what we were up to on this day last year:

We went to the Harbour Committee Halloween/bonfire dance. Craig made everyone laugh with his 'Barbie Girl' dance routine. Kate and Pete left early because Kate drank too much and felt ill. Next year I suggest no open bar!

The date has been circled, to indicate that Craig and I made love that day. Kate always thought it was hilarious that I kept 'a sex log' as she called it, and could never understand why I did such a thing. In reality it was something I started doing when we were trying for a baby, and I never got out of the habit.

I flip the diary to the back to see the final total of times we had sex during 2013. Seventy-five. In my opinion, that was a pretty excellent score for a couple in their forties, though I'd never advertise the fact, in case it's crap. I grab my current diary and tally up the times we made love before that awful September day when Craig stormed out. Twenty-one. Wow, I had no idea the number had fallen that drastically. Was it my fault for spending my evenings studying genealogy? Or was it Craig's for allowing his penis to wander elsewhere? I'll never know, but the anxiety caused by such a revelation is almost unbearable.

∽

'So, tell me the truth, you haven't done any more Helena-stalking have you?'

Kate and I are together again in my living room. She's been here a lot recently, though I suspect it's more in an effort to keep an eye on me, rather than the fact she enjoys my company. I swallow a small mouthful of Sauvignon Blanc and pretend to study a stain at the bottom of my glass, but Kate's eyes never leave me. If I lie, she'll be onto me, so I might as well come clean. I hold my finger and thumb about an inch apart.

'Just a little.'

My friend groans.

'How much is just a little, exactly?' She places her wine glass onto the coffee table, folds her arms and watches me. To be honest, I've been wondering what my behaviour has to do with her anyway, but maybe she's being an over-caring friend. I imagine that if Kate didn't have any interest at all, that would bother me as well.

'I've only been trolling her on Facebook, which we both agreed is what the platform was created for anyway. But I promise I haven't done anything that'll get me in trouble at work, so don't worry about that.'

Kate curls her feet under her bottom and sinks back into the sofa. I'm not sure if she believes that all I've done is look on Helena's social media, but she seems happy in her ignorance.

'That's a big achievement,' she says. 'Well done.'

'Actually, that's a lie. There is something else.'

'Jesus! What is it? You haven't sent her a shit through the post, have you?'

'No, it's funnier than that – at least in my opinion it is. The other day I found Craig's garage on some review site or other. I didn't even know there was such a site for mechanics, but in any case, I left him a one-star review.'

To my surprise, Kate bursts into laughter and claps her hands together.

'That I can approve of! What did you say?'

I'm relieved by her lightened mood and I carry on with my story.

'I said that I hired him to tune my engine, but after two decades of inferior attention, he chose to inspect somebody else's rusty exhaust pipe instead.'

Kate takes a sip of wine and almost chokes on it.

'Bloody hell, that's fantastic... Wait, you were being sexual in that review, weren't you?'

'Of course!'

'Fabulous.'

We clink glasses together and laugh until our eyes water. I'm a funny friend who played out a teeny bit of revenge on her ex-husband, and that's fine with Kate. I won't tell her, therefore, that on the bookshelf two feet away from where she's sitting, my Helena notes and observations journal is bulging at the seams.

Because – as they say – what she doesn't know won't hurt her.

31

2014

I read the WhatsApp message for the ninth time.

Listen, something's happened and I wanted you to hear it from me. Craig and Helena have asked Pete and I round for dinner tonight. I know you're gonna freak out but I promise it wasn't my idea. Craig asked Pete and the stupid bastard said yes! You know what he's like! Anyway, don't worry about it. We still love you and being in Helena's house at least means I can spy on what she's up to and report back to you tomorrow. Please don't worry. I'm sorry about this. It's really not my fault. Lots of love, Kate. xx

Kate and I talk about many things via messages, but out of all the topics we've ever discussed, this is by far the last thing I ever expected her to mention. When I received the message twenty minutes ago, I thought it was a prank. However, after reading it for the second time, I realised it couldn't be someone's interpretation of a joke. Who would make light of such a terrible subject? Nobody. Nobody I know, anyway.

Kate's words have shocked me, and you know the worst part? I have just arrived home after working with her all bloody day! Why didn't she tell me about it then? I know the answer to that question already! Kate was afraid I'd kick off in the middle of the library, and that would not do. That would not do AT ALL! She must be a great actress, that's all I can say, because in the eight hours that we spent together, she wasn't strange or anxious in any way. Quite the opposite in fact.

My first reaction is to bang out a reply filled with venom:

How can you do this to me? You're supposed to be my friend! And what the fuck do you mean you can spy on her? You've been telling me not to do that for weeks, you hypocrite!

I end by calling Kate a traitorous bitch and hope she chokes on whatever swill Helena serves up for dinner this evening. However, as my finger hovers above the send button, it occurs to me that this kind of response is exactly what Kate expects from me. I imagine her and Pete crouched over the phone and Pete snorting. 'Well I did warn you, you should never have told her,' and then her replying with a, 'Yeah, she must be even more psycho than I thought. Shame.' The idea that they could talk about my reaction – and maybe even pass it along to Craig and his slut, fills me with terror. I delete the text and reply in a kinder voice:

Wow, I didn't expect that, but I really do appreciate you letting me know. Don't worry about it. I know it's not your fault. Give Pete a slap from me LOL and try to enjoy yourself

tonight. Make sure you gather as much scandal as you can.
I'll hear about it tomorrow. :-)

Kate replies within minutes, relieved no doubt that I am calm about it all. It amuses and enrages me that she believes I am okay with the obvious betrayal of our friendship. For Pete to accept a dinner invitation from his best friend is one thing, but for Kate to go along with it? That's a stab in the back as far as I'm concerned. And she can pretend she's going for my benefit as much as she likes, but I know the truth and she does, too. The reason Kate is going to that dinner party is to make sure she keeps in with Pete and his mate. If she refused to hang out in the new foursome, Pete would start going out on his own and Kate would be left out. That development would drive her bonkers.

I am bundled up from the November drizzle, shivering once again at the bottom of Helena Love's driveway. I've been watching the goings on inside the house for the past ten minutes, but I know that I'll need to move on soon, because my loitering is bound to attract a nosey neighbour or two. I had a close call last week when an old lady wandered past and straight out asked what I was doing. My well-rehearsed contingency plan went straight out of my mind, so I told her I was waiting for my son to come out of his friend's house. She stared for a moment and then crossed the road. I don't know if she believed me, but it got me thinking that I need to line up a better story in future – especially since my presence on this estate is becoming ever more regular.

Perhaps the most sensible thing to do is to stop coming here altogether, but how can I move away from this? Helena seems to have an adverse reaction to closing her curtains, even when it's dark, so she must expect people to stare in, otherwise why do it? I do wonder what Craig thinks about this little habit of hers, since he was always the first person to close the blinds in our house. He despised the idea of someone staring in as they passed, which is funny, because here I am – staring in but not passing.

The new fab foursome are seated at the table in the window and I can see Helena and Kate in deep conversation. They must be discussing the wallpaper, because both keep pointing to the wall and nodding their heads. At one point, Kate even runs her fingers down the paper, and then waves her hands in the air. She must be saying something oh-so amusing and enlightening, because Helena throws her head back and then they both burst into laughter.

To hell with Kate.

To hell with them all.

As if reading my earlier thoughts, Craig's arm shoots out from his corner of the table, and reaches for the thick, velvety curtain. It glides its way over to the middle, and then Kate responds by pulling on the other side. The two pieces of fabric meet like theatre curtains at the end of a performance. Now what? How can I see what's going on when there's no window to stare through?

In the distance, a dog walker enters the estate via Smuggler's Steps. He hasn't seen me but if he gets any closer, I'll be in full view. More alarmingly, if the dog makes a fuss, my presence will be revealed for sure.

I look from the house to the walker and back again.

And it is at that moment I decide to wander down the driveway, unclip the side gate, and pay Helena and Craig a surprise visit.

~

Helena Love's back door is pale pink. I know this because there is a security light above my head, glowing right onto it. I've never seen a pink door and I'm not sure where you'd even buy outdoor paint that colour, but perhaps that's the last thing I should be obsessing about right now.

I know I need to be careful because Helena's door is in direct view of the neighbouring property, with a trimmed hedge in-between. Her neighbours' names are Trevor and Julia Buckfast. I discovered this after I obtained a copy of the electoral roll and they were listed on there. So too were John and Joan MacFarlane at number forty-eight and Linda and Bruce Hollies at number fifty.

The neighbour across the road is Derek Lindell: he isn't married, has lived on his own since his mother passed away in 2010 and enjoys posting photographs of his six-year-old cat on Facebook. The feline's name is Sparkles, which is a bloody stupid name if you ask me, but Derek's social media companions seem to like it. Derek is a *Doctor Who* fan (he's a member of the Cromwey chapter of the fan club) and he's been banned from the local bus station for tormenting passengers on the number eight bus. I found this out when I googled him last week, along with Trevor and Julia Buckfast, though the only interesting thing they've done this year is to start a line-dancing class at the harbour club. It was cancelled after five weeks because a local schoolteacher sprained her ankle and threatened to sue. A sign in the post office informs me that they're looking into teaching private classes in their back garden – weather permitting.

My hand hovers over Helena's door handle, but before I can try it, a cat makes an impromptu appearance from under the hedge. Thanks to Derek's Facebook page, I recognise it as Sparkles. He stares at me for the briefest of seconds, and then rubs his tail around my calves, purring as he does so. I wave my arms around and try to shoo him away, but he's too intrigued by my presence. Instead of sauntering off, he collapses next to my foot, hoists his back legs in the air and proceeds to give himself a wash.

I can't allow an animal to disturb my plans, and I turn my attention back to the door. My heart thunders in my chest and my mouth feels as though it's filled with cotton wool. My subconscious invades my head and asks what I'm doing; assures me that I should not be in this situation and begs me to leave. It's right – I'm a fool for even walking to the estate, never mind wandering into the back garden. Yet even though I am aware of what I'm doing and know I can stop at any time, I don't want to. My husband is on the other side of that door with his new lover and my so-called best friend. I need to feel the terrible pain of that reality because it is the only connection I have with Craig at this moment.

And that fucking sucks.

I press down on the handle and I'm shocked to discover that instead of meeting resistance, it glides open straight away. Who doesn't lock their back door in this day and age? Mine's locked all day and night, because you don't know who could be hanging around – especially at night.

A whoosh of warm air hits me from the gap I've created. It's filled with the rich, sweet smell of beef bourguignon and roast potatoes, and despite my best intentions, my mouth fills with saliva. I haven't eaten a thing since breakfast and I'm ashamed that my starving body craves Helena's cooking.

Since I didn't expect the door to be unlocked, I'm hesitant as to what I should do next. Do I go in? Do I confront them all for being the traitors, cheaters and thieves that they are? My mind whirrs, as Sparkles the cat whips past me, straight into the kitchen and then down the hall. The gasps and cries of 'Jesus Christ' and 'shoo' that resonate from the living room, alert me to the fact that the cat has made an unscheduled appearance at the dinner party. Two seconds later, the hall light flashes on and I hear Craig's voice heading towards the kitchen. He's been given the job of discharging the cat and if I don't move fast, we'll be face to face whether we like it or not.

I bound over to an outdoor storage unit and fold myself as small as I can behind it. Moments later, the cat dashes out of the back door in a series of hisses and complaints.

'And don't come back!' shouts Craig, as though the stupid cat can understand him.

Unapologetic, Sparkles sniffs me as he trots past, but doesn't give away my location. My toes throb in my shoes and my ankles and knees complain at the unpleasant position they find them-selves in. I shift in an effort to lessen the weight and as I do so, I catch sight of Craig perched at the back door. He lights a cigarette, takes a long drag in and an even longer release out. When did he start smoking again? He had a twenty-a-day habit when I first met him, but lack of finances and my constant complaining soon kicked that into the past. It would seem that now he's rid of me, his dirty little habit is back. I hope it kills him.

I keep my head down as far as I can and pray that when Craig extinguishes his cigarette, he doesn't throw it into the corner where I'm hiding. The cement and pebble path is crunchy and bumpy beneath my feet, but because my knees are painful from squatting, I have no choice but to shift my weight forward and allow them to come into contact with the ground. The sharp pieces of stone and grit grind into my legs and I grimace, but there's no way I can release my position without Craig spotting me, so I'm stuck here. Thank goodness I wore a dark coat and hat; otherwise he would have seen me.

But would that be such a bad thing?

Yes. Yes, it would.

I try to blink away my tears. What has happened to me; to the person I used to be? I don't even recognise myself anymore. I shuffle as far as I can without giving myself away, and just as I can bear the agony no longer, Kate appears at the door. She's giggling, giddy and flushed; the obvious result of having a few too many glasses of Sauvignon Blanc. To appear generous to their hosts, Kate and Pete will have brought two bottles with them this evening: one for the table, and the other in the hopes it will not be drunk, so that it can return home with them later. I know her well. I know her *too* well.

'All okay on the cat front?' she asks.

'Yeah, it's gone now,' Craig says. 'Bloody thing lives next door, I think. It's always shitting in our garden.'

A couple of things irritate me about this sentence. First of all, the cat doesn't live next door; it lives with Derek in the sad, unloved house across the road. Craig would know this if he'd bothered to research. Also, how can my husband describe this obscure patch of lawn and hedges as 'our garden'? This isn't his garden. His garden is at home with me on the harbour. It has a greenhouse and tomato bushes and yellow roses in the corner! It has two gnomes and a pond and a wooden bench that creaks if we dare sit on it. This isn't his garden! This isn't his estate! This isn't his life!!

'It's quite a good size, this garden.' Kate lights her own cigarette and takes a drag.

'Yeah, better than my old one,' Craig replies.

This sentence cuts straight through me. We worked hard to create our beautiful space: we dug flower beds; hung baskets filled with daisies and pansies, and even built the greenhouse all on our own. He thinks this one is better, does he? And does he think his new woman is better than his old one? That goes without saying, really. The wind bites at my face and stings my eyes. I blink and try to steady my breathing, because I need to say something to him. I need to tell him that this situation isn't fair. That none of this is fair.

I breathe a mouthful of freezing air and close my eyes. Seconds later I'm on my feet, I snap my eyes open, and expect to see Craig and Kate in front of me. To my astonishment, my husband has gone and only my friend remains. She squints, stares at me, and then jolts her head to look over her shoulder. Confirming that we're alone, Kate steps out onto the path and holds the door closed behind her.

'Jenny!' she snarls through gritted teeth.

'Hello,' I reply.

Kate drags me through the front garden so quickly that I don't even remember going through the side gate. However, before we reach the end of the drive, a familiar voice grinds into my ears, and lands with a thud in my brain.

'Jenny! What the hell are you doing here?'

I spin around and there is Craig, in all his dinner party glory. His nostrils are flared and he's wringing his hands so hard it's a wonder his bones don't shatter. He comes straight into my personal space, so I push his shoulder and he takes a step backwards.

'Don't come near me, you bastard!' I scream. 'How dare you?! How dare you invite our friends over to your slut's home?! And for a dinner party as well! A dinner party just like the one we were meant to have, on the night you left me!'

'Have you been drinking?'

Craig's voice is more of a snarl, and he glowers at me as though he's never hated anyone as much as he hates me. Maybe he hasn't. Kate throws her arms out and Craig looks behind him.

'Aww, what's the matter? Scared your little slut will see us talking?'

'Jenny, please!' Kate snaps. 'Let's get you a taxi, shall we?'

Kate pulls me behind the bush at the end of the drive; out of sight of dear little Helena. God forbid she should see me on her big night!

'Oh, shut up, Kate. It's your fault that I'm here in the first place!'

'My fault?'

My friend throws her hand to her chest, as though she is in a corny 1930s movie.

'Yes, your fault! If you hadn't said yes to spending time with these two... these two sex maniacs... I wouldn't be here in the first place!'

My arms thrash around like a baby bird trying to fly, and I hate myself for not being able to come up with something wittier than 'sex maniacs'.

'I hate every bloody one of you!' My voice falters and I stare at the ground, praying that my legs continue to hold me upright. Kate and Craig don't respond to my disclosure, and instead, everyone stays quiet, tucked behind the bush and safely out of Helena's sight.

The night air is so cold I can see my breath, and unwelcome tears sting my eyes. I wipe them away with the back of my hand, and hope that no one notices.

'Why did you leave me for her?' The words shoot out of my mouth, and my companions jump at the unexpected sound. There's no disguising my tears anymore, and as they fall down my cheeks, my chest contracts and shudders.

'I said, why did you leave me for her?!'

Craig throws his arms around his middle, but doesn't reply. When I look up at him, I manage to catch his eye for a second, and then the connection is gone.

'How about I go into that house and have it out with your lover? Eh? Maybe she can tell me what's so good about her!'

I push Craig's chest, but he stands firm. I won't be able to get past him without a fight.

'Craig? Kate? Where did you go?'

Helena's voice booms through the night, and from a tiny gap through the bush, I can just make her out, illuminated by the light at the back door. I want to run straight at her and pull her bloody hair out, but as though reading my thoughts, Kate plants herself in front of me.

'Shit.' Craig steps into Helena's view and waves.

'Won't be a minute,' he stutters. 'That bloody cat ran up the tree, and I'm making sure it's not stuck.'

Kate pats Craig on the arm.

'You go in,' she says. 'I'll stay here and keep an eye on *the cat*.'

'Please go home, Jenny,' Craig hisses. 'And don't come here again.'

Craig disappears and I try my hardest to speak; to send a barrage of words into Helena's ears, but it's no good. My breath is so short that I can't move my mouth, and a rainbow of colours swirls like a kaleidoscope before my eyes.

Kate's voice begs me to stay with her, and then my knees buckle, and I head for the ground.

The *dinner party incident*, as I always refer to it, is the last straw for my fragile mental health. The doctor tells me I am suffering from nervous exhaustion, but it doesn't take a genius to work that one out. I am forced to take a few weeks off work, and Rebecca phones me every evening. I look forward to her daily calls – they remind me that I am still alive – even though there are times when I don't want to be.

Craig has been nowhere near me, but that's hardly surprising, given the circumstances. He's probably now convinced himself that his old wife is a psycho, therefore proving that he was right to move on in the first place.

Things between Kate and I are awkward to say the least. After she made sure that I was okay on the night of the party, she dusted me down and phoned a cab. I was lucky to get away with just a few scrapes and bruises, but Kate didn't stick around long enough to know that. She was more concerned with getting me out of Helena's domain to really care about my welfare, and that hurts much more than my physical injuries. Still, since then, she's consistently questioned my whereabouts, and bombarded me with positive quotes about letting go of the past and moving forward. Well, Kate is an expert at moving forward, I'll give her that much.

But in spite of all the anger I hold for my friend's hypocrisy and betrayal, I continue to assure her that I am done with my stalking. Instead, I promise that from now on I will concentrate on returning to a state of normality.

Whatever the hell that is.

32

2019

'Do you want tea or coffee?'

'Tea please, with sugar.'

It's Monday morning and I'm supposed to be preparing another family tree, but instead I've been interrupted by an impromptu visit from Kate. She's dressed in faded jeans and a 'True Blue' Madonna T-shirt, giving her the air of someone who has stepped out of the 1980s. Her dyed, blonde hair is pulled away from her face with a thick black band and if she's wearing any makeup, it's pretty hard to see.

I pour the tea into mugs and stir in two spoons of sugar for Kate. I cringe whenever my friend requests sweet tea, but I sense that this is not the time to lecture her about type 2 diabetes, or tooth decay.

'Are you on your way to work?'

Kate grabs a choc-chip cookie from the tin, and half of it disappears into her mouth.

'I took today off,' she says, as crumbs spray out of her mouth. 'Pete and I are supposed to be playing tennis this afternoon.'

I hand her a mug and she nods her approval.

'Supposed to be?'

Kate shrugs and we both move to the living room with our drinks. The sun was so bright earlier that I closed the curtains. Now it must have gone behind a cloud, because the room is dull, except for a sliver of brightness coming through a crack in the drapes.

'We had another argument.' She sighs. 'Things aren't going great for us right now.'

'Bloody hell, I wish you two could work things out. I'd hate you to end up like Craig and me.'

I plonk my mug onto the sideboard and throw open the curtains. There is a woman sitting on the harbour wall, eating a sausage roll while dressed in a short lace dress and a denim jacket. Her hair is rumpled and even from this distance, I can see that her makeup has seen better days.

'Ha, come and look at this woman! She's taking a rest after doing the walk of shame, though to be honest there doesn't seem to be any shame involved.'

Kate doesn't reply, and I presume she hasn't heard me. I swing round to repeat my observation, but I'm stopped before I can utter a word. My friend stands in front of my old coffee table, clutching my current Helena journal, and scowling. She flicks through a few pages, clicks her tongue, shakes her head and then stares at me.

'Jenny,' she says. 'You're doing it again, aren't you?'

I am desperate to snatch my journal from Kate's hands, but I'm too far away and besides, it would make me look even guiltier than I already am. I revert to my go-to tactic and deny all knowledge.

'Doing what?' I say in the most innocent voice I can muster, but Kate doesn't answer. She's too busy flicking through the pages. We stand in silence for a few seconds, and then Kate gasps and reads out loud:

'Phoned the health inspector to report a rat at Helena's café. Stole one of Helena's wedding photos and threw it in the harbour. Stole Craig's locket, so that he'll hate Helena even more than he does already.' Kate steals her gaze away from the book and blinks at me. 'For fuck's sake, Jenny! What are you doing?'

I stroll up to my friend and take my journal back. I clutch it to my chest and gulp with such force that I'm convinced Mrs Moore must have heard it next door. Kate frowns and bites her lip. She's waiting for an explanation, but I'm not sure I have one. Not one she'll believe in any case.

'It's just a joke. Don't be so serious!'

'Just a joke?!' Kate points to my notebook and rolls her eyes. 'But you did all of these things and hundreds more by the looks of it. Jesus, when you told me about the hair removal cream incident, I thought it was a one-off, but this – this is crazy. Does Rebecca know?'

I throw the book onto my cabinet and turn to face Kate.

'No, she doesn't, and don't you dare tell her! She'll take it the wrong way, like you have.'

My friend falls onto the couch and grabs her head as though she's about to pop it off.

'The wrong way? What other way is there to take it, Jenny?'

The phone rings. It's a woman in a call centre, telling me I've had an accident that wasn't my fault.

'Fuck off,' I shout, and throw the phone onto the sofa.

'It all makes sense now. All of it!' Kate rubs her cheeks. Her mouth turns up at the corners and she makes a gloating, puffing sound as though she's uncovered the secrets of Stonehenge. 'That's why you've been friendly to Helena, isn't it? It's got nothing to do with helping her find information about Annabelle. You wanted to torment her!' Kate taps her mouth with her finger as though playing a tune. 'Bloody hell, I should have known after the last time you stalked her, but I thought that you'd come to your senses by now. Obviously not. You're obsessed!'

'Look, it's not like that! Yes, I'll admit that I'm being friendly to play around with her a little, but I'm not obsessed!' I sit down next to my friend and she recoils.

'But the journal!' Kate jumps up, and snatches the book from the cabinet. 'Even the fact that you're noting down these bits of revenge or whatever you call them... even that is crazy. What if the police see it? What will happen then?'

I burst into laughter and Kate's mouth hangs open in disgust.

'The police? They didn't want to know when Mrs Moore's house was broken into last year. What makes you think they'll be interested that I stole some crappy mementoes or signed Helena up for a dating site? Don't be absurd!'

'Wait a minute! You signed her up for a dating site? Are you insane?'

I cross my arms and stare at the wall behind Kate's head.

'You're taking everything out of context,' I say. 'Every little thing I've done to Helena is because of stuff she's done to me!'

'Okay, like what?'

My mouth hangs slack and I scratch my jaw in disbelief. How can Kate question what Helena has done to me?

'She stole my husband!' I scream and Kate throws her arms in the air and grabs her handbag from the back of the chair.

'Not this again?! It was five years ago, Jenny! And he's not even with her anymore! Maybe it's time for you to let it go!' Kate hands me the notebook. 'Take this. You'll need it when they come looking for you.'

I jump up, throw open a drawer and ram the journal inside. Kate storms down the hall, pausing only to push her feet into her trainers. I hurry after her, but my friend is in no mood to stay.

'Stop! Please! Please don't go – we need to talk.'

She ignores my pleas and opens the door.

'You need to look at yourself in the mirror,' she says. 'You've lost the plot.'

Kate turns to leave and almost bumps straight into Helena, who is standing on my doorstep, holding two takeaway cups of coffee in her hands.

'Hey, Kate. Is everything all right?'

'Ask your friend,' she says, and then pushes past Helena, and out into the harbour.

33

Another day, another family tree, and this time it's for Mrs Tyler – a woman whose great, great-aunt Lillian was murdered in London during the late 1800s. Family legend has it that the woman was killed by Jack the Ripper, and now it's my job to tell them that it's all a pile of crap. Studying the Ripper case files is gory and obscene, but also addictive and helpful for keeping my mind off Kate and her crazy notion that I'm... well... crazy.

Just as I'm tracing the footsteps of Lillian on the night of her fateful murder, my phone pings. It's Helena.

Is it okay if I come round? I've got some news. It's about Kate.

I want to say no. I'm far too busy with this job to get involved with petty gossip – real or otherwise. However, despite our recent argument – and the fact that Kate has ignored every text and message I've sent – I still care, and I'm curious to know what kind of news Helena might have about her.

I hit reply and tell her to come over. As I contemplate our

conversation, I'm appalled to discover crumbs of toast and other debris scattered all over the living room carpet. How long has it been since I cleaned in here? A week? Two? My mum would be ashamed. I dart to the understairs cupboard, drag out the vacuum and whizz it round the downstairs area. Helena shouldn't have any reason to trek upstairs, but then you never can tell with her. Just in case, I clean the first few steps, then spring up to close the bedroom doors. The dimmer it is up there, the less she'll be able to see.

I hate myself sometimes.

Helena dances around on the doorstep like a toddler in a baby gymnastics club. Her eyes are red-rimmed and her hair is dishevelled and uncombed. She's wearing dungarees that have been cut off at the bottom, and her green T-shirt is faded and unironed. My gran would have said she looked as though she'd been dragged through a hedge backwards, and she'd have been right.

'What on earth's wrong?' I ask, but when Helena opens her mouth, no words come out. Whatever has happened appears to be huge and I'm not sure I'm prepared for it. I step back and Helena shoves past me and straight into the living room, without taking her shoes off first. I follow her in, my mind whirring.

'Do you want something to drink? Orange juice? Tea?'

'No, thank you.'

Helena stands next to my Victorian cabinet, playing with a tiny ceramic pig that I bought from a local antiques centre. She turns to face me, the ornament still clutched in her hand. I pray she doesn't drop it.

'Is it true that you used to call me Miss Piggy?'

Her words land in my chest. Is this why she wanted to speak to me? Because I gave her a stupid nickname? Surely not. I laugh and scratch my face.

'That was a long time ago.' I reach over, take the pig from her grasp and place it back onto the cabinet. 'It was just a joke – y'know, like when you used to slag me off to your yoga teacher?'

Helena squirms, ignores my comment and then examines her hair in the mirror and groans.

'Have you got a brush? I forgot to do my hair this morning.' I nod and hand her mine, but I'll have to destroy it when she's gone. She runs it over the top of her head, but it does nothing to tame her curls. 'Kate mentioned it when I saw her last night. But you're right, I'm sure I've called you far worse.'

She flashes a smile, crosses to my bookshelf and rummages around, tidying some volumes and staring at others. I'm relieved that I took the decision to burn my journal, because if I hadn't, it might have been tucked on that shelf right now. Who knows what kind of shit that would result in? Helena picks up a copy of *Pride and Prejudice* and holds it out to me.

'Would you mind if I borrow this? I've never read it and I've heard only great things about it.'

'You can have it if you want. I bought it years ago from a car boot sale, but never got around to reading it.'

Helena thanks me and hugs the book to her chest. Then she leans back into the sofa and stares at me so hard that I lower my eyes. We both stay in silence for the longest time: her on the couch, me hovering between the door and the window, wondering if I should pretend that I've got an important meeting to go to.

'Helena, are you okay?' I ask. 'You didn't come here to question me about some stupid nickname, did you? I can't even remember calling you it, but if I did, I sincerely apologise.'

'No, I didn't come over because of that. I was curious, that's all.'

'So, what is it then? To be honest, you're acting a little odd this morning.'

Helena threads her fingers together, cracks her knuckles and then takes a deep breath.

'Kate told me that you've been faking our friendship, so that you can take revenge on me for stealing Craig. Is that true?'

34

'How could you?' I shout. 'How could you tell Helena about what I've been doing?'

Kate looks up at me from behind a pile of hardbacks. Her mouth hangs open and her eyes are as big as planets. Guilty, disgusting, unfaithful planets.

'You were supposed to be my friend!'

There is a pensioner reading group going on in the centre of the library, and the participants stare at Kate and me in wonderment.

'Let's get back to the book, shall we?' asks the coordinator, though nobody is interested.

'This sounds like it'll be better than the book,' laughs one old man, and the woman next to him nods and turns up her hearing aid.

Kate's face flushes red as she stands up, grabs the books and storms past me.

'Jenny,' she says through weary eyes, 'what are you doing here? Please don't make a scene!'

I follow my friend towards the bookshelves, but before I can say anything else, Liz sprints out of the back room, her eyes ablaze.

'What on earth is going on here?' She throws us a dirty look. 'No, on second thoughts, don't bother telling me. Just take it outside. Now!'

My ears are ringing and my legs feel detached from my body, but somehow Kate and I manage to stumble out of the library and into the street. Outside, there is a demonstration going on to try and save the indoor market next door. The building has been empty for so long that the bottom of the door is damp and has been chewed away by vermin, but the demonstrators don't seem to care.

'Save our market! Save our market!' they shout, while marching up and down with placards and flags. An old woman wearing a huge straw hat thrusts a leaflet into my hands, but they're shaking so much that the paper flutters down to the ground.

'Follow me!' I can just about hear Kate's voice through the chants, and although it takes every ounce of my strength, I manage to go after her. We end up at the library fire door at the back of the building. We've had many conversations here over the years, but never anything like this. Kate turns her back to the door and presses her elbows into the side of her body. Whereas minutes ago her face was red, now her skin is ashen and she has beads of sweat on her top lip. I lean on the wall next to her; the bricks hard and sharp on my bare arms.

'Why?' I ask. 'Why did you do it?'

The wind blows a cloud of dust into the air, and some of it scatters into our faces. I brush it away with the back of my fingers, while Kate rubs the corner of her eye.

'Look.' She sighs. 'Last night I was walking past Helena's house and she was at the window, looking as though her whole world was falling apart. So, I felt obliged to go and see what was wrong.'

'And?'

'And... we got talking and Helena was so upset about the way her life is going, and how everything seems to be falling to pieces. I know she's an attention-seeker, but she was so upset that I thought she deserved to know exactly why bad things are happening to her.'

'But you're supposed to be *my* friend, not hers!'

'I'm friends with both of you! But I was so angry about the way you've been behaving, that I figured the only way to get you to stop, was to tell her. I thought maybe that jolt would be what you needed, to finally let the whole thing go.'

I lean in towards her and sneer.

'But now Helena will probably go to the police! It'll ruin my life even more than it's ruined already.'

My friend stares at me through narrow eyes.

'Helena's not going to the police,' Kate says. 'Did she tell you she was?'

'No, but...'

'Exactly. She's just relieved to know the truth, so that she can finally get her life back together. And this should prompt you to do the same!'

Before I can say anything else, Liz bounds around the corner. She's out of breath and panting by the time she reaches us.

'Are you ladies all right now?' she asks in her best boss voice. Kate nods, but I keep quiet. 'When you're ready Kate, please could you come back inside? The market demonstrators are handing out leaflets to the book club and I suspect it's not going to end well.'

Kate assures her boss that she will be there in a second, and Liz ambles off around the corner.

'I've got to go.' Kate rubs her temples, and I notice that she isn't wearing her wedding ring.

I grab her hand.

'What now?'

'Why aren't you wearing your wedding ring? You always wear your wedding ring.'

Kate picks at a bit of fluff on her trousers.

'Pete's left me, Jenny. Our marriage hasn't been working for a long time, and after many – many – painful conversations, we decided the best thing to do was to separate.'

Tears spring to my eyes, but I blink them back down.

'I knew you were having problems,' I say, 'but I had no idea that things were that bad.'

'How could you?' Kate replies. 'You've been too obsessed with Helena to notice.'

35

It's Sunday: five days since I heard from Helena, and I feel pretty okay about that. I'm woken by the sun shining through the curtains, and Rebecca stands next to my bed with a breakfast tray in her hands. She's home for the weekend and I couldn't be happier to see my girl. Last night we enjoyed a quiet evening together, where I told her that I'd broken contact with Helena and fallen out with Kate. I didn't give details and Rebecca didn't ask for any, which is just as well.

I heave myself up to a sitting position and rub my eyes.

'You made me breakfast in bed? To what do I owe this pleasure?'

Rebecca places the tray onto my lap and then sits next to me. There are two mugs of tea, four croissants, a bowl of yoghurt and a heap of strawberries. I recognise that these are the same berries that have sat in the fridge for the past four days and are past their sell-by date, but it's the thought that counts. I'll try to avoid the squidgy ones.

'I thought you deserved it.' Rebecca picks up her mug of tea and blows on it. 'You want me to open the curtains?'

I take a bite of croissant, and strawberry jam oozes out onto my tongue.

'No, the sun shines right in here in the morning. I'll be too blind to see my breakfast if you open them.'

I pick up my phone to see the time. 9.45am. How on earth did I sleep this long? It's a good job Rebecca woke me when she did. I scroll down the list of notifications – three from Facebook, one from Instagram and a missed call... from Helena.

'Ugh, what does she want?'

'Who?' I hand Rebecca my phone and she grimaces. 'Oh dear, it looks like things are not quite finished between you after all.'

I swipe to delete the notification, turn on my ringer and then get back to my breakfast. The trouble is, the moment I see that somebody has tried to call me I can't relax until I find out what they want.

'Are you going to call her back?' Rebecca speaks through a mouthful of croissant, and a heap of crumbs scatter onto my duvet. 'I don't think you should.'

'Don't talk with your mouth full,' I say, only half-joking. 'You're right though. It's time for me to stay away.'

Rebecca nods and we continue to lounge in comfortable companionship. My pyjama-clad daughter educates me on what it's like to live and work in London, and I share stories of how her dad and I used to go there at least once a month when we were in our early twenties. It's a fun conversation, and just as I'm about to tell Rebecca about meeting Sarah Jessica Parker in Covent Garden, the phone rings. It's Helena.

'Hello?'

There is silence and then Helena's familiar squeaky voice comes through. I press the speaker button so that Rebecca can hear it too.

'Jenny? Can you come over? We need to talk.'

I want to say no, as I'm sure the reason she wants to see me is to go over what Kate revealed to her. No good can possibly come from that.

'To be honest, Helena, I don't think I can. Rebecca's home and we're having breakfast and a catch-up before we hit the beach.'

'Please! It's important.'

I roll my eyes at Rebecca. Everything Helena does is important. Why is today any different?

'We're not even dressed yet,' I say. 'It isn't a good time.'

'Please,' Helena begs. 'I don't care what you're wearing; I need to see you. Can you come over as soon as possible?'

There's a peculiar urgency in her voice that is somewhat concerning, and Rebecca must sense it, because she prods me in the shoulder and pulls a face.

'Tell her we'll come over,' she whispers, and then she springs off the bed.

Rebecca is not at all fazed by the creepiness of Smuggler's Steps. She used to play down here as a teenager, she tells me, and her friends would dare each other to climb up them in the dead of night.

'I only ever got as far as the thirteenth step,' she says, 'but Garry Lowry once got almost to the top. He had to stop because his mother phoned and said she knew what he was up to and he needed to get back home straight away!' Rebecca laughs at the memory. 'I wonder whatever happened to him. I haven't seen him since school.'

I grip onto the wooden banister, though I'm not sure if that makes the stairs more or less dangerous. I take one step at a time and navigate my way through the stingy nettles, brambles and odd rusty nail.

'Garry Lowry?' I ask. 'He works in advertising now. I saw him and his mother in town a little while back and we had a nice chat. He was wearing a suit and tie and looked pretty smart. He's single, you know.'

Rebecca stops climbing and turns to scowl at me.

'Mother, you're the only person I know who could try and fix me up with someone while we're on a mercy dash to a heart-broken woman's house!'

I tut and then pull my arm away from a wild blackberry bush.

'Helena's not heartbroken! Just the other week she was brag-ging about this one night stand she'd had, and I think she might have seen him again after that. If she was that distraught, sex would be the last thing on her mind, don't you think?'

We reach the top of the steps and Rebecca turns to offer her hand.

'Here, let me do my bit to help the aged,' she says, and I play-fully slap her away. 'Who was this bloke anyway? Knowing Helena, she invented him to make herself look popular.'

I bend down to tighten my shoelace and also acclimatise myself after the long trek up. No matter how fit I think I am, Smuggler's Steps are always on hand to prove otherwise.

'I don't know who he was,' I say. 'She met him in the café, they went out for drinks and then they ended up at her house, in bed. According to her, he was the best sex she'd ever had, even though she had no idea what his name was!'

Rebecca's lip curls and she wrinkles her nose.

'Ugh, don't tell me anymore.' She throws her hands up. 'The idea of my wicked stepmother doing it with anyone is disgusting – let alone a complete stranger.'

'I couldn't tell you anything else even if I wanted to,' I say. 'That's the only information I have – and thank God for that!'

Moments later we reach Helena's house and I knock on the door.

And then all hell breaks loose.

36

The sun shines straight through Helena's front window and blinds me to the point where the only thing I can see is the dark shadow of a man, lurking beside the open curtains. When Helena opened the door to us just seconds ago, her eyes were red-rimmed, her hair matted and her cheeks sallow. As soon as I saw her, I knew that this was more than Helena's usual attempts at attention seeking, but when Rebecca asked what was wrong, she was met by silence.

Now my daughter and I pause at the living room door, trying to make out who the man is, while Helena hovers behind us, breathing onto the back of my neck. The stranger reaches round, glides the curtain to block out the light, and I then see who it is: Stuart Wilson-Price, Annabelle's father.

'Nice to see you again, Jenny.' Stuart bounds towards me and shakes my hand as though I've entered a bizarre job interview. He then turns to Rebecca and squeezes her hand too.

'This must be Rebecca! Wow, you've changed since I last saw you. You've chopped off your hair!' He throws his hands to his head and traces an imaginary ponytail down to his bottom. 'Annabelle was jealous of your hair, but I think hers is longer than yours now! Well, that's if she hasn't had it cut off since I last saw her. Your dad has made her do so much in the past few months that I can't keep up with it all!'

Stuart sniggers, but Rebecca gawps at him. This is the first time she has laid eyes on the man since 2007, and she must be more confused than I am at this point. I have many questions. Why is Annabelle's father in Helena's living room? How does he even know her? Before I have chance to figure anything out, I see it.

Stuart Wilson-Price is holding a knife in his left hand. An enormous, glinting, threatening knife.

I have no idea what's going on, but my first instinct is to get my daughter away from danger, so I grab her arm and spin towards the living room door. Helena is standing right in front of us, trembling and chewing on the skin around her fingernails. I try to navigate a way round her, but she's as rigid as a porcelain doll and blocks our path.

'What's your hurry?'

Stuart brushes past all three of us and is out into the hall before I have the chance to take a breath. His broad frame takes up much of the space between the wall and staircase, and he waggles the knife close to Helena's face.

'I'm afraid I can't let you go,' he says in a sinister voice. 'And I'll need to take your phones, for your own protection, you understand. I'd hate for there to be any dangerous misunderstandings.'

I want to be brave enough to fight against this order, and maybe if I was on my own I would. However, there's no way I can take a risk with my daughter here, so instead of protesting, I slide my hand into my pocket, retrieve my phone and give it to him. I turn to tell Rebecca to do the same, but hers is already out and she presents it to Stuart without uttering a word.

'Good girls.' He swirls the knife in a circle. 'Let's go back into the living room, shall we? That way we should all stay safe and hopefully nobody will get hurt.'

My daughter grabs hold of my hand and the little girl she once was is brought back to life. It's funny but it doesn't matter how old you are, you still need your mum in times of distress or danger. I could do with mine, but even she can't help us now. Stuart directs us all back into the living room and once there we stand in a row, like the three little pigs, contemplating the big bad wolf. Our captor hovers in front of us; his hand wrapped around the knife. Helena seems incapable of speech, and as terrified as I am, I take it upon myself to try and negotiate.

'Stuart,' I say through tight lips, 'I'm not sure why you're here or why we're here, but whatever it is, there's no need to use a knife. Please can you get rid of it? You're scaring my daughter.'

In the few times I've seen Stuart Wilson-Price this year, he has always dressed smart. Today, however, his crumpled shirt is untucked from his trousers, and the buttons strain across his chest, revealing strands of untidy hair.

'Your daughter is scared?' he screams, and grabs me by the hair. The pain feels like a thousand ants nipping at my scalp, and I jerk my head back in an effort to relieve the agony. He throws me onto the floor, and my wrist bends backwards under my body. I cry out, but I'm shocked when my voice merges with Rebecca's. I look up in time to see my daughter lying on the couch, with Stuart on top of her. He turns his head to look at me.

'My daughter's been seduced by your ex, and you think I care that yours is *scared*? What about if I have my way with her, eh? Do you think she'll be scared then?'

I jump up with the intention of ripping Stuart from the sofa, but then I see the knife at Rebecca's throat and it's clear that there's nothing I can do to help. My entire body shakes, and I look over at Helena. My husband's ex has her hands clasped over her face, like a toddler playing hide and seek with friends. I turn my attention back to Stuart, as he fumbles with Rebecca's clothes. I can't bear the petrified look in my daughter's eyes.

'Leave her alone! Please, just get off her!'

Stuart laughs and rolls himself off the couch. Rebecca shuffles up to a sitting position, wheezing and grunting as she tries to get her breath.

'Calm down, I'm not gonna do anything to your precious offspring. Unlike your ex, I'm not that way inclined.' Stuart pulls himself upright, straightens his clothes and laughs as though he's here for our entertainment. 'Come on, you two, sit down. You're going to be exhausted standing around all day long.'

I collapse onto the sofa and Rebecca glues herself to my side. I throw my arms around her and I can feel her trembling body relax into mine. Helena tries to sit next to us, but Stuart instructs her to take the armchair instead.

'You'll end up looking like the three witches from *Macbeth* if you sit together.' He laughs. 'Though let's be honest, you do a pretty good impression of them even sitting apart!'

Stuart closes the living room door and lugs a dining chair across it. Then he pulls out another and sits in the middle of the room, giving a perfect impersonation of a deranged teacher surveying his class. The knife waggles as he talks and although it's several feet away, we all recoil from the sharp blade.

'Rebecca.' He beams. 'I haven't seen you in what is it? Eleven years? Twelve? The last time I saw you, you were at the canoe club, dressed in your little wetsuit and goggles. I never could work out why you needed googles for canoeing, but I'm sure you had your reasons. How have you been keeping? You been well?'

Rebecca's leg is pressed up against mine and I feel it tighten as Stuart speaks to her. I want to yell at him to stop talking to her, but I can't. Instead, I make sure my leg is held even closer to hers, so she knows that I'm here. That mummy is always here.

'I'm fine.'

'Still living in Cromwey?'

'London.'

Stuart whistles as though that's the most impressive thing he's ever heard.

'London, eh? In that case you should be used to seeing people dashing around with knives!' He runs his finger down the length of the blade and chuckles at his inappropriate joke. This man is horrendous. I knew it when we drank tea on the promenade, and my opinion hasn't changed now that he's keeping us hostage.

I glower over at Helena. She's slouched on the chair with her feet curled up under her. Her skin is grey, and she looks as though she hasn't slept in months. Her mouth vibrates as she watches Stuart from the corner of her eye.

'Look.' I lean forward and place my hands together. 'I have no idea how you got into my friend's house, but if you leave now, we promise not to tell anyone. We'll all forget this ever happened and you can go back to Bournemouth before you do something you'll regret.'

I hate to be submissive to this revolting man, but I figure if we're going to get out of here unscathed, what other choice do we have? Unfortunately for all of us, Stuart isn't about to fall for my pleas. He smiles, reaches forward and places his hand on Helena's knee. She flinches but still remains mute.

'Your friend? Come on now, we both know that's not a word you'd use to describe the woman who fucked your husband behind your back!' He stands up and then perches on the edge of the armchair, throwing his knife-free arm around Helena's shoulder. Her entire body tenses, and who can blame her?

'Look, I know you want to get out of here, but you shouldn't resort to lying. Is that what you want to teach your daughter? That dishonesty is acceptable? Tut, tut! I thought better of you, Jenny.'

'You don't even know me,' I snap. 'How could you think anything about me at all?'

'Believe me I think a lot about you... especially when I'm in bed with this one.' He squeezes Helena's shoulder and she squeaks like a small rodent.

So that's how he got in here. It all makes sense now. Stuart must be the bloke Helena's been having a fling with! But why him? Why did she have to get involved with Annabelle's bloody father? I always knew she was stupid, but this takes it to another level.

'Please tell me what you want from us,' I beg. 'You can't keep us here for no reason at all.'

'You're smart and you're also correct.' Stuart gets up and inspects his teeth in the mirror above the fireplace. 'I do want something from you. I want you to phone my daughter and that gormless ex-husband of yours and get them round here. Then maybe we can talk about leaving.'

He watches me in the reflection of the mirror, and I make sure that my eyes never leave his.

'I can't do that. Craig and Annabelle will know there's something wrong, since I never call them. Besides which, while some people might be happy setting others up, I can't do that. I'm sorry.'

My eyes dart over to Helena, but if she captured my dig at her moral standards, she doesn't make it apparent.

'I'm going to the loo,' Stuart barks. 'When I get back, I'll expect you to have changed your mind.' He points the knife at Rebecca, and she squirms closer to me. 'You – you can come with me. You can be my insurance policy, in case mama bear tries to leave.'

'She's not going anywhere,' I snarl. 'If you need the toilet, off you go but my daughter stays here.'

I drape my arm around Rebecca's shoulder, but it's no good.

Stuart marches over, grabs her by the arm and hoists her up. She makes a screeching sound but I can't do anything about it, the knife is held to her throat and tears fall from my beautiful girl's eyes.

'And in case you do consider leaving, you should know that I've locked the windows and I'll be doing the same to the front door when I go past. If I see you've tampered with anything, I'll slit your daughter from ear to ear, right in front of you. Understand?'

I nod and hate myself for it.

37

'I can't believe you slept with Annabelle's father!' I hiss at Helena. I don't know how much of this business involves her, but at this point I'm willing to bet it's a fair chunk. Helena wipes her mouth on the arm of her hoodie and curls up even smaller than before; her head resting on her trembling knees. If she heard my comment, she's not about to address it any time soon, but from the rattling sound coming from her chest, I fear she's about to have a nervous breakdown. I check the living room door to make sure that Stuart isn't on his way down the stairs and then almost throw myself at Helena's chair.

'Listen, I need you to stay calm, okay? If Stuart sees that you're upset, it'll make him even crazier, and that's not going to help any of us. Do you understand?'

Helena nods, but continues to gasp for breath.

'I can't... breathe...' She clasps a hand to her neck and her eyes water. I check the door once more and then grab her hands. They're freezing.

'Yes, you can. Just breathe in slowly, and out slowly... in and out... in and out... that's it.'

Helena does as instructed, and her gasping subsides.

Helping this woman is the last thing I want to do, and I'm furious that she tricked us into coming over this morning. However, if I'm going to get any helpful information out of her, I have to be as friendly as I can.

'He made me call you.' She stares at me through wide, frazzled eyes.

'We can talk about all the details later. But listen, for now I need you to tell me one thing, okay?' Helena nods. 'Did you know he was Annabelle's father when you slept with him? Or did he trick you into thinking he was an innocent bloke who happened to be passing?' Helena shakes her head as though it's the most complicated question I could have asked her. 'It's okay, he flirted with me too, but I'm jaded enough to turn him down. He told me he was in town to persuade Annabelle to come home with him, but I need to know what he told you, because it might be important as to why he's keeping us here.'

Helena picks at the arms of the flaking leather armchair with her fingernails. Some of the leather cracks and deteriorates into tiny slivers, and she flicks them onto the floor.

'I did know who he was,' she stutters. 'I found him on Facebook and sent him a message.'

'For Christ's sake!' I spit. 'How did you even find him?'

'I'm not as stupid as you think! It was that time when me, you and Rebecca were in the café. Rebecca mentioned seeing Stuart in the school assembly, so I put his name into my phone and checked him out that night.'

I want to scream about her stupidity, but it's too late to say anything now. Stuart's footsteps on the stairs tell me it's time to go back to my position on the sofa. I leave Helena where she is, and scuttle across the living room, making it seconds before the door opens. Stuart and Rebecca come in and the monster holds his knife close to my daughter's back.

'This one decided she needed to go to the toilet too.' Stuart laughs. 'But don't worry, ladies; I still have her phone, so there was no risk of any unwanted, outgoing calls!' He holds up the handset and gives it a shake. 'Lovely photos on here by the way. It must be nice to still have a family. By the way, Rebecca, you should think about getting a lock on your phone. You never know who might look through it when it's unoccupied.'

He shoves my daughter onto the sofa, then moves to Helena, grabs her chin and stares into her face.

'Calmed down yet?' he asks, and when she doesn't reply, he leans down and kisses her. When she doesn't reciprocate, he pulls back. 'Open your mouth, bitch.' Helena stares at him through terrified eyes, and he sticks his fingers between her lips and prises open her mouth. She gags, but that doesn't stop him from kissing her again. I can't bear to watch. It's all too horrifying. When he's finished, Helena coughs and rubs her lips on the sleeve of her hoodie. Stuart sniggers and then turns to Rebecca and me.

'She doesn't usually complain,' he mutters. 'She normally opens her mouth for more than my tongue, don't you, sweetheart? Jeez, is it me or is it getting hot in here?'

Stuart folds up the sleeves of his shirt and passes the knife back and forth between his hands as he does so. He's got a huge gold sovereign ring on his little finger, and I can't help but stare at it. I once had a boyfriend in the 1980s that had a silver ring similar to that, and I haven't seen one in about thirty years. But obsessing about Stuart's fashion choices is the least of my worries right now. I need to get us out of here without the need for body bags, but without my phone and everything locked, I have no bloody clue how to do that.

Stuart holds out Rebecca's handset and motions to my daughter.

'Right,' he says. 'Just like we discussed upstairs, you're going to call your father and tell him to come over to Helena's house.

Understand?' Rebecca nods. 'Good girl. You're a really good girl. And don't forget – if he asks, just say that you want to see him and Annabelle before you head back to London, okay?'

'But what will I do if he wonders why I want to meet here? My dad will never believe I want to see him at his old wife's house, because I'd never have any reason to be here.'

Stuart lifts the knife to his mouth and taps his lips as though trying to find a solution to the problem. It's all play-acting. This man loves drama even more than Helena does. I'm shocked they didn't make a proper go of things.

'I'm sure you'll think of something sufficient,' he says in a soft voice. 'But if you get it wrong, you'll need to suffer the consequences. Understand?'

'Yes.' Rebecca holds out her hand to retrieve the phone, but Stuart doesn't give it to her.

'Wait a minute,' he says. 'I'll dial the number myself. We wouldn't want you to dial 999 by mistake, would we?'

He presses a few buttons and hands the phone back to Rebecca. She stares down at the handset and then holds it close to her ear. At the same time, Stuart lounges next to me on the sofa, and holds the knife to the side of my face. I can feel his hot breath on my right temple. He smells like coffee and cigarettes and reminds me of a teacher I had at school. Mr Hewitt his name was and I didn't like him either.

'Remember what I said,' Stuart crows, 'or your mum will receive an impromptu facelift.'

The panic on Rebecca's face is heartbreaking, but I use my eyes to assure her that everything will be okay. I wish I could believe that.

After a few rings, the phone is answered and Craig's voice glides into the room.

'Rebecca! How you doing, baby?'

My daughter stares at Stuart and he urges her to keep talking. All the time I can feel the coldness of the blade on my cheek and when Rebecca pauses for a second, Stuart clasps his hand over my mouth, pinches my nose and sticks the tip of the knife into my face. It feels as though I've been stung by a wasp, and my first instinct is to scream, but I'm in some kind of stranglehold, so all I can do is make an agonising grinding sound. It scratches the back of my throat and I can feel the pressured heat rushing to my eyes. The thick wet blood trickles down my face, my head feels fuzzy and I beg myself not to faint.

'Do it,' Stuart mouths to Rebecca, and my eyes widen in agreement.

'Rebecca, are you still there?' Craig's voice sounds confused, worried even, but Rebecca knows not to cause a scene. Instead, she coughs and takes a deep but haltering breath.

'Yes, I'm here. I popped by Helena's house to return the spare key, but she's gone out. I've let myself in and thought you might like to come and retrieve all those things she's still hoarding here. I've found the sunglasses you were missing, and also the leather jacket. Do you want to come over and get them?'

There's a pause on the other end of the line and Rebecca scowls at Stuart. He releases my nose so that I can take a breath, and then moves the knife close to my forehead.

'Make sure he says yes,' he mouths, and Rebecca nods.

'I'm not sure that's a great idea,' Craig says. 'It's all in the hands of the solicitors now.'

Stuart clasps my mouth and nose even tighter and I feel the tip of the knife stab into the middle of my forehead. Every nerve in my body begs me to fight him off, but I can't because who knows what he's capable of? Blood trickles down the bridge of my nose and pools at the corner of my eye. There's a new panic on Rebecca's face, but Stuart lets go of my nose and urges her to keep going.

'I know that, Dad,' she says. 'But to be honest, I'd love to see you. And Annabelle too. It's... It's just that the last time I saw you both, we were fighting in the gallery and I don't want to leave things like that.' She starts to cry, and Stuart's breath gets slower and deeper. My eyes flit over to Helena. She has her face buried in her hands, but no noise comes from her at all. Thank goodness.

Craig speaks again.

'Hey, there's no need to cry, silly.' He talks to his daughter as though she's twelve years old, but I find it comforting.

'Okay,' he says, 'we'll come over for a minute, but I can't risk staying any longer than that, in case Helena comes home.'

'Okay, I understand.' Rebecca bids her father goodbye and presses the end call button.

Stuart releases me, reaches over and kisses my daughter on the top of her head.'Good girl.' He smiles. 'I knew you could do it!' Rebecca recoils, but Stuart leers and playfully slaps her arm. 'This is fun, don't you think? I'm enjoying us all hanging out like this, and believe me, after spending time with this one, I've been craving some stimulating company. She's not the juiciest strawberry in the fruit bowl, is she?'

He points the knife at Helena, and she uncurls from the foetal position, launches herself forward and beats her fists on Stuart's chest. From this position, he could stab her straight in the back, but instead he holds the knife away from her body and throws her into the chair.

'You bastard!' she screams, her face contorted and twisted. 'I wish I'd never met you!'

Stuart reaches over to the coffee table and retrieves a box of tissues. He hurls it at my already-burning cheek.

'Here, clean yourself up. Drying congealed blood is not a good look on you.' He turns to Helena. 'And you can shut the hell up. If you hadn't contacted me in the first place, I'd never have come here, so no use crying about it now!'

I wipe at the blood with a tissue, but without a mirror it's hard to see what's mopped up and what isn't. Rebecca lifts her hand to help, but Stuart screams at her not to interfere.

'So why don't you tell everyone why you contacted me, Helena? Was it out of the goodness of your heart? Was it because you were concerned about my daughter and wanted me to come rescue her?'

Helena shakes her head and her dangling earrings hit off the sides of her face.

'You know it wasn't.'

'I do, but these people don't!'

Helena goes back into her curled-up position, and Stuart grabs a small wooden owl from the mantelpiece and tosses it at her. The ornament bounces off her head and pings straight over the back of the chair. She wails and throws her hands up to her scalp.

'Bingo!!' Stuart shouts. 'So anyway, where were we? Yes, Helena's compassionate message. I had no idea that Annabelle had moved in with that piece of shit Craig, until I received a contact request on Facebook from someone called Helena Love. I thought that was a made-up name if ever there was one, but when I read it, I discovered that Ms Love is Craig's wife, even though they don't share a name. But that's modern women for you! They want your money, they want your gifts, but they don't want your fucking name!' Stuart's phone pings from the depths of his pocket, but he ignores it.

'Anyway, Helena kindly informed me that Craig was involved with my daughter, and encouraged me to come down and – how did she put it? Oh yes, "unleash holy hell on their perfect new lives."' He laughs at the memory. 'With an invitation like that, how could I refuse? So here I am, ready to unleash it!'

What a stupid bitch! I throw dirty looks at Helena, but she doesn't notice. She's too busy glowering at Stuart.

'I didn't mean that! I wanted you to come down here and talk some sense into your daughter. That's all I ever wanted!'

'Of course it was.' Stuart sniggers. He shoves the handle of the knife under his arm, and lights up a cigarette. He takes a deep drag and then stubs it out on Helena's wallpaper. It makes a sizzling sound and leaves behind a black charcoal dot. I can't stop staring at it.

'Helena, how long does it take to get from Annabelle's house to here?'

She shrugs.

'I don't know, I've never made the journey.'

'Ha! Get over yourself! I bet you've travelled that route more times than the postman! Oops, excuse me ladies, I should have said post person. Forgive me!'

Stuart doffs an imaginary cap, as though he's a refined country gentleman. I have no idea how long it takes to get from Annabelle's home to here, and I'm not sure what would be better – fast or slow. On the one hand, Stuart might calm down when he sees his daughter, but on the other, I can't imagine Craig bringing any kind of tranquillity to this situation.

As we wait for Annabelle and Craig to show up, I scour my brains for memories of Stuart from twelve years ago. I figure if I can recall something personal, then I can find some kind of level playing field for which to open negotiations. But it's hard to come up with any memories at all because for the most part, he was another faceless parent picking his kid up from school, a party or a club. Most grown-ups blend into the background at these events and while you may nod or greet each other with a hello sometimes, there's a tendency to bury yourself in your phone and ignore each other. Sad, but that's the truth of it.

I remember Annabelle's mother better than Stuart, because she stood out from the crowd. She was a small woman, kind of chubby, if we're still allowed to say that. She was well into her thirties, but still fancied herself as a Goth, in large black boots and a long coat that skimmed her ankles. I don't think I remember her wearing anything except black or deep red, and her head was often shaved at one side and crimson on the other.

When the girls were in year five, they had a spat in the playground and ended up falling out, as kids that age are prone to do. Rebecca had decided (temporarily as it turned out) that Annabelle was not worthy of her friendship because she was a telltale, or a whinger or some bloody thing. I accepted that the girls were going through a phase, but Annabelle's mother did not. One damp afternoon while waiting for them to come out of class, she marched up to me and exclaimed that she 'needed a word'.

I kind of nodded and the mother – what the hell was her name? Karen? Deborah? I don't know, but she lectured me about how I needed to force Rebecca to be friends with Annabelle once again. I was a great believer – and still am – that you can't ever force a friendship, so I declined the demand and the children made up anyway. What the mother thought about it remains unknown, but I made sure to avoid her in the future. I wish I could have done the same with Stuart.

The clock ticks from the other side of the living room. It's 11.35am, but it feels more like midnight. How can it be that under two hours ago I was in bed, gossiping with my daughter and sharing croissants and tea? Now we're being held hostage by a psychopathic father and the croissants are a distant memory.

'Where the fuck are they?'

Stuart's booming voice brings me out of my head and back into the room. He's gazing out of a gap in the curtains, but there's still no sign of Annabelle and Craig. Maybe Craig recognised the horror in Rebecca's voice, and we'll get lucky. Perhaps the police are on their way as we speak, sirens blaring and tasers poised for action. How I wish that could be true.

'Maybe they're not coming.' Helena is perkier than she was five minutes ago, and I wonder how that's possible, until I see her bony hand clutched around the neck of an empty wine bottle. She must have found it at the side of the chair, and now she's going to try and smash it over Stuart's head while his back is turned. And she's going to miss and he's going to kill her, and then he'll kill Rebecca and me, as well.

Stuart continues to stare out of the window, his back towards Helena. I wave my arms to catch her attention, but instead of understanding the danger she's putting us all in, she holds her finger to her mouth and then lifts herself out of the chair. Rebecca and I both stiffen on the sofa as Helena raises the bottle above her head and drifts towards Stuart. She's going to do it. She's really going to do it! I am motionless, and desperate for Stuart not to notice that something is occurring, but when Helena is within feet of him, he spins round and catches her with the bottle.

Stuart twists the object out of Helena's fingers, throws her down and then smashes the bottle into the fireplace. Shards of glass ricochet off the wall and rain down onto the floor. All that's left is the broken stem and Stuart is not in any hurry to let it go. Now thanks to Helena, he has two lethal weapons instead of one, and he points both of them at her.

'Didn't they ever teach you about reflections at school?' he asks, pointing at the wall mirror adjacent to the window. 'I saw you coming before your pathetic, tiny mind decided to get up out of the chair. Now sit down and shut up or I'll lose my patience and use this for what it's intended for.'

Stuart holds the knife high as Helena crawls towards the chair, but she only goes a few feet before Stuart puts the knife and bottle in one hand and grabs her by the back of her hoodie.

'Not there. Here!' He points to the piece of carpet that has glass scattered all over it. Helena's face falls, and she leaps to her feet.

'No. No, I'm not going to sit there. It's covered in glass.'

'Nothing gets past you, does it? Now come on, sit.'

Stuart pushes on Helena's back until her knees buckle, and then he drags her towards the fireplace. She resists and screams for help, but it's no good. If she lived in a terrace, the neighbours could have phoned the police by now, but there's little hope of anyone hearing us in a detached house.

As I watch Helena's knees make contact with the broken glass, my jaw contracts. I can almost feel the shards going into my own knees and it makes me feel sick. Seeing another woman in physical pain is not something I relish, but seeing this particular woman in agony brings me a guilty and unexpected pleasure. I should relieve her pain. I should beg Stuart to leave her alone. I should and I would...

Had she not brought such agony into our lives.

Just as I am wondering what will happen next, the doorbell rings. We all peer at the living room door, and the bell goes again. And again. Stuart throws what's left of the broken bottle into the fire. The thought of having two weapons in a room with so many people must have made even him nervous.

'Right,' Stuart shouts. 'No more funny business. Helena, shut up and don't move. Rebecca, you get the door and bring your dad and Annabelle in here.' He throws the keys at my daughter, and then grabs my wrist and forces me to stand up. My legs shake as he places his arm around me and holds the knife to my throat. 'Remember, if I hear one wrong word while you're out there, your mother will be as broken as that bottle. Got it?'

Rebecca nods her head, wipes her nose on the back of her hand and moves into the hall. I stay still, trying to get as far away from the knife as I can. Stuart's mouth is right next to my ear, and his vile, smoke-filled breath filters into my nostrils.

'I'll always wish it was you who fucked me, instead of that one.' He motions to Helena, who is crying on the floor. 'Maybe there's still time.' He bites my earlobe and the feeling of his teeth touching my flesh is horrifying. I don't say anything and instead strain to hear what's going on in the hall. Craig greets my daughter with an excited, high-pitched voice, and Annabelle giggles at some little joke he's cracked. They're happy that Rebecca wants to talk to them at last, but they're in for a terrible surprise.

38

As I try to keep as far away as I can from Stuart's knife, I'm aware of the blurred outlines of Craig, Rebecca and Annabelle through the frosted glass in the living room door. Stuart breathes into my ear and I can feel his hands tremble against my neck. I wish I knew what was coming next, so that I could prepare myself, but since that's not an option, all I can do is stay silent and pray for a miracle.

'Don't forget, we can only stay for a minute,' Craig bellows from the hallway, 'but you can come out for lunch with us if you like. My treat!'

The door opens and Craig and Annabelle appear. I watch my ex-husband as his smile fades and his eyes dart from me, to Stuart, to Helena and back again. Nothing on earth could have prepared him for this situation when he left his house this morning. It's all beyond words.

'Come in! Come in! We've been waiting for you.' Stuart waves the knife as though directing traffic, and then holds it back to my throat. Craig is rooted to the spot, and Annabelle squeezes past him to face her father.

'Dad! What... What's going on? Why are you here?'

Annabelle's eyes are wide, and her glowing complexion turns flushed and blotchy. She stares at her father for a moment and then her gaze falls to me. When she notices the knife, her hand shoots up to her mouth and she gasps.

'Dad, what are you doing? What the fuck is going on?'

'Watch your language, Annabelle.' Stuart snorts. 'You know you're not allowed to swear in my presence.' He holds the blade even closer to me, so that everyone can witness his intentions. 'Now come on in and make yourselves at home. But I have to ask you not to scream or do anything stupid, because as you can see, we're in a bit of a situation here.'

He releases me from his grasp and instructs me to sit back down on the couch. 'Okay, Rebecca, give me back the door keys, and then sit down where you were.' My daughter drops them into Stuart's hand and then takes her place next to me on the sofa. 'That's it, good girl.' He wags the knife at Annabelle. 'Right, I'll need you to give me your phones, and then, Annabelle, you can sit on the armchair and Craig can make do with a dining chair.'

My ex-husband stares at Stuart in silence, and then drags a wooden seat over to the armchair. Once seated, he gazes over at Helena. She still has her back to the room, but from where I sit, I can see tiny spots of blood coming through the legs of her jeans.

'Don't worry about her,' Stuart tells Craig. 'She's in the naughty corner. But you're learning how to be a good girl, aren't you, sweetie?' Stuart thrusts his hands onto Helena's shoulders and pushes her down into the glass. She shrieks as the shards crunch beneath her knees, which amuses Stuart so much that he does it again.

And again.

And again.

Helena's wails are excruciating, and Stuart is revelling in every horrendous, terrifying moment.

'Do shut up,' he shouts. 'It's only a bit of glass!' He laughs and then turns to the rest of us. 'Can you believe this shit?' We all stay quiet; unsure whether it's a question that requires an answer, but in the end Annabelle speaks.

'Dad,' she begs, 'I know you're angry at Craig and I, but please don't punish Helena for it. She's completely innocent in all this.'

'You're wrong there, I'm afraid,' Stuart replies. 'It was Helena who informed me about you and this paedophile in the first place. As I was just telling these folks, she wanted me to destroy his life, the way he's destroyed hers. So here I am.'

Helena sobs again and none of us can take our eyes off her. The blood on her jeans is getting worse with every passing minute, and I know it'll be ten times worse from the front.

'Okay.' Annabelle sighs. 'But still, no matter what she's done, Helena shouldn't be forced to kneel on all that glass. Look at her! Her knees are bleeding. She needs to be treated.'

I'm impressed by Annabelle's ability to stay calm in such an intense atmosphere, and Stuart seems to be listening to her pleas. He smiles at his daughter and I feel myself relax a little, until he raises his hand, and belts Helena on the side of the head. She cries out and her back vibrates as though having trouble breathing again. I hope she doesn't pass out and hit her head on the hearth. What the hell would happen then?

'Right, you!' Stuart barks at Helena. 'Annabelle seems to have forgiven you for unleashing hell on her life, though why she's done that, I'll never know. I'd guess she's gone soft in the head, but I think that happened months ago when she shacked up with your husband! Never mind. Come on, stand up, or are you gonna stay down there all day? It doesn't matter to me either way; make your choice.'

Helena tries to rise, but the shards of glass embedded in her knees cause her to flinch and gasp.

'I'll help her.' Before any of us have time to digest where the voice is coming from, Rebecca is up from the sofa and at Helena's side. Stuart doesn't attempt to make her sit down again, and instead he just stares as my daughter takes over the care of her stepmother. 'Come on, you can do this. It's all right; we can get all this cleared up, okay?'

Helena allows Rebecca to slide her hands underneath her armpits and together they move until Helena is in something resembling a standing position. She falters for a moment and then turns to reveal a sight that is almost overwhelming. Her jeans are soaked in blood from the knees down and splinters of sharp, painful glass stick out at right angles from the fabric.

'That looks painful!' Stuart hisses in mock sympathy. 'Rebecca, can I trust you to take her to the kitchen and clean her up?' My daughter nods. 'Now don't forget – everything's locked up in there, so please don't attempt to do anything stupid, okay?'

'Okay.'

'I wish I'd never contacted you,' Helena stutters through watery eyes. 'I should never have trusted you to help.'

'Look at it this way.' Stuart sniggers. 'If you hadn't messaged me, you'd have missed out on all those brilliant orgasms. Hate to tell you, Craig, but according to your wife, she was sexually frustrated throughout your entire relationship. Isn't that right, love?'

Helena doesn't reply, but Craig opens his mouth, hesitates and then closes it again. Rebecca helps a hobbling Helena out of the room, leaving tiny fragments of glass in her wake.

'Keep the kitchen door open,' Stuart shouts, as he sits cross-legged on the floor. 'That way I'll know what's going on in there.'

As soon as Helena leaves the room, Craig sits up straight.

'So, what do you want from us?' he asks. 'Just let me know and I'm sure we can come to an arrangement.'

My ex-husband's voice is firm and unfeeling, but inside I know he will be shitting himself. Some years ago, a gang of yobs forced their way into his garage one afternoon. Not content with money found in the little cash tin, they then held Craig at knife-point and demanded he open the safe. He came out unscathed and afterwards the police praised him for dealing with the incident in such a calm way. But Craig confessed to me that while he was like a robot on the outside, inside he was terrified for his life. It took him a long time to recover from his ordeal, and he installed a panic button – and a good old-fashioned baseball bat – not long after. I wish we had either of those today.

'Some kind of arrangement?' Stuart laughs. 'You say that as though I want money, but believe me I have more than you ever will! That's why it's hard for me to understand why Annabelle left. She could have had anyone she wanted – men who have real money and social standing – but instead she chose a filthy twat! Cromwey's answer to Jimmy Fucking Savile!'

Annabelle lurches up from her chair.

'That's it,' she shouts. 'We're going home! You can't keep us here anymore. Come on, Craig.'

I look on as Craig's new love trots towards the living room door, like a disgruntled teenager. My ex-husband starts to get up, but Stuart laughs and pushes past him.

'For fuck's sake, let's stop with the dramatics. You're not fifteen anymore.'

'I'm not listening.'

Annabelle carries on walking out to the hall, but instead of following, Stuart takes out his phone and flicks his finger across the screen.

'Before you go, would you like to see a new photo of your mother? I took it this morning.'

Stuart waggles his phone towards his daughter, and she returns to the living room.

'What do you mean, you took a photo of Mum this morning? You know you're not supposed to be anywhere near her house.'

'Yeah, that's what she said, right before I strangled her.'

'You're lying,' Annabelle cries, but the terror in her eyes is apparent.

Stuart ignores his daughter, and Craig takes her arm and guides her back onto the chair.

'What is it they say? It takes about four minutes to strangle a fully-grown woman? Something like that.' Stuart lights a cigarette and blows the smoke into my face. The stench catches in my throat and stings my eyes. 'Anyway, I'm not sure it took that long, but it probably wasn't far off. It was hard work though, I'll tell you that. Great streams of mascara all down her face... puffed out cheeks... But when I felt her windpipe crunch beneath my fingers, I knew I was almost there.'

Annabelle's nostrils flare and she holds a protective hand to her throat. Stuart blows out another long stream of smoke, and laughs.

'Y'know, the strangest thing though? When it was over, a blue bruise appeared above her left eye. One little bruise! So bizarre! In all the years I'd imagined strangling that woman, I never pictured anything like that above her eye. Below it maybe, but not above. Here, have a look.'

Stuart offers the phone to Annabelle. She stares at the screen and then bursts into great, gulping tears. She throws her head into Craig's chest and for a moment he and I make eye contact. In that one look, I know what that photo must have revealed. I feel like I'm about to throw up, and shuffle in my seat to relieve the pressure on my stomach. Stuart notices my discomfort and shoves his phone back into his pocket.

'Don't you sit there in judgement!' He points his finger at me. 'Didn't you tell me the other week that you wanted to kill Helena when she stole Craig from you? Full of rage and anger you were, so don't pretend you're above strangling someone, because you're not.'

I'm floored. It's obvious he's looking to provoke me, but it's not a situation I want to be involved with. Instead of answering his accusation, I concentrate on what's going on in the kitchen, though I can't hear much above Helena's groans in there, and Annabelle's sobs in here.

Craig licks his lips. His mouth must be dry, and I have an urge to fetch him a drink. But then I remember it's not my job and hasn't been for some time, so I let the feeling go.

Stuart ignores his broken daughter and pokes his head around the living room door.

'Hurry up in there,' he shouts, and Helena responds with a series of yelps and moans.

'I'm going as fast as I can,' Rebecca yells. 'She's pretty cut up. She needs some real medical treatment.'

'Good try, but no,' Stuart replies. 'No doctors, no hospital. If you can't patch her up here, she'll have to bleed to death. It's her own stupid fault she got cut in the first place.'

'What happened to her?' Craig whispers to me.

'She tried to smack him with a bottle,' I reply, and Stuart shushes me.

'No talking; no sharing information. Be quiet or you'll find yourself in the naughty corner. Understand?'

I nod, but in my head, I curse this creature with the foul breath and the intrusive hands. I have no idea where this is all going to end, but I know one thing – I won't go down without a fight.

39

Helena's irritating cuckoo clock announces that it's 4pm. We've been here for five hours now, and the likelihood of leaving anytime soon is zero. I have to give Annabelle credit though, because despite her despair for the past two hours, she's done everything she can to bring an end to this situation: she's talked; she's begged; she's even brought up childhood memories, but Stuart just laughed; told her to stop being stupid and flung her back onto the chair.

Outside, there are children playing at the end of the driveway. Helena told me a while ago that she's had to complain about them swinging on her gate, but today I imagine she welcomes the sound – if only to indicate that there are people close by. I appreciate them being there, because maybe it will provoke the kids' mother to pop in and apologise about the noise. Maybe she'll poke her head through the tiny gap in the front window curtain and ring the police or fetch help.

Or maybe not.

Helena's eyes are swollen and the blood from her knees has soaked her tracksuit bottoms. I offer to patch her up again – if only to get out of the room for a few minutes – but Stuart refuses.

'She doesn't need any more attention,' he says. 'But if you feel the need to be helpful, there's something you can do for me.'

Stuart motions for me to get up, but I freeze. A sharp pain shoots through my head and Rebecca grabs onto my hand.

'Mum's not going anywhere,' she yells, but Stuart prises my daughter off me and waves the knife in her face.

'Do shut up.' He rolls his eyes, and then instructs Annabelle to get up out of her chair.

'No, I'm not going anywhere with you.'

'Look, mate, let us go, okay?' Craig's voice rings around the room and I cringe. His habit of calling everyone 'mate' has gained him a few negative comments in the past, but I fear this one could be the worst.

'I'm not your mate, mate!' Stuart shouts. 'Okay, I've had enough of this shit. All of you get up. Come on, get up now!'

Stuart waves the knife around and I fear that someone is going to be slashed at any moment. We stay still, but then his blade goes too close to Annabelle's throat, and it's clear that he isn't scared to use it, even on his own daughter. We all pull ourselves up from our chairs; fragile shells of the people we were just hours ago. My hips ache and my bottom tingles as the blood rushes in after hours of sitting.

'So, you can follow instructions when you need to,' Stuart barks. 'Right, everyone into the hall. Quick as you can.'

We all obey Stuart's orders like five pathetic little sheep. I hate myself for being overpowered by this bastard. I hate all of us for being overpowered by him.

For some bizarre reason, Helena's understairs cupboard has an open padlock on the top of the door. She once told me that it's because she stores her jewellery in there when she goes on holiday, though I'm sure any self-respecting burglar could get through it with a good pair of bolt cutters. Today, however, the padlock is not going to keep people out, it's going to keep them in. Stuart holds open the door and instructs everyone to go inside. When it's my turn, he grabs my arm and squeezes it so hard I flinch.

'Not you. You're coming with me.'

He makes sure everyone is packed in tight, and then slams the door and applies the padlock. The key sticks out of the bottom of it, though it's no use to anyone inside.

'Right, you, get upstairs and into the bedroom; first on the right.'

The glint of the knife's metal shines into my eyes. My knees quiver all the way up the stairs because I know what's going to happen to me in Helena's spare room. I was once in a position like this when I was seventeen years old. My teenage boyfriend raped me in my own bedroom while my parents were downstairs, because he said he wanted to prove that sex wasn't painful at all. He was wrong about that, but despite my agony, I didn't scream; didn't fight him off or make a fuss, because I was too scared of what my parents would say. I just lay there until he had finished, and then wiped his tears as he cried and told me how sorry he was. For years I didn't even know if I'd been assaulted, because back then you never heard of such a thing as date rape – it was a case of your boyfriend going too far and that was the end of it.

But today we are in different times. I will not be quiet today; I will never be quiet again. As I enter the room, I search for something that could help me deal with Stuart Wilson-Price. I can't see anything, because as luck would have it, this seems to be the only room in Helena's house that's clean and free of chintz.

'Get on the bed and take your top off,' he demands. 'Hurry up.'

He licks his bottom lip and his nostrils flare. He's enjoying this far too much and I know I need to move fast, if I'm going to get out of this.

And then I remember.

When we were teenagers, my friend Joanne was attacked on her way home from school, by a bloke who grabbed her from behind. At first, she thought it was an over-enthusiastic friend playing a trick on her, but it wasn't until she managed to turn around that she realised that wasn't the case at all. The attacker tried to drag her into a copse but Joanne made such a racket that it attracted the attention of a woman in a nearby house. She bolted out clutching a frying pan and the would-be rapist gave up and fled.

A week later our school had a visit from a female police officer, who told us that in a situation like that, we should try and do as much damage to the attacker as possible. The idea, she said, was not to hurt, but to paralyse. Whether this was official police advice or woman-to-woman counsel I have no idea, but one of the techniques she demonstrated has stuck in my mind ever since. I was too scared to use it when I was seventeen, but I'm not scared anymore.

I remove my blouse and Stuart stands at the bottom of the bed and ogles my breasts as though they're the first he's ever seen. He disgusts me but I can't let him see that. I'm in a vulnerable position on the bed, so if my plan is going to work, Stuart needs to imagine I'm compliant. I throw my top onto the floor, and in the next breath, he's on me, hoisting my bra over my breasts and pawing at me like a horny boy at a high-school disco.

'Wait... Wait...' I try to shuffle up the bed, away from his grasp.

'Don't fight this,' he snarls. 'It will make things worse for you.'

I turn my head, but he grabs my mouth and kisses me. His lips are rough, and he rams his tongue into my mouth. It takes all my strength not to bite down on it, or vomit, or both. His kiss gets deeper and more aggressive until he bites down on my lip with such force that I squeal. This excites Stuart further and he drops the knife onto the floor and his hands are on my fly, tugging it down and popping open the button. His fingers dart straight into my underwear and I know that it's now or never with my plan. As he makes a grunting sound, I push at his shoulder in what I hope isn't a too aggressive manner. I need him to trust me.

'Wait a minute. Let me get you out of these.'

I grab the top of his trousers and he eyeballs me. He can't believe that I'm into this and seems to believe I fancy him.

Stupid, stupid man.

'You're even naughtier than I hoped you'd be.' He laughs and I cringe.

'It's been a long time,' I say and Stuart hoots again, as though he's about to do me a favour.

He gets off me and kneels back on the bed, allowing me to unbutton his fly and push his trousers down. He's not wearing any boxer shorts and his erection stares out at me like a weapon. A weapon that will not come anywhere near my body.

I reach down and stroke him between his legs. As predicted, he closes his eyes and leans his head back as though he's starring in an adult film. I give him a few moments of fun, to make sure he's out of it, and then I grab his testicles, twist them ninety degrees and drag them down as far as I can. Stuart screams in agony and his hands dart to his wounded genitals. I somehow manage to knee him as he hugs his groin and then I dive off the bed, grabbing the knife from the floor as I go.

'Fucking bitch!' he screams, but I'm out of the room before

he knows what's happened. I slam the door and then push Helena's pine blanket box across it. It'll slow Stuart down for five seconds at most, but those seconds might make all the difference.

I yank my bra back over my breasts, and then I take the stairs two at a time, and arrive at the understairs cupboard. I dump the knife on the hall table and although my hands are shaking and I suspect I'm going to vomit at any moment, I somehow manage to unlock the padlock. The door bursts open and my four companions pile out, all gasping for breath.

'Quickly! Quickly!' The words stumble out through my swollen lips, and I'm aware that tears are streaming down my face. Craig throws his arms round me.

'Are you okay? What did he do to you?'

'I'm fine, but we haven't got long. We need to get out of here. He'll be down any second.'

From upstairs comes the rumble of Stuart smashing his way out of the bedroom. The front door beckons, but while we all get there quickly, there is no sign of the key for the deadlock.

'Stuart took it,' Helena cries. 'He hid it in his trouser pocket.'

The panic in Helena's voice is nothing compared to how I feel inside. I have just had my hands on his trousers and it didn't even occur to me that the keys were in there. I feel like such a twat. How could I have done all that in the bedroom, and yet we still can't get out of this house? As soon as he gets out of that room, Stuart is going to kill me.

'Does the back door have a deadlock?' Rebecca asks. Helena nods, and then Annabelle flies at the front door and pounds on it with her fist.

'Let us out of here!! Let us out of here!!'

It gives me an idea.

'The kids! They might still be on the gate!' I gallop into the living room and fling open the curtains, but the annoying chil-dren from down the road are gone. Shit. I rattle the windows but as Stuart promised, they're locked. I turn to go back into the hall, but as I do, I am aware of Stuart's feet clomping on the stairs.

He's out.

40

As soon as I hear Stuart stumble down the stairs, I know everything will reach a climax, one way or the other. The man was unhinged already, but after being kneed in the balls and barricaded into a room, he is now deranged. Craig retrieves the knife, but he has never been violent in his life. A womaniser he may be, but able to use a weapon? No.

The end comes quickly.

Stuart marches up to my ex-husband as though the knife is the least of his problems. Craig fights back, and the action – if you can call it that – spirals from the hall to the living room in a matter of moments. But in the end, with the sound of metal whizzing through the air, coupled with the screams, the sobs and the blood, there can be only one winner.

And it is not Craig.

In the movies, stab victims tend to grab their wound, make some profound last statement, and then slide down the wall to their death. I don't know if that's true to real life or not, but I can tell you that when Stuart's knife finds Craig's chest, his passing is immediate. There is no stumbling around, no trying to reach for his attacker and no final words. Instead, my ex-husband clatters to the floor before any of us even know what has happened. The only evidence that an attack has occurred is the body in front of us, and the blood-soaked knife in Stuart's hand.

When Rebecca sees what has happened to her dad, she dives at Stuart with all the rage of a tiger protecting her child. Stuart ignores her for several seconds, and then grabs her by the neck and throws her into the fireplace. Seeing my daughter's head crack on the unforgiving stone slabs, I let out a sound so agonising, that it's doubtful I'll ever make it again.

At least I hope I don't.

Ignoring the glass ground into the carpet, I kneel down to help Rebecca, but my hands turn to mush and my fingers refuse to cooperate in my efforts.

'Don't move her,' Helena shouts from behind me. 'You might do more harm than good.'

'More harm than good?' I scream. 'If you hadn't tricked us into coming here, this would never have happened!'

And then I see it.

Stuart Wilson-Price is hovering over me, his face distorted into a rage-filled mask.

'Look what you made me do!!' he screams. 'You fucking bitch!'

He holds the knife above my head and drops of blood drip off and land in a glassy pool next to my knees. Blood that had come from deep inside the man I once loved is now soaking into Helena's carpet. Soon it will be photographed and a yellow tape will declare it to be a crime scene.

I am aware that I'll soon be another statistic, but I have no more fight to give. I close my eyes and await my fate, but no blow comes. Instead, there is a thick, glugging sound, followed by the exhalation of a deep and faltering breath. I glance up and see Stuart's face as red as an old-fashioned phone box. His eyes are bulging, and from my position on the floor, his face appears to have swelled to twice its normal size. I scramble to my feet and there behind him is Annabelle, holding a knife she's found in the depths of Helena's kitchen. She's already plunged it into her father's back once, and now she holds it high above her head, ready to thrust it again.

I don't tell her to stop.

The ambulance smells like a mix of antiseptic, cleaning supplies and old urine. The lights glare into my eyes and the air is stifling and thick. It's as though years of trauma have permeated the walls and fixtures, and now they refuse to leave. A thin blue blanket is all that separates me from my daughter, but it might as well be a cement wall.

'Rebecca. Rebecca, Mummy's here. We'll be at the hospital soon, okay? Please hold on.'

The paramedic pats my shoulder. She has a warm smile and reassuring eyes.

'That's good,' she says. 'Just keep talking. It'll comfort her to hear your voice.'

'Is she going to be okay?' I ask. 'Please let her be okay!' Tears stream down my face and the paramedic purses her lips and nods.

'We're doing all we can,' she replies.

Rebecca stirs beneath the oxygen mask and she rubs it on the blanket in an effort to free herself. Her eyes flicker and roll, but she's unable to focus and in the end her eyelids fall again.

'Hush,' I whisper. 'Don't try to speak. It's okay, I'm here. I'm always here.'

The police want to interview me, but the nurses inform them that I'm too busy taking care of my daughter to speak with them right now. I appreciate their care, but I know they can't protect me forever. Soon, I'll need to give my side of the story and so will Rebecca.

My daughter opens her eyes, and her lips turn up at the sides in a brave attempt at a smile. The crisp white pillowcase is stark against her skin, but I'm thankful that she's regained some colour in the last few hours. When we arrived, she was so pale she blended into her surroundings. I was more terrified than I've ever been in my life.

'How are you feeling?' I ask.

'Like I've been thrown into a fireplace,' she replies, and then grimaces.

'Just lay still,' I say. 'Don't even talk if it's not comfortable.'

'I'm okay. Well, not okay, but you know what I mean.'

I hold my daughter's hand and pray she doesn't ask the inevitable question about her dad. Except she does, and I can only tell her what she already knows.

Craig is gone.

The coffee machine makes a juddering sound as though it's about to break down at any moment. As the water spurts from the tap, it spits tiny drops over the side of the cup and I step back and hope that it doesn't end up on the floor.

'Hey.'

Helena hobbles up behind me and gives a half-hearted wave. Her sweatpants have been cut above the knees and her legs have been cleaned and bandaged, though some blood is still visible through the material. She uses a crutch, though I'm not sure her injuries are bad enough to warrant one.

'Hi.'

I turn to retrieve my cup and take a tentative sip. The liquid is warm and tastes vaguely like coffee, but that's about it.

'You want one?'

Helena throws up her hands.

'I couldn't face anything,' she says. 'They've flushed my wounds with some kind of stinging solution, and given me a dozen stitches. The pain meds are supposed to make me feel better, but at the moment they're making me nauseous.'

I carry my drink to a nearby chair and Helena sits next to me. She's shaking as though cold, but I can feel the heat coming through her clothes and out of her body. It must be shock. We are all suffering with that this evening.

'How's Rebecca?'

'She's awake. Loaded up on meds and she's had some stitches to her forehead, but the doctor says she'll be fine. They're keeping her in for the next few days though, for observation.'

'That's good. And what about you?'

Helena points to the grazes on my face, but I shrug off her concern.

'I'm okay.' I stroke the scab on my temple. 'They're surface scars, thankfully. Compared to everyone else, I got off lightly.'

Helena grabs my hand, but I whip it away and pretend to do up a loose button.

'I loved Craig with all my heart.' She sighs. 'I don't think I'll ever get over it... none of it.'

I sip my coffee and contemplate the fact that no matter how heartbroken everyone is around her; everything is always about Helena.

And that will never change.

41

ONE MONTH LATER

The police caught up with me for a statement, and I told them everything I knew. It turns out that Stuart Wilson-Price had been an abusive bastard his entire life. He once beat his wife while she was pregnant with Annabelle, and then continued to abuse her when the kids were young. When her family flew the nest, she did too – rescued by one of Stuart's colleagues who saw the bruises on her arms during an office Christmas party. On the morning of the hostage situation, Stuart had travelled to his wife's new home, forced his way inside and strangled the poor woman in her living room. When her new partner arrived home from the supermarket, Stuart was long gone – on his way to extend his demented rage onto our family.

It's odd that in all the years of seeing both Stuart and his wife at the school gates, it never occurred to me that one was abused and the other was an abuser. That's the thing when you see someone from afar for five minutes a day. You make up your mind as to what they're like based on their clothes, their appearance and even their children, but I guess we never really know anyone we see in the playground. Not unless we take the time to socialise with them out of school, but even then, who can tell what goes on behind closed doors? Not me.

As it happens, Annabelle had witnessed Stuart's attacks and had tried on several occasions to cut ties with him. Her move to Cromwey was going to be a clean start, until Stuart came to town at Helena's invitation. Now, thanks to that intervention, poor Annabelle is in custody, awaiting her fate, and all we can do is hope she'll get an empathetic judge, with a warm heart.

Rebecca and I sit on her favourite bench, on the stone pier. My beautiful daughter is pale and fragile, but she's alive, thank God. She's alive.

'Are you feeling okay? Warm enough? Do you want to go home?'

Rebecca laughs and shakes her head.

'I'm fine, Mum! I promise I'm not about to fall to pieces, so you can stop fussing.'

'Well, fussing is my job as a mother, so I can't give that up. But I'll promise to keep it to a minimum for the next hour or two.'

'Thank you.'

Rebecca links her arm through mine, and rests her head on my shoulder. Her hair tickles my neck, but I resist the urge to brush it away. I almost lost my baby last month, so as far as I'm concerned, it's a privilege to feel her so close.

'I wish I could remember every moment Dad and I sat on this bench. I'd relive every one if I could!'

'You guys were down here almost every evening during the summer months, even when you were a toddler. I can't tell you how nervous I was at the thought of you bounding along this pier aged two! I insisted you wear your reins, and followed you once or twice, just to make sure you were!'

Rebecca lifts her head off my shoulder and wipes the salt spray from her face.

'Really? You followed us?'

'Definitely! And sure enough, you didn't have your reins on – until Dad spotted me marching towards him and you were restrained immediately!'

'That's funny. One time we had an argument on this bench, because Dad wouldn't let me go to Lisa Matthew's house party, without him meeting her parents first. I told him he was ruining my life, and stormed home without him!'

I remember that incident well. Rebecca was only thirteen, but acted twenty-five. Craig did insist on going with her, but when they arrived at the party, there were a dozen 'big kids' banging down the door. Rebecca took one look, grabbed Craig's hand and trotted back home. Much to his relief.

'Your dad loved spending time with you,' I say. 'He always looked forward it.'

Rebecca pulls a red woollen hat out of her handbag, and slides it onto her head. I wish I'd thought to bring one as well. No matter how pleasant the weather is inland, the temperature on the stone pier is never particularly welcoming.

'After he moved in with *her*, we never came down to the pier again,' she says. 'Don't you think that's sad?'

'Yes. Yes, I do.'

We sit in silence for a moment, contemplating the past, the present and what our future could have been, if not for the actions of one woman. As if reading my mind, Rebecca turns and stares straight into my eyes.

'I hate Helena so much, Mum. Everything bad that's happened in my life, is all because of her.'

The ferocity of the way Rebecca spits out the words hits me

hard. I could contribute my own feelings to the conversation, but I think my daughter already knows. I squeeze her hand and let her continue to rant.

'If Helena hadn't come into our lives, we'd have still been a family. Dad and I would be putting the world to rights on this bench every other week, and you'd still be playing Scrabble with him on a Sunday afternoon.'

'And we'd be celebrating our silver wedding,' I say. 'What a peculiar thought that is.'

A young family – Mum, Dad and toddler daughter – stride past us. The little girl laughs and points at the squabbling gulls, while her parents stop her from chasing them straight off the edge of the pier. I miss those days. I miss my family.

'It should have been Helena who died that day,' Rebecca says. 'She was the one who destroyed us, and she should have been the one who paid for it.'

I blow a long stream of air out of my nose.

'I can't argue about that,' I say, and we both stare out to sea.

Kate shivers at my front door, soaked through from an unexpected shower. She's wearing a baseball cap, and the water drips off the peak, straight onto her Blondie T-shirt. Her lips quiver, but I don't know whether that is as a result of nerves, the rain or both. Apart from Craig's funeral, this is the first time I've seen my friend since our confrontation behind the library, and her arrival at my front door is unexpected, but not altogether unwelcome.

'Please... please can... we talk?'

Kate's voice stutters and she avoids all eye contact, but when I step back from the front door, she smiles and comes in.

'You're soaked,' I say, stating the obvious. 'Do you want me to lend you some clothes, while I stick these in the dryer?'

'Yes please. I have no idea where the rain came from. It was sunny when I stepped out of my house.'

I nod, close the door and then turn to dash upstairs to retrieve some clothes. I make it to the second stair and Kate grabs my arm.

'I'm so sorry.' She sniffs, and then bursts into tears.

Kate and I drink tea in my kitchen, just as we have done hundreds of times in the past. This thick pine table used to belong to my parents, and when I was still living at home, Kate and I would huddle around it and eat custard creams and gossip about Liz. When our kids were small, we made cookies and muffins here, while our dog Sam gobbled up any crumbs that fell in his direction. When Craig ran off with Helena, we nursed wine and plotted his downfall, and after I'd been on a disastrous blind date with a would-be suiter, we sat with my laptop and made fun of his Facebook page. Yes, this table has seen everything since the beginning of our friendship, and now it's seeing the end.

We've come full circle.

'It was a lovely funeral,' Kate says. 'I know it's stupid to attribute the word *lovely* to someone's passing, but it was respectful and kind. Craig would have been thrilled.'

My friend is right. If my gran was still around, she'd say that there'd been a good turnout and the vicar had given him a great send-off. Since my ex-husband was not a churchgoer, the minister didn't know him, but he heard plenty of stories from me and Helena, in order to present a decent memorial. I left out the womanising parts of Craig's life, but with Helena and I sitting in the front row and rumours flying around town, the vicar got the idea. The music was provided by a Queen CD and everyone wore bright and colourful clothes, because whatever Craig was, he was never dull.

'Liz told me you're leaving Cromwey. Is that true?' I'm not sure if I am supposed to mention this piece of news from our old boss, but since Kate doesn't seem too forthcoming about it, I feel as though I have no choice. She picks up a digestive biscuit, holds it to her mouth and then returns it.

'I've got no appetite at the moment,' she says.

'That's what a break-up does to you,' I reply. 'I can see you've lost weight in your face.'

Kate's hands shoot up to her cheeks and she pokes at them as though kneading dough.

'How is Rebecca?' she asks, avoiding my earlier question.

'She's doing okay – better than I expected. She's devastated, but back in London. The thought of her being in the city by herself is terrifying, but as Rebecca likes to remind me, it was in small-town Cromwey where the attack took place, so she thinks I'm worrying needlessly.'

Kate nods and takes a gulp of tea.

'She'll be fine. She's a good girl and I'm proud of her.'

'Me too.'

'I've decided to go up to Aberdeen,' Kate says. 'My parents have a spare room in the pub, so I'm going to make a fresh start and see how I get on. I might even find myself a kilt-wearing laddie while I'm at it.'

I smile. If it was anyone else contemplating a new man while going through a divorce, I'd think they were joking, but with Kate you can never be too sure. I take her hand in mine.

'I wish you all the luck in the world with your new adventure,' I say.

'And I wish all the same for you.'

42

The harbour at night is a beautiful space. During the autumn it is often bathed in this glorious golden light, which gives the place an enchanted atmosphere. Add to that the twinkling lights of the resting boats, and the excited voices of tourists departing restaurants, and it is my idea of heaven. Sometimes I sit in my tiny front garden and watch the harbour life go by, and I'll walk up towards the bridge and encounter a dog walker or two. However, it would never occur to me to head south towards Smuggler's Steps and the stone pier, because I'm creeped out by the late-night ambience down there.

Recent cutbacks have ensured that every other lamp post in that area has been turned off, which means that on the stretch of pathway leading from the steps to the beginning of the pier, there are probably ten instances of light, if that. I'd imagine that the only people crazy enough to head in that direction would be daredevil teenagers and the odd psychopathic killer.

When Helena asked if I'd accompany her to the stone pier in order to scatter Craig's ashes, my first reaction was to refuse. Going to his funeral was a depressing experience, but at the same time it gave me a degree of closure. However, helping his wife with the next part of the process seemed intrusive and inappropriate to me; particularly as she was now aware of the tricks I'd been playing on her already fragile life. Turning down Helena's invitation was the correct thing to do, and to me the matter was closed – that is until the woman herself turned up on my doorstep twenty minutes ago, and begged me to change my mind.

It was 11.40pm and I was about to get into bed, but how could I refuse the distraught woman loitering on my doorstep? Clutching a wooden urn and dressed in a long black smock dress, with a navy-blue shawl, Helena looked every inch the weeping widow.

'Please,' she said. 'Please do this with me. I can't do it on my own.'

I told her that it was nonsense to even contemplate such an activity in the dead of night, but Helena wept and said that the council had refused her request to scatter the ashes from the pier.

'Doing it under the cover of darkness is my only option,' she said. 'Otherwise it will never happen.'

And so here we are, Helena and I, wandering past Smuggler's Steps and heading towards the stone pier. There's not another soul around, and as the cliffs loom in front of us, I have a distinct feeling of dread. It's extraordinary the sounds you presume to hear when wandering around late at night.

After stumbling several times in the darkness, we reach the pier. It is bathed in a shadowy light made possible only by a handful of small Victorian lamp posts, scattered at irregular intervals. We inch past the concrete benches and the old bandstand peeks out at us from the shadows. Beyond that there are the old rusting railings, and below, the unforgiving English Channel. As we move towards our final destination, my body quivers and my teeth chatter, but it has little to do with being cold.

I lean over the railings and gaze out towards the mainland. The lights of the Royal Hotel stare back through the darkness, as though beckoning me to take refuge there. I wish I could. I'd do anything to be in there right now. It is creepy and disturbing on the pier, and I contemplate running away at least a dozen times, but after what seems like hours of silence, Helena turns to me. In her arms she still holds the urn which houses Craig's ashes, and even in the dim light I can see that her eyes are red, swollen and full of pain. Despite my better judgement, I feel sorry for her.

'Do you think Craig would approve of this?' she asks.

I look towards one of the stone seats, where my ex-husband and my daughter spent hours throwing lines off the pier in order to catch crabs. I miss those days. I miss that life.

'I think he would,' I reply. 'He loved it here.'

'Do you want to scatter them?' Helena asks, and she holds the urn towards me.

'No, you do it. He was your husband after all.'

I almost choke on the words, but whatever I feel about my companion, my statement is the truth. Craig had left me in body and mind long ago, and I've spent the past weeks wondering if I'm even allowed to grieve his loss at all – except as the mother of his child.

'Okay, here we go.' Helena turns to face the railings, and struggles to remove the top from the urn. I've seen too many movies to know how wrong this moment could go, so I step in and together we manipulate the lid until it gives way.

'Ready?'

'Ready.'

'Together,' Helena says, and we turn the urn upside down and observe the dusty remains of our husband scatter down towards the Channel. From the golden light of the old lamp post, I watch the ashes reach the water; floating, spreading and weaving their way out to sea. I say no words out loud, but inside I thank Craig for giving me the best gift he could ever have given – my daughter. My ex-love was a complicated man and life together was not always easy, but I loved him regardless.

And perhaps I always will.

The moon shines through the scattered clouds, and creates a horror film impression on the surface of the water. Helena is still gazing over the railings, lost in her own thoughts, but nothing remains for us to do now.

'Shall we go?' I ask. 'We've done what we came to do.'

'You know when I fell down Smuggler's Steps?'

Helena's question is so random that it floors me.

'Yes. At least I know of it anyway.'

Helena turns and gazes straight into my face. Her eyes are wide, as she licks and bites her cracked lips.

'Did you push me?' she asks.

My mind whirs, and I'm confused by the sudden change in conversation.

'What do you mean?'

'It's a simple enough question, Jenny. Did you push me down Smuggler's Steps?'

I grip onto the railings and all colour drains from my knuckles.

'What would make you think that?'

Helena turns to watch the ashes once again, but there's nothing to be seen. They've all gone now, swept under by the current, and will be eaten by the fish and crabs that Craig once coveted.

'After Kate told me about the stuff you'd been doing recently, I kind of worked it out. Over the years, little things have come back to me about the day I went down those steps. There was a particular perfume wafting around. It was floral with something else... cinnamon maybe. I could never fathom what perfume it was – until you wore it the day the incident happened at my house. It was the same scent that had haunted me since the day of my fall. It was you who was wearing it, wasn't it? It was you who was there at the steps, and you pushed me.'

I laugh, but I do not feel joyful in any way.

'Are you insane? Lots of people wear the same perfume! If only one person wore it, the whole industry would collapse.'

A faraway clap of thunder brings us both back to the present with a shuddering jolt. Helena sighs and rubs her head.

'You're right,' she says. 'Of course you're right. I'm sorry; I must still be in shock I suppose. Just forget what I said – I'm having a nervous breakdown.' Helena holds her hands over her face and grunts. 'Everything's getting on top of me right now.'

I watch as ripples of water splash and shimmer against the deep concrete pier. This night is peculiar, but memories need to be confronted and words must be said. It's the only way that either of us can move forward.

'Helena?'

'Yes?'

'You're right. I did push you.'

43

2014

Despite being caught hiding in the garden during the dinner party, my obsession with Helena and my husband continued for a little while. Nobody knew, because stalking is not something you boast about, and whenever Kate asked me, I'd deny all knowledge. Who was she to ask anyway? Someone who became friends with my husband's new woman gave up any right she had to question my intentions.

And no matter how hard I tried, I could not keep away from Helena's street and her house. I was no longer naïve, however, so instead of risking being caught at the end of her drive, I made friends with Derek, the guy who owned the cat that got into Helena's house during that fateful evening. He was an idiot – he had nothing to say at all, unless it was related to *Doctor Who* and some 1970s band I'd never heard of. I'm all for a bit of fan-worship, but Derek took it to extremes. It was little wonder he had no real-life friends, but since his front window faced onto Helena's, he was the most suitable candidate for my attention.

One afternoon, as Derek explained why Tom Baker was the

most successful of all the Doctors, I saw Craig and Helena come out of their front door and head towards Craig's BMW. The two were in the midst of an animated conversation, but it was impossible to know what it was about. After talking for a minute or two, Craig jumped into his car and slammed it into reverse. Helena waved at my husband from the driveway, but he didn't return the gesture.

After watching my rival trot back into the house, I knew it was pointless to stay in Derek's company a moment longer, so I made my excuses and left. I pulled my hood down low and had a good gander into Helena's house as I passed, but she was nowhere to be seen.

My heart was heavy and I wondered why I insisted on tormenting myself in such a way. Maybe Kate was right. Maybe I should give it up once and for all, but the problem with obsessions is that they're all-consuming, and hard to let go of.

But I made myself a promise.

Just one more week of watching, and then I'd be done.

Or two.

Or three.

I ambled past the row of houses that led to Smuggler's Steps, but as I reached the top, I noticed how shiny they were. It was coming into winter and I knew that while the stones may appear wet, in reality they would be icy – a result of the hurtling temperatures we'd had in recent days, and brain-dead teenagers tossing buckets of water to create deathtrap slides. I'd heard all about that in a disgruntled post on the *Cromwey Chats Back* Facebook page.

I wondered if I dared risk a descent, but then heard footsteps coming straight towards me: the clip, clip, clip of stilettos on concrete. Who would wear high heels on such a revolting day? I gazed down the gloomy, darkening street and was shocked to discover that the person was Helena.

Craig's new love had her head down, but I could see the headphones covering her ears. She was singing along to a Robbie Williams song. She had not seen me, so I stepped behind a giant oak tree and then peeked out just long enough to see her reach the top of Smuggler's Steps. Helena wavered, slid her high-heeled boot over the stone, and then grasped hold of the wooden banister. I couldn't believe she was contemplating going down there. What was wrong with this woman? She could slip and break her neck!

She could slip... and break her neck!

Adrenaline rushed into my chest and I swear in that moment, my heartbeat could be heard for miles away.

Boomp... Boomp... Boomp...

I'd like to say that it was not a premeditated decision; that I simply stepped out and accidentally tripped Helena Love. But the truth was, even though I only had seconds to think about it, the decision to push my rival was entirely premeditated, and they'd say so in a court of law.

The icy wind flew straight through my coat and froze me from the inside out, and yet not even that could calm the rage that stirred inside of me. A little voice – my subconscious perhaps – whispered in my ear.

Just one little tap.

Just a tiny one behind her knee.

That's really nothing when you think of what she did to you.

Is it?

And that was it really.

I came out of my hiding place for a matter of seconds, stepped forward, pushed the back of her knee with my foot, and watched it give way under the pressure.

Helena went down with far more force than I ever imagined she would. The fall came so quickly that she barely had time to scream, so instead her mouth released a grunting, savage sound, the likes of which you might hear on a wildlife programme. With her arms spread out like a giant starfish, Helena fell five steps and then came to a halt as she reached the sixth. She groaned for a fraction of a second, tried to lift her head and then that was it.

Just silence.

And stillness.

While I couldn't see Helena's face, her curls stuck out above her head and hung bat-like towards the steps below. Her winter coat was so thick that it was impossible to see if she was still breathing, and my own breath came in short, sharp bursts as I shuffled forward to get a clearer look. For a brief moment I contemplated going down the steps, but a voice screeched from inside my head.

You did this. You pushed her and now she's dead.

No matter what you do, you'll be blamed.

You're the one with the motive.

Didn't you want her dead, after all?

Well, now you've got your wish.

I stuffed my hands into my pockets, turned away from Helena's crumpled body and headed into the maze of streets on her estate. From there I could make my way down the hill and back to my house on the harbour without anyone knowing what had happened. I needed to get away, because this situation was none of my concern.

Absolutely none of my concern.

By the time I got home, I could hardly breathe and my whole body felt as though it was filled with thousands of tiny icicles. Every one of them prodded and spiked into my bones with such ferocity that I wondered if I'd ever feel warm again. I took a hot shower and as I grabbed my towel, I could hear the faint sounds of the air ambulance and what seemed like a million sirens, dashing up the hill.

What had I done?

I had pushed a fellow human being down the worst steps you could tumble down, and then I had done nothing to help her! I had left her like an unwanted bag of rags, not knowing if anyone else would come along to help. That action was shameful and evil, and something I'd never have contemplated just a few short months ago.

It was the worst thing I could have done.

Why then, did it feel so right?

In the end, Helena's injuries weren't life-threatening, and I was glad. Not because I wished her good health, but because I knew that if she was left incapacitated, it wouldn't be long before somebody knocked on my door. I didn't wish to have my life destroyed even more than it was already, so I vowed that my stalking days were over. From then on, I concentrated on my own life and what remained of my family, and I was doing okay – more than okay – until Craig abandoned Helena and she came marching into my life.

For the last time.

44

The night has turned stormy in more ways than one. The wind whistles around my head and my ears cry in agony, while my hair whips up and ties in knots at the back of my head. Helena balances on the second rung of the railings in front of me, her head turned to examine my clouded face. She blinks and under the glow of the lamp post, her eyes are illuminated – other-worldly almost.

'I was pregnant,' Helena says. 'And after you pushed me, I wasn't anymore.'

Helena's words feel like a slap to the face and it takes all my strength not to throw up right here on the pier. She was pregnant? How did I not know?! Why didn't anybody tell me?

'Are you sure?' I ask, though I know that's a stupid question.

'I was two months gone. Craig wasn't happy about it, I'm sorry to say. He said he'd never even thought about having another child after Rebecca, and that we should have been more careful. He even wondered if we should... if we should have it at all. We'd quarrelled about it that day in fact, because I wanted to tell my parents the happy news. He said we couldn't tell anyone until we knew what we were going to do, but for me there was never any question. I wanted that baby more than anything. I felt as though it was my last chance, and as it turned out, it was.'

'Helena, I had no idea you were pregnant, and I really am sorry for your loss.'

For once I'm not lying.

She shrugs and drops the empty urn onto the ground. It makes a cracking sound as the corner makes contact with the concrete, but if Helena cares, she doesn't show it. On the horizon a strip of light reveals a ship heading to places unknown, carrying goods, people or both. I wish I was with them. I wish I could sail far away from here, far away from Helena and all the agony she's brought into my life.

'It's okay. It's all in the past now – just like me and Craig. And now it's just me and you left. Funny how things work out, isn't it? I stole your husband and you stole my child. Maybe that means we're even and can start over again.'

Did I steal her child? Maybe I did. But then five years later, she indirectly killed my ex-husband and injured my daughter.

I hadn't forgotten about that.

Helena's feet slip on the railings, and she grabs hold of the top. I jerk forward to steady her, but she shrugs me away.

'When I first got together with Craig, I wished I had your life,' Helena declares.

Her words startle me.

'My life? You got my husband, wasn't that enough?'

'I know that! But when we lost the baby, I became depressed that all I got was a middle-aged man who had been there, done that. I was jealous of the life you had, because Craig got all his firsts with you – every single one – and I didn't even get a baby. I had nothing, Jenny. I felt as though you'd got it all!!'

A wave of hilarity sweeps over me and escapes out of my mouth.

'I got it all? I got it all?!! If you didn't want a second-hand man in your life, then perhaps you should have found someone new to the game. You could have left my husband with me, where he belonged. It's not my fault you had an affair. You knew his situation when you chose to sleep with him!'

My words pass Helena's ears and float out over the water like a fog. The people on the ship probably hear more of what I say than Helena does, but it always has been about her, hasn't it? Nobody else ever matters in Helena's little world.

'You don't understand.' She sighs. 'That's how I felt after I'd had the miscarriage. I wondered if we'd ever be happy. You see, the trouble with being unfaithful is that it doesn't teach you how to be domesticated; it teaches you to be devious. If you remove all the sneaking around, the lying and the hotel rooms – those bloody airless hotel rooms... what do you have? I worried that the only thing we were left with was the knowledge that we'd never feel the same kind of excitement again – now that it was all legal.'

In that moment, my heart breaks all over again. Isn't it enough that Helena stole my husband in the first place? Should I now be subjected to hearing all the details of hotel rooms and excitement?

'I'm sorry you felt that way,' I sneer. 'That really is the biggest tragedy of this entire story.'

'Listen to me,' she shouts. 'I *did* feel that way, but then something magical happened, a month after I lost the baby. One evening Craig and I were strolling along the pier – this pier – holding hands. There were fairy lights all around because it was Christmas, and I was gazing out at the ocean. When I turned around Craig was down on one knee! He told me that he'd never felt like this about anyone in his whole life, and that while I fretted that he'd had every first with you, I had no reason to worry. As far as he was concerned, the real first was happening right in that second, because that was the first time he'd ever been in love.'

Helena smiles at the memory, but all I'm left with is despair. What is happening? Why is this woman telling me such lies? And then a little voice whispers in my head.

Maybe it isn't lies.

Maybe Craig didn't love you.

Wouldn't that explain everything?

Anger and loathing etch their way into every pore of my face and I want to fall to my knees and cry my bloody eyes out. But I don't, because I need to keep calm. I need this night to be over.

'I'm sorry,' Helena says. 'I know that must be hard to hear.'

'If you were such a great love, then how come he left you for Annabelle?'

My words come out like bullets and I hope they kill her, but instead Helena purses her lips into a thin, almost invisible line.

'He never would have stayed with that little tart,' she snaps. 'That was an opportunity that presented itself to him, and he couldn't resist. What man could, let's face it! But I have no doubt that Craig would have come to his senses – if he'd been given the chance.'

My husband's deluded, great love leans over the railings, trying to catch one last glimpse of the floating ashes. They're long gone though, just like the love Craig once held for her – and the love he pretended to have for me.

As I watch Helena lament her loss, the obsessive rage that seeped into my body five years ago, rises up again. My head feels as though it belongs to somebody else and I can no longer quiet the screams of the shattered woman who still lives inside me.

There can be no more lies.

No more obsessions.

No more heartbreak.

Not anymore.

I step forward and shove Helena with all my might. The wind helps in my efforts and at the last moment she twists her head and our eyes meet. Her flailing arms rise up, and her hand makes contact with my wrist, gouging scratches with those bloody blue nails of hers.

Down she goes.

Down, down, down.

Her skinny frame pirouettes and loops, and then Helena's head smashes into the concrete wall of the pier. The only sound after that is the splintering and splitting of her skull on the cold, unforgiving cement, before her body cracks into the sea below. For the briefest moment she floats there, like a character from a Victorian Gothic novel. Her long mourning dress stretches out from her body and her limbs float with it. She's a starfish, a beautiful, curly-haired starfish, illuminated in the moonlight.

Until a wave engulfs her body and she is swallowed up by the sea.

There's one thing left to do. I raise my foot and kick the empty urn over the side of the pier, so that it can join Helena and Craig on their final journeys.

'Good riddance to the both of you,' I shout, as I amble back up the pier, and into the darkness.

THE END

ACKNOWLEDGEMENTS

This book has had a long journey to publication, and I could never have done it without the support and love of my family and friends. In that regard, I'd like to thank the following:

Mum, Dad, Paul, Wendy and Angelina, for always being there for me, and for being as excited about this novel as I am. Also, thank you to my dad for reading an early draft, and acting as my sounding board!

My friends, Helen and Claire, for encouraging me to write this book. Hopefully by the time it comes out, we'll be able to see each other again.

My husband, Richard, deserves a million hugs for going through my manuscript and deleting all of my 'inwardly, downwardly' moments. This book could never have been finished without him.

My beautiful daughter, Daisy, for being the light of my life and biggest champion of this book. Daisy – all my dreams came true because of you.

Betsy Reavley, my editor, Ian Skewis, and everyone at Bloodhound Books, for believing in this book and giving me a chance.

It was one of the proudest moments of my life when Betsy offered me a two-book deal, and I will remain forever grateful and excited.

Made in the USA
Middletown, DE
30 September 2020